HARRIET ASHER

iUniverse, Inc.
Bloomington

Hope Farm

iUniverse books may be ordered through booksellers or by contacting:

iUniverse
1663 Liberty Drive
Bloomington, IN 47403
www.iuniverse.com
1-800-Authors (1-800-288-4677)

Because of the dynamic nature of the Internet, any web addresses or links contained in this book may have changed since publication and may no longer be valid. The views expressed in this work are solely those of the author and do not necessarily reflect the views of the publisher, and the publisher hereby disclaims any responsibility for them.

Any people depicted in stock imagery provided by Thinkstock are models, and such images are being used for illustrative purposes only.
Certain stock imagery © Thinkstock.

ISBN: 978-1-4759-1167-1 (sc)
ISBN: 978-1-4759-1168-8 (ebk)

Printed in the United States of America

iUniverse rev. date: 4/18/2012

DEDICATION

To my husband Barrie, my three children Barry, John and Katie, and also my grandson, Alfie.

My heartfelt thanks go to my dear friends and acquaintances, both past and present, for their input to my story, intentional or otherwise.

People can take everything away from you but never your memories. Thanks to all of you, for all of them!

Harriet Asher

PREFACE

Many friends and relatives have informed me that the stories I have relayed over the years are both engaging and thought provoking. I am often seen with our two chocolate Labradors on our beautiful beaches in Nova Scotia and in my local community enjoying the space and the great outdoors. This is mainly where I dream up my stories, adding life's experiences to the mix.

The story begins with Nanny, Grampy and their wonderful staff who run a busy country stables and riding school. One day Nanny noticed when she entered the Old Barn that something magical and mysterious happened. An owl she had named Katherine is the cause. The animals are able to converse with Nanny and Katherine after the wise old owl scatters her veil of magic dust. The effect of the owl's magic soon spreads. Hope Farm goes from strength to strength. Only Nanny realizes the magic is happening, and who causes the changes for the better. Nanny, Grampy and their staff face many challenges along the way to make the stables successful. There are twists of fate and surprises galore for everyone on Hope Farm.

CHAPTER 1

Flames leap from the burning trash barrel in the farmyard. Barry Gordon, the farm manager, is in charge of the fire, though at this particular moment leaping flames are winning the battle. He shouts at the top of his voice to Jay-Jay Lewis, a farmhand, "Please help me. Nanny will be angry with me if she sees this. She advised me not to burn anything today because it's too windy! Quick, get some brooms and soak that old blanket in the trough."

Dry fall leaves blow about the yard resembling huge gray flakes of snow. They whirl around and gather in large piles by the corners of the outbuildings. What a fool Barry is to defy the boss, Jay-Jay thinks. His skinny arms pump vigorously as he runs across the yard to Barry's aid. He runs his long thin fingers through his dirty blond wavy hair trying to keep it off his long thin shaped face. "I'm on it!" Jay-Jay yells with panic rising in his chest. He runs over to the storeroom just inside the barn door. He grabs two brooms together with a large hose hanging on a hook beside them. He quickly turns back towards the fire where Barry is throwing a bucket of water onto the roaring blaze now spewing sparks. A look of panic crosses his face as he uncoils the hose while running towards the fire. Jay-Jay tosses the old blanket draped over the rail by the horse trough into the water then hands a broom to Barry's outstretched hand. Turning back to the now soaked blanket, he pulls it from the trough. Flicking it open with one swift movement like a matador, he throws it over the flames. It lands neatly covering the top of the barrel and successfully contains the flames.

Kate Nelson, the stable girl, having smelled the smoke drifting towards the open barn door, emerges to see where the pungent smell is coming from. Barry calls to her, "Turn the water on!" as he points to the hose snaking across the dusty ground. Turning to where the hose connects to the fire hydrant beside her, she turns the handle and water starts to flow. She runs over to help the boys. Her braided auburn hair swishes in the wind, resembling a horse's tail.

Barry sprays water on the barrel to cool it down as Jay-Jay beats the small sparks still burning on the uneven ground surrounding it. "Grab that bucket and get some more water from the trough behind you," Barry instructs Kate who turns and grabs the rusty old bucket filling it with one quick scoop before handing it to Jay-Jay.

"Thanks, Kate. It's a good think that you're so strong," Jay-Jay comments, his voice dripping with sarcasm.

"Eh? What are you implying, skinny-ribs?" she asks with an indignant look on her square and freckled face. Placing her hands on her curvy hips, she pulls her shoulders back quickly. The top button of her checked shirt flies off, much to Jay-Jay's amusement. Kate turns away so that he cannot see the smirk spreading across her face.

"Sorry. I didn't mean to insult you." Jay-Jay replies, trying his best to sound at least a little sincere.

Kate's head whips round towards the now extinguished fire. "I think I can hear Nanny's Kubota mule driving up from the gallops."

"I hope not!" the men say in unison, "or we will all be in big trouble," Barry adds.

"Less of the 'we'. This was entirely your fault, not ours," Jay-Jay quickly reminds him. "We helped you put the fire out you were told not to start."

"Yeah, yeah. I suppose you're right," Barry replies looking rather sheepish.

Kate and Jay-Jay look at one another and scramble towards the barn, leaving Barry alone to explain the scene to Nanny.

She drives up on her brightly colored Kubota mule, the large all-terrain wheels whipping up the leaves which swirl in circles of color behind her. She carefully parks the vehicle in its slot beside the Old Barn. Slowly removing her silver and black open-faced helmet, she places it on the bench seat beside her before staring at her manager. Her hazel eyes flash a look of anger at the mess in the farmyard. She is a formidable woman. On realizing that Barry has gone against her strict instructions, her Scottish accent becomes very prominent when she speaks. "Well?" she asks, followed by a pregnant pause. "I hope you have a good explanation for this mess." Her windswept curly blonde hair partially obscures her vision as the wind whips around the farmyard.

He lowers his heart-shaped face and begins to apologize for his mistake when, much to his surprise, Nanny interrupts him by saying, "I realize you wanted to get the trash burned and you thought I would be out of your way for a much longer time, so we will say no more about it on this occasion. I hope you have learned your lesson though."

Barry stares at her in surprise. He was expecting her to give him a sharp dressing-down. His brown leather chaps and highly polished boots are now completely soaked. He adjusts his wax jacket, which had started to slip from his narrow shoulders. His usual smart appearance and immaculately styled dark brown hair now look the worse for wear. "Sorry, Nanny. I should have listened to you, and yes, I will not be starting any more fires on windy days. Thanks for being so understanding about this."

Nanny nods her head in acknowledgement, her thin lips starting to rise at the corners of her mouth. She is just about to speak when a loud bang, followed by a crash, comes from behind the stable doors. Nanny wonders what on earth is going on in there. She lifts her ever-present cougar print bronze cane from her mule, and toddles towards the noise as quickly as her short legs can carry her. Nanny used to be quick on agile feet, even quicker in mind. Everywhere she had ever lived, people loved her for her quick sense of humour. Nanny is slightly plump because of her love of cheese not to mention her love of pop! That, together with her waning will power over the years, had caused a steady weight gain. Nanny always smiled through expressive fine lines on a plump and cheery face. Her lively eyes sparkled in the morning sunshine, although sadly they were not as sharp as they had once been.

Nanny is proud to be known for her generosity, whether that be with time, listening to others, or with offering money on the odd occasion if she is able to help a genuine cause. However, if you ever cross, bully, or in any way deliberately belittle her, then you had better watch out! She would wait patiently for years to get her revenge, something of which she was not proud. Nanny is also a very sympathetic and affectionate person. She is a survivor with ferocious determination. She is a chatterbox, always eager to talk and talk and talk, usually accompanying her speech with expressive arm movements, much to the amusement of others. Her sense of humor is her armor.

Nanny enters the barn to discover that Sophie, her eleven-year-old brown mare, is the cause of the commotion. This horse has big broad shoulders and is built like a tank. Its wavy black mane and tail swish around vigorously. Its green eyes are so beautiful that you could easily drown in their lure. If one of the dozen or so horses living on Nanny and Grampy's farm irritated Sophie, it would become very vocal and had recently taken to kicking with its sturdy hind legs. This trait, which Nanny did not appreciate, had become a great concern. Nanny calms Sophie by speaking to her in a low, calm voice saying, "There, there, Sophie. Be a good girl for Nanny."

She rubs Sophie's muzzle and softly blows up its nostrils. The horse responds by blowing out hot breath which has an almost overpowering stink of hay. An unwelcomed spray of wetness accompanies it, much to the amusement of Sophie's owner. She laughs loudly as she wipes the mess away with the sleeve of her favorite black hoodie. Hobbling down the barn to get fresh water for her horse, she gives it a sugar lump from her jacket pocket in passing. Sophie neighs in appreciation as Nanny hands it the treat. It is no wonder that we look the way we do old girl, thinks Nanny.

An owl with beautiful white feathers often visited the farm. Nanny named it Katherine. She liked to name most of the animals living there. "They are part of my family," she had once remarked to Barry. Nanny sees Katherine fly into the Old Barn through the open door. She watches it with intent curiosity to discover what the owl is up to. She suddenly feels a change come over her. She now feels as if she can read the horses' thoughts. Knowing that this is impossible it makes her a little afraid, in fact considerably afraid. She stumbles out of the barn to get some fresh air and to clear her mind. These unusual feelings are so strong that she decides to re-enter the building to confirm that she is not losing her mind. She tries very hard to rationalize the strange thoughts now invading her mind. A soothing calm immediately descends on her as soon as her plump hands with their painted nails touch the loose old door handle.

"I must remind Grampy to fix this or it will fall off. If it does, then we will all be in big trouble!" she says to Kate who is now up to her ample chest in dust and hay, sneezing almost continuously into her sleeve.

"You do that," Kate replies. I'm terrified I will get stuck in here by myself someday."

Carefully turning the handle Nanny comes face to face with her stallion named Aitch. She had purchased Aitch many years ago. Together they had been through a great deal. They had ridden together as a team periodically in cross-country competitions. They had been very successful together in show jumping circles. The former had not been Nanny's strong point, so she had decided to concentrate on her show jumping skills. They used to have a great time going for hacks in the woods together. They loved to gallop along the long sandy beach chasing the seagulls along the shore. Aitch loved the water, but Nanny did not. Nothing seemed to give Aitch more pleasure than bucking her off into the waves. She had always meant to ask Aitch's previous owner how it had been given its name. Aitch stands for Haughty, Horrid, Hairpiece or Handcuffs, but none of these applies to this handsome stallion. Its coat was the color of nutmeg, and in a certain light it possessed a wonderful sheen. It had a short tail and its head was shorter than you would expect for a horse of its size, but Aitch certainly knew how to use what it had. Annoying flies did not stand a chance. One flick of that strong short tail and they were history. Aitch is kind to the horses around him but likes to be the boss, always in full control, or so it seemed.

On moving further down the barn corridor, a grey mare named Jumper is shuffling around in her stall. Nanny stops to speak to it. "What beautiful blue eyes you have, Jumper," she says as she strokes its neck. She is very surprised at the strength of its muscles under its thick soft coat. Kate has exercised the horse a lot that day, so Nanny thinks Jumper might need its legs rubbing down, as it appears to be a little lame. "Kate, pass me the sheepskin mitt please. I am going to rub Jumper's legs as I think they may be a little sore. You have ridden her too much today."

"Okay Nanny. Here you are," Kate says passing her the mitt. "That will be a great help and yes, I think you are right about the lameness." Kate has a great affinity with Jumper. In a peculiar way, they have a similar nature. They both have a short attention span and are easily distracted. The farmhands were of the conclusion that Jumper got its name because if anything could be jumped, she would try to jump it. All riders needed to be aware of its eagerness to jump. Grampy was always afraid that Jumper might try to jump over his precious Jeep, leaving hoof prints and dents behind.

A clever horse, standing 16 hands high, Jumpers' long legs made it a very graceful looking animal with a great presence. The downfall to this vision of beauty is that it does not possess a good gait. At times, it looked clumsy. This is disappointing as potentially it could have been a good dressage horse. Jumper is capable of clearing six feet high walls with ease, is a good sprinter but lacks the stamina for distance. This was a great disappointment to Kate in particular, as she enjoys dressage. Inclined to be a selfish horse, Jumper is very determined and gives a fantastic ride when treated with respect. The team had recently reported to Nanny that more and more respect and patience is required as Jumper's advancing years are beginning to take their toll.

Although it was still able to attack a ditch or fence with gusto, Jumper appeared to punish its rider by becoming uncooperative if a fence fell, although it pricked its ears up showing enthusiasm if the obstacle was cleared. Jumper's clear blue eyes have dulled a little in later life notices Nanny but you can see they still have a story to tell. She loved the single curly hair above its right eye which ruined the perfect line in which its hair grew. She always had a compulsion to smooth it down or cut it off, but then if she did, it would spoil the appeal. It was all part of Jumper's being Jumper.

Nanny suddenly feels her chest tighten, so she sits down on a bail of damp hay to take the weight off her feet. A slight tickle rises in her throat. "I wish I had brought my inhaler," she says to herself. Her allergies are getting much worse with age, another problem that she continues to deny.

She then feels a tingling sensation on the tip of her button nose. Wondering what is creating the feeling, she looks up towards the rafters where she spies the owl, Katherine, staring down at her through a veil of falling dust sparkling in a beam of daylight shining through the gap in the wall of the Old Barn. Nanny suddenly gets the feeling that both Aitch and Jumper, although confident on the outside, are inwardly insecure. After patting them both affectionately, she leaves the barn, worrying that on top of all her other health issues, she is now losing her mind. She decides to go and spend a little time watching a movie with Grampy before retiring for the night, trying desperately to push these odd thoughts from her mind.

On returning to the house, Nanny observes Grampy hunched over his beloved computer as usual, after a long day working in town. He is probably checking the prices of a new Jeep, she muses. Rubbing his bald patch she affectionately says, "Now dear, you know we can't afford that right now, so let's have a cup of hot chocolate instead."

"Uh-huh," he utters, pretending to switch off his computer while brushing his moustache with his arthritic fingers. Nanny knows it will be at least another hour or so before he returns to the family room. No doubt he will then shower, before checking his iPod Touch. On a good night, he might watch an hour of TV with the family before retiring for the night.

CHAPTER 2

The next morning brings beautiful sunshine accompanied by a clear blue sky. A little sprinkling of snow has fallen during the night, giving the appearance over the fields of icing sugar on a cake. Passing Flossie and Alfie the donkeys, Nanny throws them each half a carrot. The duck pond looks exceptionally beautiful today as does the surrounding field, which is edged with spruce trees and is covered with colorful wild flowers. The donkeys love splashing and annoying the many ducks living there. Skipper is Nanny's favorite duck. She had found the little black and white duck with a broken wing on the farm the previous year. After being nursed back to health, it now lives happily with the other ducks on the pond. It always gives a loud quack whenever Nanny passes by. Bullfrogs croak loudly from the bulrushes standing in line like soldiers on parade.

Barry watches Jay-Jay arrive in his rusty old car bright and early as always. Barry shouts to him, "How does that heap stay in one piece the way you drive it around? I've always wondered how it stays together."

"Skill, Barry, skill. I'm a professional driver," Jay-Jay replies in all seriousness. He stretches his lanky frame after closing the car door. He seemed to spend most of his wages keeping it on the road. Both he and Nanny have a wicked sense of humor. This has carried them through many a problem on the farm. Jay-Jay always worked hard, as Nanny had been able to do in previous years, and he was equally adept at both giving and following orders.

Barry stares at Jay-Jay in silence. The first job of their day was always to get the arena ready in preparation for riding lessons. Barry is excellent at his job, being extremely organized, articulate, and over the years, he has become a more patient, thoughtful, and caring employee. Barry enjoyed his important position as manager on the farm and was never happier than when telling people what to do. Very kind to the children who visit the farm, he always answers their many questions clearly and precisely. Barry, Jay-Jay and Kate regularly organize several visits from local schools in amongst what was a very busy schedule for them all.

Barry watches Nanny load her mule with bottles of nectar and bags of birdseed. He waves to her as she goes on her way to fill up the various bird feeders she has spread around the farm. It is really too early in the year to fill the bottles, but Nanny, being the eternal optimist, can hardly wait. A hummingbird she named Ella entertained her so much the previous year that she hoped by filling up the feeders early, it would return with its' family. Nanny placed a feeder on either side of the entrance to the Old Barn.

She turns to observe Katherine the owl fly overhead disappearing into the Old Barn through a gap in the wall. Today is a not a good day for Nanny's painfully twisted fingers. It is with a feeling of anticipation that she follows the owl into the Old Barn once more. On entering, she feels strangely drawn towards Jumper's stall, where the horse leans its head towards her looking deeply into her eyes. Jumper bares its teeth and whispers, "Place your hands on either side of my neck under my mane and rub them up and down. It will help ease your pain."

Nanny immediately does as she is invited, delighting in the comfort Jumper offers. The pain evaporates into thin air and her fingers are, for a while at least, flexible and nimble once more. Jumper whinnies loudly, knowing it has helped.

It flicks its tail wildly and bounces its head from side to side in joy, accidentally hitting Nanny on the forehead. They pause and look at one another in shock. Nanny bursts into fits of laughter. She looks up to see the owl perched directly above her head staring down at her with large amber eyes. A thin veil of dust is once again descending from the owl.

Looking around she notices that two cracked windows in the exercise arena have been replaced. In the background, she hears the noise of washing machines running in the laundry. That is odd, thinks Nanny. Barry had informed her that it would be the following Tuesday before the repairman would be able to fix the machines. Striding as quickly as she can down the corridor towards the laundry, she forgets her cane resting on the bales of hay beside Jumper's stall. Her feet are pain-free at this particular moment. On entering the laundry, she sees the driers are spinning furiously and the washing machines are all full. There must be some magic in the air, muses Nanny. She smiles to herself as the owl glides past silently, its wing lightly touching her hair. "Thank you so very much, Katherine. What would I do without you?" asks Nanny. Katherine pauses at the gap in the wall, turns, and winks before hooting, before flying away into the distance.

Nanny returns to retrieve her cane and notices how discolored Jumper's teeth are as she passes its stall. "Gosh, they are the same color as my own, but at least we still have them. We'll have to settle for that," remarks Nanny. "I must phone Paddy Lovett, our local veterinarian, to come over with his rasp and play at being a dentist. Perhaps he could do something for me while he's here!" She laughs to herself as she exits the barn, cane in hand.

Flossie and Alfie, the donkeys, bray at Nanny as she tries to sneak past them to feed the ducks. Skipper quacks at her as she hobbles along. Observing that the donkeys are putting on a little too much weight, she wonders if it is crazy to think of putting them into the Old Barn, so that the wise old owl can spread some of her magic on them as well.

*   *   *

Today's riding lessons begin with a class for people with special needs. Barry, Jay-Jay and Kate work very well together with this group. They carefully select a horse for each person in the class to match his or her ability. They patiently help each individual to groom, tack up, and ride around the arena. Whenever possible they have the lessons outdoors. The main aim is for everybody to have fun. After each lesson, Jay-Jay and Kate supervise the return of the tack while Barry returns to deal with the numerous messages and his many other duties in the office. Everybody wonders how he manages to fit everything into his day. Nanny laughs to herself as she watches him strut across the yard in his leather chaps and boots, glancing at his own passing reflection in the window. He checks that his hair gel is still doing its job as the day progresses. Nanny's voice is heard saying, "Thank you all for your patience in that class. I could see that every single person in the arena had a good time."

"No problem," Barry replies with a huge smile on his face. "We all enjoy the pleasure it gives the riders and their caregivers."

Later that afternoon, Nanny hears the sound of a car coming down the long tree lined gravel driveway. It is Grampy in his pumpkin colored Jeep. In the fall, it is difficult to see him approach as his car blends in with the glorious canopy of colors created by the trees. Nanny chuckles at this thought. She watches him take out his heavy briefcase before emptying the trunk full of the grocery shopping he has purchased on his way home. He grins his crooked smile at Nanny, asking, "Hi how was your day?" kissing her affectionately on her flushed cheek.

Before she has the chance to reply, he turns, doing what Nanny refers to as "the Military Strut" towards his office where no doubt he will stay for most of the evening after supper.

Nanny decides to lead both donkeys into the Old Barn. She leads them into the stall next to Jumper. Turning around she sees Jumper bow forward, leaning towards her. Their eyes are at the same level. She does not know what it is doing and is unsure if the horse is in pain or maybe it just wants to play with her. An old straw hat hangs on the peg beside the stall. She lifts it off the peg and stretches up on tiptoes to place the hat carefully on Jumper's head, thinking how cute it looks with its ears sticking out through the holes in the top. Jumper quietly whinnies back in gratitude while Nanny attends to the other horses, humming contentedly to herself. She feels this strange contentment for the remainder of her day. An added bonus is that she feels no pain whatsoever in her aging body. How very odd, she thinks, but she is very grateful for it. She cannot help but wonder what that old owl is spreading around, but something is definitely happening in the Old Barn. More of this, whatever it is, will be welcomed.

Nanny takes a few minutes to rest in the Old Barn after hosing all the animals down to cool them off before retiring them for the night. She thinks, or rather knows, she has heard someone speak to her, but nobody is around. She is alone as she walks up and down checking every single stall twice. She checks thoroughly where she thought the voice had come from. Nobody is there. The horses do not stir at all. Poor Nanny begins to feel very afraid.

Her father had been a crazy man who heard voices. Ever since she became an adult a long time ago, one of her biggest fears was that she would end up like him. "Is this the start of hearing things that aren't real?" she asks herself. Trying to dismiss these thoughts, she puts away the soft bridles, followed by the saddle pads, in preparation for stocktaking the following day. She pats the horses that are facing her, and speaks to each of them in a low gentle voice. As she passes Jumper's stall she says, "Sweet dreams, Jumper."

You can imagine her disbelief when the grey mare replies in a very loud voice, "Sweet dreams to you too. I'll see you in the morning."

The floor seems to move under Nanny's unsteady feet. She feels as if her legs are made of marshmallow and that her feet are now made of lead. She looks Jumper right between the eyes and says, as if it was a perfectly normal question, "Did you speak to me?" unsure if she wanted the horse to reply or not. One thing she is certain of is that she is not dreaming. She is very much wide-awake and very afraid. She tries to shout for Grampy or anyone who may be around, but her throat is now dry and her voice diminishes to a tiny squeak. No one appears to be around the Old Barn. She knows better than to go back to the house and say, "Hey guess what? The horses spoke to me."

Aitch is the first horse to look at Nanny after she has a fitful few minutes. To her horror, after staring at each other for what seems like an age, Aitch says, "Well, well Nanny. What are you going to do now?"

Her mouth falls open in disbelief as she faints, crashing to the floor with a dull thud. Brushing herself off after wakening up with a start, she stumbles out of the barn, and heads back to the farmhouse. She bathes for what seems like an eternity in her soaker tub, staring blankly at the plain washroom wall. She is so stunned by the events in the barn that she forgets to turn on the jets which ease her aches and pains on a daily basis. Understandably, she does not sleep at all well that night.

*   *   *

Nanny wakes to the sound of Ronnie the Rooster crowing. It always likes to make a noise and be seen as much as possible, all the while being adored by a harem of hens. It lives the life of Riley on the farm. A few years ago Grampy rebuilt the hen house after Hurricane Dave blew the doors off the old one. Ronnie takes great pride in making sure that everyone who passes by knows it is his domain. Chris Harrold, the farm cook, always welcomes the fresh organic eggs. If the hens' egg laying is plentiful, each of the staff take turns to take a tray of eggs home. Kate is in charge of this plan which she posts behind the office door every week.

"My turn next," she reminds Barry as she enters the office with a basket full of freshly laid brown eggs.

"It's actually my turn," he gently reminds her, "but I had to buy a box yesterday so you can take the next tray."

"You are just too kind to me," she jests sarcastically. "Chris requires two dozen for the farm house. She told me she is going to be baking today. I'll take them over to her now." Kate leaves the office, basket in hand, her hips swaying back and forth as she walks slowly across the farmyard.

A wonderful aroma drifts from the house. It smells like one of Chris's secret recipes she had inherited from her good friend Millie who had won many awards for her baking at various agricultural and craft shows. Chris does a wonderful job in the farm kitchen. She cooks the most marvelous meals and is like a mother figure to Nanny, the mother she never had. Chris gives her opinion where she feels it necessary, but is careful never to overstep her position of housekeeper, despite also being a good friend. Nanny both appreciates and respects Chris's opinion, taking onboard most things she offers her opinion on, after giving them her careful consideration. One of Nanny's many problems is that she could sometimes be impulsive. She does not possess as much patience as you might expect someone of her years to have. Chris could see a lot of herself in her boss so she understood how Nanny operated. She always appreciates, and respects, that Nanny is her employer and is careful never to overstep that line. They would have many a chat in Nanny's private apartments where there is an unwritten rule that they can discuss absolutely anything in total confidence. It was as if these conversations never, ever, took place.

"Before you go to attend to your horses," Chris says, as Nanny swings the heavy kitchen door open for Kate to enter with the eggs, "can you give me a list of meals you would like me to prepare for Grampy and yourself, please? I intend to stock up your freezer today."

Nanny smiles back gratefully before replying, "I have left it on the side of the glass cabinet for you, Chris. Thanks for reminding me."

"Okay, no problem. I would also like to have the requirements for the staff meals by tomorrow, if that is possible," she adds hopefully, tucking a stray piece of her pale blonde hair back into her hairnet. A smile spreads across her deeply lined face.

"I can only promise that I will do my best to remember to ask what they would like as I see each of them in my travels today," replies Nanny, filling her travel mug with freshly brewed coffee.

"That would be great," Chris replies, adding, "I will ask anyone I see also."

"Good plan if it works," Nanny says as she closes the door behind her after putting on her heavy boots. Chris watches through the kitchen windows as Nanny wraps her purple cashmere scarf around her neck twice as she walks unsteadily towards her beloved animals.

*   *   *

As a new day dawns, the schedule shows that the tack needs soaping. Some horses require shaving, a job that the men from F&V Blacksmith's do extremely well. Effy is an old blacksmith of French ancestry. He wears a leather apron that looks as old as he is, and usually wears blue pants. He ties the long strings on his apron around his waist three times before beginning many hours of backbreaking work. Nanny always wanted to ask him why he did not just cut the strings or, better still, get a new apron that fitted. However, she never did. Effy liked to accompany Nanny in collecting eggs after finishing his long day. He finds it very relaxing, as does she. They use this time to catch up on local gossip.

Nanny has left her reading glasses in the Old Barn by mistake, so she hobbles across the farmyard to retrieve them. She is surprised and delighted to see that the barn has been cleaned already, but she could not remember leaving any instructions for this to be done. She calls Barry on his iPhone to ask if he knew anything about it. Nanny doubts her own mind now, after her horses spoke to her in the Old Barn. Barry answers her call, replying with slight annoyance in his voice, "I have too much to do in the main barn. I had not even thought about the old one yet."

"Okay. Just as I thought, Barry. Thank you. Sorry to have troubled you."

"It's quite alright. I'll speak to you later."

"This is a real mystery," Nanny says to herself.

Nanny looks at the luxurious stall being prepared for a seventeen hand high black stallion named Sir Gareth. The stall is next to the main office. This elegant horse belongs to a local bookmaker named Alistair Alexander. Nanny used to be very dependent on the income he provided when she only had two horses stabled. Thankfully, the farm is no longer as dependent on clients' income as in previous times. Alistair's broad smile, the way he flicks his hair to the side and his expensive soft leather jackets, along with his large wallet, endeared him to her many moons ago. He had been a good friend to her for many years.

The entire team feels that the farm needed to move forward and expand, so they are looking for more clients like Alistair. In years gone by Nanny and Grampy played darts with him and his wife at the local pub. Alistair always played out on double seven where possible and Nanny on double seventeen. It is funny the things you remember, she thought to herself as she collected her glasses.

On her way out of the barn, Nanny pauses by the arena window, observing Jumper being lunged by Jay-Jay and

Kate. Nanny thinks that Paddy, the vet, advised them to rest Jumper for two weeks and this was only the second day. Astounded by this, she walks as quickly as she can towards Kate and asks, "Has Jumper been given her medication? What do you think you are doing by exercising her now? I thought Paddy's instructions were for Jumper to be rested."

Kate hesitates slightly, her neck flushing brightly, before replying, "Jumper is no longer lame. I phoned Paddy and he is on his way here to check it out for himself. We are being exceptionally careful with Jumper until he gets here."

"Just hold on to her and keep her still until he arrives. I will go and get a carrot and her blanket. I don't want her moved until she has been checked over," orders Nanny, pulling her shoulders back in dismay at the pair.

"I told you we shouldn't have taken Jumper out, but you wouldn't listen," Jay-Jay spits through gritted teeth. Kate glares back at him before handing him the reigns, then storming off towards the stalls.

On her return to the tack room, Nanny notices that it has all been cleaned. All the metal is sparkling and everything hangs neatly side by side on the correct pegs. The freshly laundered saddle pads are stacked neatly on the shelves. To the best of her knowledge this has never happened before. Even the hay nets are filled with dampened hay and hang over each horses stall door.

"Something strange is definitely happening in this building," she says aloud before glancing up to witness the owl ruffling her feathers directly above her head. "Twit-to-woo," she hoots as her amber eyes meet with hers. Mesmerized, she returns Katherine's gaze and whispers, "thank you very much," to the kind bird. The owl winks back at her and appears to bow before flying out through the open doors.

Nanny's cell phone rings. It is Alistair on the line. "Can Sir Gareth be entered in a cross-country competition in two months' time?" he enquires politely.

"Absolutely," she replies excitedly. Alistair drops names casually into their conversation as usual. Immediately Nanny recognizes one of them. She hopes that this will mean big business will be coming her way. She hopes that Sir Gareth will be the first of many horses from the barn to compete in big competitions. The publicity will be fantastic to encourage others to board with us, she thinks. Alastair promises that he will give personal recommendations for Hope Farm to the other competitors. "Thank you very much, Alistair. Consider your request done. I will see to it myself right away."

"You are a sweetheart," Alistair replies. "I will see you soon and thanks for dealing with this personally."

"You are too kind. I do not forget all the help you gave me in the past."

"It's all water under the bridge, Nanny. I know you appreciate it," he quips before saying, "You have a good day."

Nanny hangs up and places her glittery cell phone back in her jacket pocket. Picking up the thickest horse blanket she can find, she heads towards the sack of carrots lying in the corner of the grain store. Opening the sack, she fills the other ripped pocket of her jacket with small juicy carrots. She turns and heads back into the arena as she hears a familiar voice coming from the end of the corridor.

"Hey Nanny, how are you today?" Paddy Lovett asks in a cheerful voice.

"Hi Paddy, it's good to see you again. I am very well, thank you. Come with me and see if you can explain this miracle," she commands wryly.

"What miracle? What on earth are you talking about, Nanny?" he asks, swinging his battered old black Gladstone bag, which contains his equipment.

"Jumper appears to have made a remarkable recovery," remarks Nanny.

She escorts Paddy over to where Jay-Jay is standing. He is rubbing Jumper's shoulders in large circular motions. As they approach, Jay-Jay looks pensively at them expecting the worst. Nanny gently places the blanket on the horse before slipping a carrot into its eager mouth. Paddy gently examines the horse thoroughly before asking Jay-Jay to walk it slowly in a figure of eight around the arena. Nanny and Paddy look at one another intently before Paddy gives his verdict. "I have absolutely no explanation whatsoever as to how Jumper was lame two days ago and is in perfect health today. However, be careful with her for the next few days. I can confirm she is no longer lame. Continue with the medication just as a precaution."

Nanny walks Paddy back to his car, idly chatting as they go. He offers his arm for her to lean on, which she gratefully accepts. On reaching his car, they exchange a friendly hug as he bids her farewell, knowing it will not be long before he returns to Hope Farm. Lowering his window, he remarks, "There's that owl again. Isn't she beautiful?"

She turns towards where he is indicating observing Katherine perched on a large fencepost fluttering her large white wings. "Yes, she is. She seems to be following me of late. She is my lucky charm. I've named her Katherine."

Paddy laughs, shouting, "You may appear hard on the outside, but you are as soft as putty on the inside, my dear," as he drives a little too quickly down the gravel driveway, leaving clouds of grey dust behind him.

Turning back towards the office, she goes to deal with the call from Alistair and inform the others of the booking. Barry is visibly excited by the possibility of prospective wealthy clients, now that it has been confirmed that Sir Gareth will be permanently stabled at Hope Farm.

As the day progresses, the farm's routine continues. Nanny goes to the stables to see how Effy is progressing with the shaving of the horses. "I'm nearly done, Madame. Sophie is the last one," Effy informs her as she enters. Vic, his able assistant, is holding Sophie's head. She is clearly unhappy about having her hind legs shaved. Nanny walks over to her horse. Taking the halter from Vic, she speaks in a soft low voice, "Calm down, Sophie. You will look even more beautiful once Effy has finished his job. The more you move about, the longer it will take for him to shave you." Amazingly, the horse calms down immediately, allowing Effy to finish shaving her coat quickly and neatly. "There now," says Nanny in a happy voice. "You look wonderful." She gives her horse a juicy carrot from her jacket pocket.

"Vic, please take Sophie back to her stall and tidy everything up while Nanny and I discuss when our next visit will be," Effy tells his assistant.

Vic grunts an unintelligible reply before leading the beautiful horse back to its stall. Nanny walks with Effy to the farmhouse to collect the egg baskets from the mudroom. Together they stride slowly towards the hen house. Both are having a painful day with their various aches and pains but neither speaks of it.

Ronnie the Rooster crows at the top of his voice as Nanny and Effy approach. Effy usually carries fresh corn in his pocket as a treat for the hens and today is no exception. "Come and get it girls," he shouts. Ronnie is first to greet them. The hens cluck and scratch at the ground gratefully picking up Ronnie's leftovers.

Something zips past Nanny's head as they leave the henhouse. Much to her delight, it is Ella the hummingbird, closely followed by her family. A smile crosses Nanny's face as the family of birds makes a beeline for the feeders she had placed outside the Old Barn. "Things are looking up," she says to her blacksmith.

"They seem to be, old girl, they seem to be," he replies in his endearing accent.

Nanny looks at him asking herself, did he call me an old girl? She raises her arched eyebrows and for once decides to keep her mouth firmly closed. A good blacksmith is hard to find these days, she reminds herself.

* * *

The continuing fine weather enables all the horses to be outside most of the time. Purely out of curiosity, Nanny decides to check on Flossy and Alfie in the Old Barn to see if any changes had taken place. It had been a few weeks since their last weigh-in. Much to her astonishment, something obviously has happened to both donkeys. It is evident that both have lost some weight. Their ears pricked up more than they had done in the past, several staff had reported. It was noted that both donkeys had also become more vocal. This was a mystery as Flossie and Alfie are eating their regular quota of food.

The donkeys enjoy exercising with the other animals in the evening. The peculiar thing is if anything the donkeys move around less in their new surroundings than they did previously, so Nanny asks herself the question, "What has caused them to lose weight?" She, in particular, is most interested and intrigued by the mystery. I think I will sleep with the donkeys for a few weeks. I might lose some weight just as they have, she thinks wickedly. Jay-Jay enters suggesting, "The donkeys are very happy and settled here. Do you want us to move them back to their field?"

"No Jay-Jay, let sleeping dogs lie as they say. Everybody seems happy with the situation as it is."

"Yes ma'am," he says, flashing a toothy grin. "May I say that you are looking exceptionally smart in your tartan skirt today?"

"You may, Jay-Jay. What do you want?"

"Well, it's funny you should say that. I could do with leaving two hours early this afternoon, as I need to take my car to the garage. The exhaust fell off on my way to work this morning. I do not want to get another ticket."

"Your wish is granted, Jay-Jay. You must inform Barry though. I wish you would put money aside each month and buy yourself a new car."

Jay-Jay sighs, saying, "Yeah, yeah. You sound like my mother, but I do know you're right."

"Well, so is she," Nanny quips before turning smartly on her heels, her tartan skirt swirling creating a kaleidoscope of color.

CHAPTER 3

Generally speaking, Grampy does not take a great deal to do with the daily happenings on the farm, but he does come home one evening asking Nanny why she spent so much time in the Old Barn when there was so much to do elsewhere. "For some strange reason, I feel better about myself when I'm in the Old Barn," was her sharp reply. "I think there must be a spirit or something peculiar in there, as I don't feel the same way anywhere else on the farm. My mood lifts and I think more positively each time I visit. I cannot decide if this is a good thing, a bad thing, or if I am losing my mind altogether. The competitive horses are like one big happy family. I have never known anything like this in all my years. It seems unreal. I am sometimes quite afraid of the change I feel while I am in there."

"Oh," replies Grampy rising from his battered office chair, "if you are sure there is nothing more than that to worry about, I suppose it is okay. I do worry about you, though. You are not as young as you used to be." Nanny looks towards heaven, deciding not to say another word on this subject, for now. "Changing the subject totally," continues Grampy, "I spoke to Barry earlier and he is asking if we can advertise for another riding instructor to lighten his workload. He is so busy now. Even I can see we could use another pair of hands." Nanny looks at him silently, over her zebra print reading glasses, her fingers playing with the pearl chain. "We will have to advertise and I think we should offer an incentive in order to recruit the best person for the job," he says with an air of authority in his voice. "We really need someone who intends to work here for a long time. How do you feel about letting out the gatehouse for them to live in as an incentive?"

"That's a great idea, Grampy," she exclaims, "I think that is one of your better suggestions. I would also be happy to include a one percent share of the farm on completion of five years first class service in the contract to promote continuity. A knowledge of breeding would be an advantage but not necessary."

Grampy looks up in astonishment at her last remark before quickly commenting, "I think that would be a good incentive, but why are you never content with what we have already achieved? If you are going to do that, then you must consider offering a share to our current employees. I do not think breeding horses is a good idea for us at all. We have more than enough on our plates as it is!" he exclaims haughtily.

She reluctantly replies, "I suppose you're right, I didn't think my suggestion through." Nanny ponders for a moment, before a wicked smile spreads across her face. "I'll sort out the advertisement," she says without argument. Grampy suspects she is planning something, but decides not to press her on the subject; knowing her as he does, he is sure it will be entertaining and, no doubt, full of mischief. Not wanting to know any details just yet, he decides to take his dogs for a walk. As he approaches the front door, he sees his friend Tony Myers arriving with a load of feedstock.

Tony is a happy chap who drives a big green truck. Sporting his usual grin from ear to ear, his white hair resembles a halo around his head. Tony lifts slab after slab of horse feed onto the old forklift truck that Barry and Jay-Jay use on a daily basis. They had left it in the car park knowing that Tony would be making his delivery today. He is always happy to help and so eager to please everyone. Tony is also a very humorous man, always making time for a drink or two and a chat. It was a huge disappointment to both Nanny and Grampy that he was uninterested in animals. Both would have hired him at the drop of a hat in any capacity if he had been interested.

At weekends and during vacations, his four children love to help on the farm. The eldest two children help in exchange for riding lessons. The younger two girls are eager and willing to help Kate muck out the stalls. They also love to help groom all the horses. If they complete their assigned tasks on time, the stable hands accompany them to the outside arena where they watch the horses practice jumping from the safety of the bleachers, hoping that one day they too will become show jumpers.

One of the girls particularly liked to spin yarns. She assumes that nobody knows she is not telling the whole truth. With a straight face, she would say that she had mucked out a stall when it was abundantly clear that she had not done so at all. She would often be found sitting on a straw bale, or an upturned bucket, painting her nails or putting her eyeliner on, but Nanny did not mind this as she found her very entertaining and she was otherwise a good worker.

Grampy asks Tony, "Would your children be interested in coming at the weekend to help in the hen house? They are superb workers for their age but we appreciate that they can only do so much. We are acutely aware that the children need time to fulfill their own activities as well as their schoolwork."

Tony's eyebrows rise at the thought of the children being occupied, allowing him and his wife time away from them. "Rest assured, the children will be happy to help out at the weekend," Tony replies confidently. "Actually, they were hoping you would ask. I can assure you they will be here at seven a.m. sharp. They love Chris's waffles and blueberries. A flask of hot chocolate will guarantee their early arrival, making getting them out of bed a lot less painful for us," he laughs as he turns toward his truck.

"That's great stuff. I will tell Nanny they will be here to help her. She will be very relieved."

Less than five minutes pass before Tony returns with a look of shock on his face. "You are not going to believe this," he says, "but somebody has tied what I think is a Welsh mountain pony to the fence at the bottom of your driveway."

Grampy stares at him thinking Tony must be pulling his leg as he frequently does. "Thanks, Tony," he replies, realizing Tony is serious on this occasion. Grampy says, "I'll get the small horse trailer and check it out." He then calls both Nanny and Barry from his cell phone to inform them of Tony's discovery. Nanny now thinks Grampy is pulling her leg, especially when he informs her that Tony made the discovery. They hook up the trailer and they bundle into Grampy's Jeep to collect the stranded pony. When they reach the farm entrance, sure enough, a gorgeous little pony is grazing quite happily. Beside her, a small battered saddle is propped up against the fence, pommel facing up. It has a missing iron and a broken girth. Next to this, lies a trunk with a letter taped firmly to the lid. Grampy reads the letter aloud. "I cannot cope with this animal any longer. I do not want to identify myself, but I feel secure in the knowledge that she will find a good home with you, should you wish to keep her. If you do not want to keep her, please try to find a home for her. She may be of use in your special needs class. She is fourteen years old and named Pixie. I apologize for her lack of shoes. I can no longer afford to look after her. I am sure that she has many more years of life ahead of her. I received her as a gift so I do not want to sell her. I feel there is no reason to have her put down as she is in good health."

Grampy folds the note and carefully places it in his vest pocket. Nanny's eyes glaze over with tears, which she wipes away with her lace handkerchief. They load Pixie into the trailer before taking her to the field beside the duck pond.

Barry phones Paddy to ask him to come and check her over the following day. Paddy confirms he will visit first thing in the morning. He goes on to inform Barry that he might know who the rightful owner of Pixie is. Barry quickly phones Effy to make an appointment to have her shod. Effy asks, "Is that the same pony that belonged to Ethel Hartlin?"

"I have no idea who you are referring to," he replies before continuing, "Should I get in touch with her then to make inquiries?"

Before he can say anything else, Effy interrupts saying, "No, no. I am getting confused in my old age. Please forget I mentioned anything at all about the pony."

CHAPTER 4

Saturday morning comes around. The children arrive ten minutes early in eager anticipation of their breakfast feast. On getting out of the truck, they spot the farm's latest addition in the paddock. They forget about their rumbling tummies as they run excitedly towards Pixie. Tony had told them about the pony the previous evening, so they had each brought a carrot. Pixie trots towards them and eagerly eats the juicy carrots. It blows a raspberry at the children and tiny orange colored pieces spray everywhere, much to their amusement. They hear Chris shout from the kitchen window, "Last call for waffles, or I will eat them myself!" The children hurry towards the kitchen door, knowing that Chris means what she says.

After a delicious breakfast of waffles, fresh blueberries and syrup, washed down with copious amounts of hot chocolate, the children quickly put on their boots. They go into the mudroom to choose a large wicker basket to fill with eggs. At that moment, Nanny is coming down the stairs from her apartment holding on tightly to the banister. With a huge smile, she greets each child in turn warning them, "We have a very busy day ahead of us, children. First, we must collect the eggs. We then need to sort them by size into boxes and trays. After we have done that we must make a comfortable stable for our new pony, Pixie."

The youngest child, Ebony, shoots her hand up like she is reaching for the sky asking Nanny, "Can I take the purple leading rein and lead Pixie by myself to her new stall, please?"

Nanny considers this request before replying, "Whoever collects the most eggs without breaking any may have the choice of what they want to do next." With eyes wide in excitement, they all readily agree before running towards the hen house where Ronnie the Rooster is crowing loudly as usual.

This is not a good day for Nanny as she is struggling badly with her arthritis. She does not want to let anyone know how much pain she was feeling. Generally, she is not one to complain and is very grateful to be alive. Every now and then, her difficulties in moving around overwhelmed her. Sometimes she just has to accept help and she will lie low for a while. Today could well be one of those days, she thinks.

While the children are occupied and happy, Nanny seizes the opportunity to lie down for fifteen minutes on the sofa bed she had placed in the spare room behind the office. She always carried a key with her so that she can enter and exit without anybody knowing. Everybody else just assumes this was an empty unused storage room, or so she thinks.

After her rest, she checks on the children who have not quite completed collecting all the eggs. She tells them she will be back in ten minutes with milkshakes and cookies for them. They are to wait here for her return, are her strict instructions. This gives Nanny sufficient time to put in the children's treat order to Chris, and then she quickly goes into the Old Barn before returning. When visiting her horses in the Old Barn she looks deeply into their eyes. She places her hands on their necks, enjoying the feel of their warmth and strength as it soothes her troubled hands. It is of enormous comfort to her and temporarily eases her physical pain.

Nanny returns fifteen minutes later with the eagerly awaited treats for the hungry children. She smiles to herself as she notices out of the corner of her eye that Ella the hummingbird and her family are hovering nearby, taking turns to drink from the feeder by the barn door.

The children are kept busy for the entire afternoon. The oldest girl, Candice, won the competition. She chooses her favorite blue hoof pick and cleans out three of Pixie's hooves asking her older brother, Quentin, to help her with the last hoof. She then proceeds to put oil on all of the hooves. This reminds Nanny of Siobhan painting her nails when she was supposed to be mucking out stalls. Candice cuts an apple into four pieces, after carefully removing the core. Each child gives a piece of apple to Pixie before leading her into the freshly prepared stall.

Nanny smiles as Ebony runs to the end of the barn to fill the purple bucket with fresh water for the pony. The bucket is almost as heavy as she is. She walks a few meters before having to put it down. She does this several times, rejecting all offers of help. She is a very determined little girl.

Tony arrives shortly after each child receives a sealed pay packet from Nanny which brings enormous smiles to all of their faces. Tony attempts to usher them into the truck as quickly as possible as they intend to watch a movie before bedtime. The children are still excited about Pixie's arrival. "Dad, Dad! Come and see Pixie," Siobhan begs, tugging at her father's sleeve.

"Oh, okay then. I would like to see her again. Wow, you have all been very busy by the look of her shiny coat. Did you collect all these baskets of eggs today?" he asks looking at the lineup of full baskets standing by the mudroom door.

"Yep, every single one," Quentin says proudly.

*   *   *

Sunday morning starts with Ronnie the Rooster making his presence known as usual. Nanny feels as though she is in another world. She crosses the yard sprightlier than of late to seek out Katherine, the wise old owl. Sadly, she is nowhere to be seen. Unbeknown to Nanny, the owl had visited and had left just a few minutes earlier. A single white feather is stuck to the still broken handle of the Old Barn. Entering with much trepidation, Aitch is the first to stare at her. It is now or never, she thinks. "Don't you look at me like that, old boy, you are just as daft as I am," she says in a nervous tone.

The old nag nudges her elbow and speaks to her, none too clearly, but enough to know he is not whinnying like a horse should. He is speaking English. She tries to fool herself that this is a trick of the mind or, at that particular moment in time, she would have been relieved to be certified insane quite honestly, as she was so afraid of what was happening around her. The old horse is talking without a shadow of a doubt. He tells her, "Do not be afraid. All of the animals and birds who come into the Old Barn can converse with chosen people who enter."

Nanny takes the opportunity to ask the horses on either side of her how, when, and why this is happening. They just look at her in silence. She turns to Jumper looking into its eyes and asks, "Will you speak to us if I go to get Barry, Jay-Jay, or Kate if she is around? I have enough problems without craziness and lunacy as well."

"No," Jumper replies with a chuckle. "They are not chosen. It is only you."

Sophie, the brown mare, is able to sense Nanny's confusion. She is stabled half way down the barn on the right hand side, just before the tack room, which is, at the moment, full to bursting with bricks for the wall as well as jumping poles, and the cavaletti are stacked against one side of the room. Nanny keeps forgetting to ask somebody to stack these items neatly as her cane often gets caught in amongst the jumps. Sophie beckons Nanny over with her head, her right ear crinkling at the tip. Sophie's sister Heidi is listening intently to the goings on around them. Nanny hobbles down to Sophie's stall and opens the bottom half of the door. She crawls under before asking her horse, "What on earth is happening in here?"

Sophie begins to explain. "The white owl comes in through a gap in the front of the building. It flies up to the rafters then drops what feels like icing sugar over the entire length of the Old Barn. After a short time, the animals wake up, regardless of the actual time. They then adopt human voices and thoughts. It is as if by magic. The problem is most of the animals do not want this gift. Heidi pretends she is not affected by it, but when she gets agitated, excited or hyper, it is obvious that she too is under the owl's magic spell."

Nanny stands open-mouthed in astonishment. She looks intently into Sophie's green eyes and urges her to continue with a nod.

"Heidi thinks she runs the place," Sophie complains. "In some ways it is true. That mare takes up so much of the staff's time. She is such hard but pleasurable work. I know she aims to please and is as affectionate as any animal can be. It is obvious to me that she is not keen on discipline, and she pretends not to hear instructions. Jumper has offered to take Heidi under her wing. Perhaps teaching her to jump by starting with the cavaletti would be a good idea. Baby steps would be the way to go." Nanny nods in agreement at the suggestion, hoping it may make Heidi better behaved. "If not, she will have to be schooled elsewhere," Nanny says decisively.

On hearing this, Heidi asks hopefully, "Nanny, can you brush me please? The dandy brush and currycomb are in the pink bucket over there in the corner. I love the way you stroke my ears, but may I ask you not to pull on my scarred ear, please. It feels weird when you touch it."

"Of course, Heidi," Nanny gently replies, "I should know better." Pulling her shoulders back quickly while gazing at Heidi, she proceeds to brush her. Do I really want to live with this secret all on my own, she wonders. Nobody would believe me if I told them about this unless they witnessed it for themselves. Is this something I inherited from my father, or is this all Katherine's doing? Nanny is unsure whether or not she likes this type of magic.

Leaving the Old Barn to prepare for stocktaking, she checks to see if anyone is available to assist her. Jay-Jay happens to be passing and offers to help. Together, they complete the stock-taking much more quickly than they had anticipated, much to their surprise and delight. Some items they had thought lost miraculously turn up.

Nanny's staff all works very much as a team. When necessary, she firmly reminds them that there is "no 'I' in team". Expecting everybody to work together, they only need to report to her if any problems arise which they cannot sort out by themselves. There is sometimes a bit of friction between Barry and Kate as they have similar personalities and they are both very competitive individuals. Kate enjoys, and excels, in dressage. Barry excels in organizing people.

Nanny laughs to herself as she recalls an incident that happened a few years ago. Barry and Kate were having a rather animated discussion in the office. Both were waving their arms around in wild gestures when suddenly the sleeve of Kate's wool sweater caught in her train-track braces. Both stopped arguing and burst into fits of laughter, which defused the situation. "You'll have to excuse me, everyone. I am going to go and see what Chris has made for supper. Grampy will be home in an hour after his ATV ride with Tony. I would like to spend some time with him when he returns."

CHAPTER 5

The following day, Nanny conducts a series of job interviews. It is always a worry to her when interviewing potential new personnel that there is always the possibility of a new staff member upsetting the apple cart. As she is a very compassionate person, she always tries to employ at least one special needs person in the group at any given time. On this occasion when Lisa Cameron arrives for her interview, the room lights up. Nanny looks intently into her big brown eyes, partially hidden behind round brown-rimmed glasses. Her raven locks bounce as she moves. Lisa has the biggest smile Nanny has seen in years, bar her own. She mentally decides to hire Lisa on the spot. Nanny does not know how she is going to manage this young woman in the capacity required, as she has cerebral palsy, but manage she will.

Initially, she has to oversee everything little thing Lisa does. She has to redo a lot of her work without Lisa realizing so as not to hurt her feelings. To see the pleasure the job gives Lisa at the end of each week when she is handed her wages is priceless to Nanny. She is also glad in the knowledge that Lisa's mother is getting a break, saving her from becoming depressed and possibly a couch potato. This is payment enough. It gives them incentive to continue.

Over the next few weeks, Lisa's work greatly improves. She becomes more articulate and displays even more compassion, if that is possible, especially when dealing with the ponies used for the special children. Nanny invites her to come into the big house for a coffee and a chat about how she thinks her work is progressing. To Nanny's utter amazement, Lisa wearing a serious expression says, "I would love to learn to compete in competitions. I have always wanted to learn to ride and jump over the sticks for as long as I can remember."

Like Nanny, Lisa is not very steady on her feet. She has poor balance and a recurrent problematic trigger finger causes her difficulty in holding the reigns. Lisa does not have a great deal of strength in her legs either. Deliberately keeping her face expressionless, Nanny wonders how she should approach the predicament she now finds herself in. She wants with all her heart to help Lisa achieve her goals, but with the same token, she has to be realistic without hurting Lisa's feelings.

"That is a very ambitious thing to want to do," Nanny replies wondering how they can both achieve this. "Let's have a cheese sandwich and a drink," she suggests, "then we will see what we can do."

After careful consideration and their snack, Nanny knows exactly what she must do. "Let's go to the Old Barn, Lisa. I have a few ideas," she says enthusiastically. Walking unsteadily together, they enter the Old Barn. Nanny writes a list of tasks for Lisa to complete by the end of the week. "Once you have completed these tasks, we will then discuss where we go from there over milkshakes and cookies. How does that sound to you, Lisa?"

"Absolutely fantastic," is the immediate reply. "Can I have chocolate milkshake, please?"

Nanny laughs. "Of course you can. I will try my best to remember. To be able to ride competitively, you will need to build up your strength and stamina. The tasks I have listed here will help you to do that. I need to see what you are physically capable of, and then we can work out an exercise program to help you," Nanny informs her kindly.

Lisa is overjoyed. She reads the list and nods in agreement. "I can easily do that. I am not afraid of hard work and I realize I need to get much stronger. I promise I won't let you down, Nanny," she replies with enthusiasm and a sparkle in her eyes. She removes her toque from her pocket and places it on her head, carefully tucking her ears inside the hat.

*   *   *

Jay-Jay is working exceptionally hard. Nanny observes he is getting more and more tanned to the point of looking dirty as the summer changes to fall. She is so glad of his happy disposition. It sets a good example to her team. He is becoming painfully thin, she thinks, but then he never did have much of an appetite. He once confessed to her that he could live on love alone, and much to the amusement of his work colleagues he also commented that he considers dating as "an extreme sport". Jay-Jay has a string of girlfriends whom he meets during their riding lessons. He's a proper little Romeo, thinks Nanny. I can see how he attracts them with his charm and baby blue eyes, and as for those eyelashes, they have a life of their own. They belong on a giraffe.

Nanny and Grampy give him permission to employ a casual laborer to help him should he feel the need. He greatly appreciates and accepts this kind offer. He knows a chap called Andrew Baxter who can help him with the heavy lifting and the many driving jobs required around the farm. Andrew has been laid off by Boulderstone Construction the previous week. Jay-Jay phones him. He is delighted to accept the job offer. They work well together, enabling them to have a few hours spare at the end of the week to help with the horses while Barry does his paperwork in the office. This new situation suits everyone very well.

The riding lessons are very popular and the waiting list grows longer each week, so much so that Barry informs Nanny that he is thinking of closing it for the remainder of the year. "The pleasure and benefits that everybody gets from the special class, which Lisa is now in charge of, is another feather in the farm's cap, Nanny," Barry is pleased to report. "Lisa takes great pride in promoting it everywhere she goes. Word is getting around quickly, generating huge interest at local meets." A smug look creeps across his boss's face at the revelation.

Nanny has asked Major Dann, the farm's head trainer, to keep an eye on Lisa's progress. Nanny informs her manager, "Lisa is getting stronger by the day. Her stamina is improving in leaps and bounds." Barry looks up from his clipboard with sudden interest. "She has started to jump the small jumps in the arena and is slowly working her way up towards higher ones. She asked Major Dann if she could attempt the small walls the other day. The cavaletti is her favorite jump, but this is not taking her out of her comfort zone." Nanny is confident that Lisa is now ready to progress on to higher jumps.

"How about asking the Major to take her under his wing for a few days?" asks Barry. "His competitive knowledge gained whilst in the army will be beneficial to her."

"That's a super idea, Barry. Thanks for that suggestion," Nanny agrees as she tucks a few stray strands of her frizzy curls back into the straining clip at the back of her head.

Kate enters the office, so Nanny asks her to hide the cavaletti for the remainder of the month, so that Lisa will not be tempted to take it out, forcing her to aim higher and get out of her comfort zone.

"Yes, I'd be glad to. I am sick of her doing the same thing over and over again."

"Just be patient please, Kate," Nanny sympathizes. "We all have different needs. Lisa is doing very well in overcoming hers."

"I know, I don't mean to be rude. I can see she is putting a lot of effort into her balance, but she can be so forgetful. It is frustrating."

"Well, I can sympathize with her on that point," laughs Nanny.

Realizing this conversation is a waste of time, Kate retreats to the staff room for her break before Nanny has the opportunity to start talking about people not completing tasks.

*   *   *

The phone rings in Nanny's apartment. One of the trainers has mistakenly given out her private number to a potential client. This error turns out to be of good fortune to the farm. Unbeknown to her when she purchased it, the phone was an old people's phone. It has oversized buttons, flashing lights which lit up the room like a nightclub in the dark, together with a ringer that could wake the dead. Nanny's phone still provides amusement years after purchasing it. They decided to keep it, as it was proving to be very useful to both of them, much to the hilarity of their children. Nanny and Grampy only found out about the lights when someone called them during the night. They both thought they were dreaming at first, and subsequently could not return to sleep as they kept bursting into fits of laughter at the thought of their bedroom turning into a disco. Occasionally, when Grampy was grumpy, Nanny was tempted to ring the number from her cell phone to try to lighten his mood, but to date had never done so. She was afraid it might make matters worse. She vowed to herself that she would do it before the end of her days though.

The caller was a woman from the next town inquiring if the farm could accommodate her five-year-old mare for a minimum of a year while she and her family went to Dubai with her husband's work. Nanny phones Barry to make an appointment for Elizabeth Smith to come and inspect the barn the next day to get a feel for the place. Nanny tries not to pin her hopes on this woman, as no doubt she will be visiting many other premises in the area. She is the ticket to potential success. To have her competitive horse, named Lady Jane, will be hugely advantageous to Hope Farm.

Nanny tries not to make five from two plus two. She tries not to get too excited visualizing all the items that she will be able to replace with the potential new income. One step at a time, she tries to tell herself. Mrs. Smith might decide against boarding her horse here. She attempts all day to dismiss the long list of items from her mind that she will be able to purchase but fails miserably. Twisting her unruly hair through her fingers repeatedly, she smirks to herself. No wonder they call me naughty Nanny, she thinks. I am totally incorrigible.

On visiting the Old Barn before supper, she wonders what Chris has prepared for this evening. She notices the broken computer in the office is displaying pictures of Nanny's only grandson as a screensaver. Oh! Grampy must have fixed it at last, she thinks gratefully. When he eventually arrives home, she gives him a huge hug thanking him for repairing it for her. He informs her he has not touched it. "Well, somebody has," she replies before adding, "And I am happy that they did." Turning on her heels she attends to the mountain of laundry which she had allowed to accumulate.

After dealing with her chores, she takes a few moments to wander aimlessly around the Old Barn. She cannot help but notice an enormous box at the end of the corridor. This light needs replacing, she thinks as she hobbles with the aid of her cane down the dimly lit corridor towards the box. Her hair catches in a plant sticking out from a shelf which holds the hard hats, reminding her that she must get her heap of hair cut. I must get more blonde put into it, she thinks. She refers to it as her touch of glamour. Reaching into her pocket to remove her glittery cell phone to call Aimée, her hairdresser, Nanny becomes annoyed with herself when she realizes she has left it sitting on the kitchen table. That is what happens when you spend too much time chatting she reminds herself, fully aware of her many failings.

After she has blown kisses or patted (and spoken) to every horse, Nanny cuts through the tape that holds the huge box together. She hurts her fingers on the plastic and metal outer casing. On seeing the contents, she nearly falls over in amazement. It is full of brand new horse blankets. She immediately goes to the office to seek out Barry.

In the yard, the blustery wind blows her hair around her puzzled face. By the time she reaches the office it is twice its size, resembling a lion's mane. Trying to tame it as she pushes the office door open, she sees Barry laughing through the glass. Choosing to ignore his amused expression, she informs him, "There is a box in the Old Barn full of brand new horse blankets. Do you know anything about it?"

"No, Nanny," replies Barry, "but I can ask the others to see if anyone knows where it came from. Did you see if there is a label or invoice with it?"

"I did look. I even looked on the barn office desk. I can't find any sign of a delivery note or anything! There are no bills or any documents attached to it."

"How strange," Barry says, rubbing his receding hairline, "I'll check with Jay-Jay and Kate to see if they know anything about it and I will call you back as soon as I find out more, but it will be tomorrow at the earliest. How does that sound?" Nanny thanks him, safe in the knowledge that he will deal with it. She decides to say goodnight to her horses earlier than normal, hoping to be able to spend some time with Grampy after the supper Chris has prepared for them.

Nanny liked anything that was top of the range. There were many items required on the farm of a much higher importance than horse blankets, much as she was grateful for them. She is unsure of what to do for the best. It would cost a fortune to return them, and anyhow, she does not know where to return them. Something catches her eye as she turns to leave the Old Barn. It is Katherine. The owl winks at Nanny before flying out the open door. All of a sudden, the penny drops. Nanny thinks she has the answer. Somehow, the owl had gifted the box of blankets. Nanny hopes the owl has heard a grateful thank you leave her glossy lips before it disappeared.

Unexpectedly, Sir Gareth says in a sarcastic tone, "Granny—oh I mean Nanny—surely you did not think for a moment that a cheap blanket would do for either me or my friends, did you?"

"No, Gareth," Nanny replies thinking, what a cheek, "not at all. I hope to have a pleasant surprise for you very soon. Someone I hope you will befriend and pass on your many skills to."

"Don't give me half a story," Sir Gareth says as he tries to coax more information from her, but she just smiles her cute smile back at him, raising her eyebrows. "No way, Gareth, you will just have to wait," Nanny firmly tells him, adding, "Take note I didn't call you 'Sir' and what's more there's nothing you can do about it." Nanny laughs as she steps outside the Old Barn back into the normal world. The raucous whinnying emanates from Sir Gareth's stall for several minutes after she leaves.

*   *   *

Nanny, sporting her diamonds and her biggest smile, greets Elizabeth Smith when she arrives at the farm. Firm handshake, Nanny remembers, attempting to promote confidence and authority. Nanny's gaze wanders over Mrs. Smith's palomino, Lady Jane. "Wow,' she exclaims, "What a beautiful animal. It is absolutely stunning! I wish I could get hair dye in the same color." Nanny laughs. Mrs. Smith laughs with her at this thought, staring in amazement at Nanny's unruly hair.

"I prefer plain grey myself. Please call me Liz," insists Mrs. Smith. She has her straight hair cut in a stylish bob, giving her a somewhat bland and mousy appearance. Her pretty eyes complement her thin lips. Sensible brown leather shoes round off the slightly old-fashioned look. Nanny feels guilty about making early assumptions, remembering the phrase "never judge a book by its cover." I just can't help myself, she thinks.

Nanny asks Liz, "Do you mind addressing me as just Nanny?" She proceeds to explain that the only person who uses her real name is her husband, adding that, "You have to have a marriage license or the password for my real name."

Liz laughs at this absurd statement. "I think we're going to get along very well," she says with a smile.

Nanny escorts Liz around the farm. Liz asks, "What is behind the grey stone wall beside the barn?"

"I was saving that little surprise for last," Nanny informs her. She opens the gate onto an English flower garden with tall cypress bushes. Liz's jaw drops in amazement at the beautiful view in front of her. Ivy covers most of the inner wall, which is home to various birds and insects. "My staff nicknamed it 'The Secret Garden'. They use it frequently in dry weather as a meeting place on their breaks."

Liz looks across towards where a bucket of sand sits beside the picnic benches, under the weeping willow tree. She asks, "Do you mind if I smoke?" as she takes a cigarette from her packet before Nanny can reply.

Nanny is severely allergic to smoke, even when the smoker is several meters from her, so she is now put in a very awkward situation. "Of course not," she replies politely, checking her pocket for her inhaler. As the women chat politely they look across to where a swing made of tires hangs from a strong branch sticking out from the old oak tree. Nanny spots Katherine, the wise old owl, perched at the end of this big branch watching intently. "You can see the entire farm from here," Katherine tells the two squirrels playing at the foot of the tree trunk.

The women leave the garden heading back towards the Old Barn. Passing the huge old maple tree, Nanny relays the story of how Dom the Dude, one of the farm cats, liked to pounce from the tree, spooking the horses as they pass on their way to the beach for their daily exercise. "All of the horses love to gallop through the waves, usually in single file. They just get used to it. We are so fortunate to have the beach almost adjacent to our farm."

"You certainly are," Liz agrees with her newfound friend.

Nanny opens the Old Barn door, which Grampy has recently fixed. "Did I tell you my husband is called Grampy?" she asks as she turns towards Liz in an attempt to maintain the flow of conversation.

"Well, that would figure," she replies rather abruptly, making Nanny feel a little inferior. "I suppose I need the password for that too?" Liz asks smugly.

Nanny chooses to ignore the remark, as she desperately wants Liz's business. Liz likes the look and feel of where Lady Jane will be stabled. She can clearly see that the farm is a well-run business and is a friendly place to be. She loves the rapport between humans and animals which is abundantly evident throughout the property. Liz eventually asks, "Could a heater be installed above Lady Jane's head? This is my only concern. I think the stall could be too cold in the winter."

Nanny is unsure of how to respond for the best, as she knows there is no way it is appropriate to have a heater directly above any horse's head. "I guess one could be installed if it gets too cold in the barn although the stables are quite well insulated," is her cautious reply.

Within fifteen minutes of completing their tour of the premises and meeting most of the team, Liz confirms she would like to stable Lady Jane at the farm. Liz places her hand on Nanny's shoulder trying to take control of the situation, asking, "Can we go to the office to discuss business now?"

"Certainly," replies Nanny, who cannot wait to get her there to sign the necessary papers. She opens a bottle of wine after sealing the deal, but surprisingly Liz declines the offer of a glass. Nanny does not want to see the wine go to waste. This could be the start of something big, she thinks, toasting her latest bit of good luck. Liz has many good contacts.

Reminder to self, she is the ticket to future financial stability. Do not upset her. As Nanny takes a drink of wine, she thinks she hears the hoot of an owl in the distance. Picking up the spare glass and opened bottle, she takes them back to the house to celebrate her good fortune with Grampy when he returns from work.

Chapter 6

Effy has his hands full on his next visit to the farm. Even with the assistance of Vic, there is a full day of shoeing to be carried out in preparation for the start of the show jumping season. In his advancing years, he has to take more breaks than previously, telling jokes at every opportunity. He is the type of chap who only reads the front page of the newspaper, then assumes he impresses others with his worldly knowledge. Nanny knows he is totally harmless and is probably just lonely. Vic deserves every penny he earns. Nanny is aware of how little Effy pays him. She slips him an envelope with a hundred dollar bill enclosed to show her gratitude. "Thank you very much indeed, Nanny. I will put this towards my vacation," Vic assures her.

"You are more than welcome. It is yours to do with whatever you choose."

He quickly slips the envelope into the pocket of his coveralls.

Grampy decides to walk around the Old Barn to see what all the fuss is about. Nothing unusual ever seems to happen when he is present. He looks over his shoulder checking that the coast is clear before turning to Aitch asking, "What is going on in here that I don't know about?"

Aitch replies by blowing a raspberry, bares his teeth, and shakes his mane and tail fiercely.

"Well I never!" exclaims Grampy as he proceeds towards the exercise ring to see if anyone else is around. It too is empty. He walks back towards the stalls, checking again to see if the coast is clear. He fears someone will think he is losing his mind if he is caught talking to the animals. He asks Jumper, "Can you speak any English?"

Just as the words leave his mouth, the doors fly open. Lisa rushes in followed by Jay-Jay along with the team to settle the horses for the night. I'm worried that Nanny is losing her mind, thinks Grampy. He laughs holding on to the thought of her having conversations with horses, but then the reality of this hits him hard. How is he going to cope with her if she really is losing her marbles? Although she is a great deal of fun, and their marriage has been a long and happy one, he does not have the time, or the patience, to baby-sit his wife. Nor does he have any desire to, come to that. His plans do not include an ailing wife. Much as he loves her, he is getting on in years too.

Katherine feels it is time to spread her magic once more. She flies into the Old Barn just as Grampy leaves. The owl spreads a veil of happiness and magic dust as she passes every stall. Every horse looks upwards towards her. The squirrels and mice at the end of the barn jump up and they all start to speak at the same time. What a noise. The animals soon work out that if they all talk at the same time, they cannot be heard. The show horses sort out who is going to be in charge. They decide to use a points system. They judge how well they were each treated on that day and how well they have been taken care of in every other area. After adding up all of these factors, they then decide who is in charge on that particular day. There are no arguments whatsoever after this has been decided upon.

Over the next few weeks, this camaraderie among the horses pays handsomely for the farm. The show jumpers are doing extremely well and the news soon spreads. The publicity the farm receives in local and national newspapers due to the success in events precedes them. Nothing comes more easily or cheaply than word of mouth, as we all know.

* * *

The show jumping season continues. Sir Gareth, Lady Jane, Jumper, and Perrah, who is a keen novice horse, arrive at the showground. Perrah is a stunningly beautiful mare who takes an instant shine to Lady Jane. They exercise together as a rule, and love to stand side by side while being hosed down or shod. All the riders are excited and eager to display their skills. There is always friendly banter among them, but deep down the competition is fierce. Each day starts at around three a.m. and ends whenever it finishes. It is as simple as that. Nanny is so glad her days of this grueling schedule are over, but she enjoyed it immensely a very long time ago.

Sophie and Heidi are taken along to give children rides around the arena. Nanny leads her horses, raising as much money as she possibly can. She then donates the proceeds to a local children's cancer hospital. She seldom chooses to look back to her years on the circuit. Being unable to participate leaves her feeling greatly frustrated and disappointed.

On the penultimate day of the circuit, Hope Farm experiences a double disaster. Two large vehicles are reversing out of the showground. One tries to avoid the other and the drivers are not as observant as they should be, probably due to fatigue caused by a season of eighteen-hour days. A truck rams into the farm's horsebox. The box has six horses onboard. Thankfully, there are no injuries, but the horsebox takes a battering. The horses are unloaded one at a time, reassured, assessed for injury, walked around, and then they are loaded into borrowed trailers for their return journey to Hope Farm. This all sounds straightforward until you experience such an incident. The police arrive to take witness statements from everyone involved. It is dark by the time they all head for home.

Everybody is truly exhausted by the time they return to the farm. It goes without saying that this is when accidents are more likely to happen which they inevitably do. Someone drops a bridle on the way into the stall. Jay-Jay does not see it when he takes Perrah in for a well-earned rest. He trips on the reins, falling head first into the wall. He looks dazed as he stands up. He staggers for a moment before vomiting on the horse's bed and passing out. Immediately an ambulance is called to take him to hospital. The accident is worse than everybody initially thought. He remains in hospital for almost a month, but with support and perseverance, he makes a full recovery. The only tell-tale sign is a slight limp which improves greatly with physiotherapy and a great deal of determination on his part. Everyone suspects that a nurse named Julie had a lot to do with his recovery. The farm hands and trainers all went that extra mile to cover his work in his absence without complaint. Nanny and Grampy promised to throw a huge Christmas party as a thank-you for them all.

Nanny and Grampy meet up with Liz Smith in the VIP tent at the end of the jumping season. She informs them that she intends to add to her already impressive string of horses which are now all residing at Hope Farm. Neither Nanny nor Grampy dares to ask what happened to her plans to accompany her rich husband to Dubai. All that Nanny really cares about is that Liz pays on time, which she does every month, like clockwork. She is surprised that Liz had not asked for some discount as she would have gladly given some. She feels it is now too late to bring the subject up. "Perhaps I will give her a few free entries to the Willowvale show as a thank you for her business," she whispers to her balding grey-haired husband.

"Your conscience has been pricking you, my sweet, hasn't it?" asks Grampy, out of the corner of his mouth.

"I guess so," she replies quietly.

Liz's opinion matters a great deal to the circle of trainers, owners, and riders at all equestrian events. She introduces

Nanny and Grampy to an acquaintance of hers who is looking for somewhere to stable her two racehorses, one named Odds and the other Evens.

On their return journey home, Grampy turns to Nanny saying, "It all sounded a little corny to me, but what do I care. Business is business." He thinks, perhaps a brand new Jeep will be coming up the driveway sooner than I had hoped!

"I know that look," she replies as if reading his mind. "You are not getting a new Jeep!"

"I never said anything about a Jeep!" he says, wondering how she knew what he was thinking.

"You don't need to say a word! I can read you like a book."

They call a truce by hugging each other lovingly before climbing the staircase to their apartment.

CHAPTER 7

In the New Year, the newly-appointed bank manager Nigel Saunders meets with Nanny and Barry to discuss boarding his magnificent stallion. His horse is a seventeen point two hand high Arabian named The Jefster.

Nigel parks his Jaguar just outside the office window. She looks at him as he towers over her, guessing his age to be mid-forties. He stands over six feet tall with a ramrod straight back, she observes, as he introduces himself to both Barry and herself in the farm office. Nanny happens to notice his sparkly blue flirtatious eyes peer over his designer bronze-rimmed glasses, making him look very distinguished. Her first thought is, I wish I had met him a quarter of a century ago. This naughty notion makes it difficult for her to keep her face straight and her mind on business. I don't suppose I will ever change, she thinks.

Barry takes one look at her knowing that this suave, smooth and sophisticated man-about-town will definitely impair her judgment today. He has worked on the farm long enough to be certain of this.

Nanny feels very distracted and is unable to concentrate fully after the introductions. Hoping to settle her own nerves, she offers Nigel a sherry. Unfortunately for her, he firmly declines the offer, so she feels it would be inappropriate for her to pour herself a large one. She sincerely hopes that Barry can deal with the situation better than she can. Years ago, she had taught him a signal. If she was too distracted to conduct any meeting, she would indicate her discomfort by removing the hairpin securing her hair in its tight bun. He nods to her, smiling broadly, as she removes the hairpin, aware of what he must do next.

Nigel opens his wallet and hands a photo of his horse to Nanny. She studies the animal intently before saying, "I cannot ever remember having seen such a magnificent gleaming coat on any animal in my entire life."

"Thank you," Nigel replies proudly. "He is rather majestic, even though I say so myself."

Barry hands Nigel a copy of the farm's boarding terms and conditions. They all take a short tour of the Old Barn which leaves Nigel feeling very impressed. Turning to address Nanny, displaying perfect white teeth through his smile, he says, "I am pleased to inform you that I would like to board The Jefster here if you have a vacancy. I'm ready to talk money if you have the time now."

"Today is your lucky day," she informs him. "We do have two vacant stalls at the moment as it happens, so you can have the choice." Nigel smiles broadly, lowering his shoulders in relief. Nanny knows that if she takes Nigel to sign any papers at this particular moment in time, she will not be wearing her business head. She is afraid that the combination of Nigel's appearance, together with the intoxicating aroma of his cologne, will affect her judgment. She might be inclined to offer too much discount without thinking. This had happened once before; she knew it would upset both Barry and Grampy if it happened again.

Luckily for her, Barry suggests that he and Nigel go over the figures together as she is due to be supervising Lisa's jumping practice. He invites Nigel to return the following day, assuring him that all the necessary documents, together with the stall of his preference, will be ready for inspection on his arrival.

She gives Barry a grateful glance for handling the situation well, allowing her a graceful exit strategy. I must reward him for his quick thinking, she thinks en route to the arena. I will get him a bottle of something he likes as a thank you, along with some cinema tickets.

As she walks over towards Lisa, a horsebox parks outside the Old Barn. Nanny's jaw drops in amazement as she recognizes Liz unloading two of Alistair's horses. Liz walks over towards her laughing loudly as Jay-Jay, Kate, and Lisa rush towards her horses, giving them a warm welcome.

"How fortunate I am to have such a caring team around my horses," Liz says to Nanny, "not to mention my incredibly hard working husband, who conveniently works so many thousands of miles away. He is quite happy to pay for my expensive hobby without complaint or any question. For that I am very grateful as well as lucky."

She turns to the now gathering crowd saying, "Hi everyone. I'd like to introduce you to my latest additions, Fifi and Mimi. You will no doubt recognize them as Alistair's cast offs! I didn't think he would part with either of them, but one phone call from my wonderful husband apparently did the trick." The team looks at one another without uttering a single word, which Liz notices, not that she cared.

Without consulting the others, Barry invites Liz into the office to offer her a substantial discount, as she is now their biggest client. He thinks that she is entitled to a little preferential treatment. He sincerely hopes Nanny will respect his snap decision, thinking it best to phone her just to clarify the situation. "Absolutely fantastic idea, Barry," she readily agrees. "Offer that to her immediately. I will feel less guilty about not having given her discount before now."

CHAPTER 8

Nanny holds a lengthy staff meeting to ensure everybody is singing from the same page. They decide unanimously to expand the Old Barn and to introduce some new show jumpers to the farm team. Perrah is maturing well and is beginning to bring home some serious money in equestrian events. Hope Farm will soon have to buy a new cabinet to hold all the trophies the horses and riders have won this season. They have won many more than even they had expected.

Nanny goes to collect her thoughts in the Old Barn. She sits in her favorite spot on the dusty straw bales. She asks herself why she does that because it troubles her weak chest every single time, causing her to cough and cough. For some reason known only to her, it is worth the discomfort to be surrounded by her horses. She just has to accept the allergies they produce and tolerate them as best she can. She seems to forget to use her inhaler more and more as time goes by. No bill or any documents ever did arrive for the many thousands of dollars' worth of horse blankets. Nanny suspected only Katherine knew the answer to this mystery. On looking down the dimly lit corridor, she notices two size sixteen saddles sitting on the rack. There is no explanation for their arrival. It is all very strange and inexplicable. Nanny scratches her head in bewilderment as she sees the white tail feathers of an owl vanish into thin air before her eyes. Suspecting that Katherine has once more spread her magic, she tests her theory by asking Aitch if he has seen anything at all out of the ordinary.

"Neigh chance," he says mocking her Scottish accent, "but I will tell you this. That old owl is a very special bird. That is all I am prepared to say for now."

"Thank you for confirming that, Aitch. I thought I was losing my mind."

*　　*　　*

A week goes by before Nanny sees the wise old owl fly into the barn again. She follows it calling out in her soft lilting accent, "Hey Katherine ma quine, can ah hae a word with ye please?"

Katherine flies down from the rafters, landing effortlessly on the door of Jumper's stall. "You certainly can," replies the owl kindly, "what can I do for you?"

"It's more like what have you already done for us," Nanny says gratefully, walking towards the owl, leaning heavily on her cougar print cane. "How can I possible repay you for everything you have done for us on the farm?" she asks, her eyes filling with tears of gratitude.

Katherine walks towards Nanny, putting a large wing around her to protect her from the cold draft. The white owl winks back at her before saying, "You can repay me by considering becoming my trainee owl when your time comes. I need to retire in the near future and we both know what is happening to you, don't we Nanny?" the owl asks, with a sympathetic tone in her voice.

"Sadly, yes. I do not know how Grampy is going to cope with my inevitable demise. I was afraid to tell him in advance, just in case I lived longer than expected. Everybody knows I never give up or admit defeat until the bitter end," she says, laughing to her feathered companion.

Katherine nods her head in agreement. "I have a story to tell you. You must keep quiet Nanny, no interruptions, and definitely no shouting out, especially if the sentence has the word 'but' at the beginning, in the middle, or the end. Do you understand?"

Nanny laughs as her eyes fill with tears once more. Forget-Me-Not, a grey kitten, who was found under a lilac bush a few days previously, jumps onto Nanny's lap, curling up in a ball. Desperately wanting to hear the explanation, she agrees to button her thin lips, the only part of her that is thin, as she gazes into Katherine's eyes with wonder and intrigue.

The owl begins, "By chance I happened to be flying around the cove when I saw yourself and Grampy sitting together with another couple. Grampy was looking at you with his big brown eyes. They twinkled in the setting sunlight. He was thinking how fortunate he was to have you with him. You were unable to return his gaze as you were looking and feeling very pensive. You kept pulling at your top, willing it to stretch another three inches to cover your tummy. The host did not mind what you looked like because, like most people, he just enjoyed your company. You being you just as you are. His wife, now she was another matter. She was jealous of you. She had no reason to be so. We both know that, but she was obsessed. When I overheard her comment, 'Do fat people not have mirrors,' as I flew past, I circled around again in disbelief, only to hear several distasteful remarks. I was very impressed and touched by your Oscar-winning performance in pretending you were not hurt, embarrassed, or in any way bothered. You laughed, avoiding everybody's gaze. You carried on as if nothing cruel had been said. I thought to myself, 'enjoy your moment, you horrid old bat, I am going to make sure that Nanny succeeds in everything she does from now on'. In the past, you worked very hard for a long time. I knew you didn't deserve to be spoken about in such a derogatory manner."

Nanny looks into the owl's eyes through grateful tears once more. Tears flow and mucus runs down her little pointed chin. She does not dare open her mouth for more than one reason. Rising to her feet, she gives the owl a huge hug and a kiss on the cheek, appreciating what it has done for her. As she steps back, the owl vanishes into thin air. Nanny turns to put the saddles and bridles away, only to discover that this has already been done. Fresh bedding is in every stall. The entire Old Barn looks spick and span. The horses are all fast asleep, some still standing. This was all down to Katherine, of course.

* * *

The following day, with renewed determination and feeling much better, Nanny decides to advertise for another experienced horsewoman to lighten the heavy workload. The successful applicant will require a compassionate nature and be able to work some weekends. Nanny knows it is going to be difficult to find somebody who fits these requirements, but try she will. She picks up her phone and places the advertisement in the local newspaper.

Turning to Barry she says, "I am glad to see Lisa is coming on in leaps and bounds with the special class. I love the way she attacks all jobs with gusto, and she astounds everyone who encounters her wonderful nature."

"I know," he agrees readily. "She amazes so many people by how capable she really is. She is now one of the most respected new riders on the circuit. Were you aware of that?"

"No I wasn't, but I'm not surprised." Nanny is visibly impressed. "The thing that impressed me the most when we chatted the other day is that she is saving all the money she can to buy a share in Perrah. I readily agreed. It is a good incentive for her."

"Good. Giving her a target to aim for and allowing her to buy a leg of a horse is a great way to encourage her." Barry says with a slight croak in his voice. "I think I may be coming down with a cold."

"Liz left today to join her husband in Dubai after depositing many thousands of dollars into the farm's account prior to her departure." Her mind wanders, wondering what Liz's husband is really like. She smiles and bites the inside of her cheek by mistake at her naughty thoughts. As if anybody other than Grampy would fancy me. There is no fool like an old fool, she thinks as she strides across the yard.

Today is a good day for her. She feels very little pain, so therefore she delights in not having to use her cane. She accomplishes much more today than she normally does. After a hard day's work, and a delicious supper, she falls into a deep and dreamless sleep, her first good sleep in months.

CHAPTER 9

The farm is running beautifully with few changes in staff, or animals come to that, with the exception of the arrival of a new riding instructress. Ruby Weaver is a welcome addition. She fits in very well with everybody without exception. The lanky brunette was a very experienced horsewoman who drove a very hard bargain with Nanny. Her résumé, together with her letters of recommendation, left Nanny and Grampy feeling very confident in their decision to hire her. Ruby's knowledge and experience enriched the team.

Each day she would greet every single person with enthusiasm, come rain or shine. Ruby showed her appreciation in so many ways to her employers. "You don't need to keep giving us little treats, Ruby. The gatehouse is part of your contract. I know you are grateful," Nanny assures her.

"Oh, it's nothing. I want to. I especially like sharing cakes I make from new recipes. I share them because I don't want to eat them all myself."

"There will never be any shortage of tasters while you live around here, young lady."

"No, I can see that," Ruby replies with pride, looking in Jay-Jay's direction.

*　　*　　*

A welcome change is the farm's income. It is now almost tenfold in comparison to where it was three years ago. Nanny knows it is mainly due to Katherine spreading her magic.

Very little expenditure is now required for saddlery, jumps, and transportation. A noticeable decrease in veterinary fees has made an enormous difference. As a child, Nanny never believed in magic or fairies. Now she knows very differently. How she wishes she had enjoyed her childhood more. It made her sad to think back to her childhood, so she chose to concentrate on the future.

Nanny asks Jay-Jay, Kate, and Ruby to assist Barry to lead some of the horses to the new hydrotherapy pool. The installation has been a huge undertaking and a massive expense. The upkeep alone is hideously expensive, but it is so beneficial to the horses. It is a big treat for them and is very therapeutic. They all love it without exception. To help cover the costs, the farm advertises the pool to veterinary clinics throughout the province. People come from all around to utilize this luxurious facility. On the first day of advertising, Barry received seven enquiries and word soon began to spread.

It was mainly thanks to Nigel's faith and confidence in Hope Farm which enabled the construction of the pool. It is a big gamble as they could lose a great deal of money if the facility is not successful in generating new business. Thankfully, to date it is a gamble that has very definitely paid off. Nanny is always tempted to jump in with the horses, but thankfully, to everybody's relief, so far she has refrained from doing so. She used to swim in the sea with her horses many moons ago. She smiles to herself as she recalls the night someone dared her to skinny dip. Anyway, back to the business in hand, she thinks smirking, all the while relishing the memory of that particular night.

Katherine notices that Nanny is losing weight. By the end of the fall, she looks absolutely fabulous. It is a great novelty for her to go into any store to buy whatever she fancies off the peg. One day she came home laden with bags containing six news tops, four pairs of pants, a couple of skirts, and some dresses. However, Nanny is keeping a secret. She wishes the reason she has regained her once good figure was due to self-restraint and will power, but sadly, it is not. She is very proud of having built a fair business into a great one at her late stage in life, albeit with the help of a little magic. She is very grateful to have lived much longer than she had expected. Over the last twenty years in particular, she feels privileged to have been able to help people less physically able than she.

Nanny has an idea. She decides to hold a competition. The prize is a trophy filled to the brim with hundred dollar bills. Beside it, she places a sealed envelope. Inside the envelope is a secret prize. The winning recipient has to choose between the cash or the envelope, which she states might contain as little as ten bucks. It actually contains a certificate granting a one percent share of the entire farm. This competition will provide her with another opportunity to reward the genuine caring animal lovers for their dedication which she and Grampy greatly appreciates.

On a wall in her apartment, she places a chart together with a box of ballot papers. Every employee is asked to fill out a ballot paper each evening, handing it to her before going home. The ballot is for whoever in their opinion, had consistently gone the extra mile that day. Nanny recorded the results on the chart. It becomes apparent very early that her manager, as she suspected, is going that extra mile on a regular basis. Nanny has just wanted to have her suspicions confirmed by her entire team.

When she announces the results, Barry is amazed that he won the competition by a huge margin. Much to Nanny's surprise, he chooses the sealed envelope. She felt sure whoever the lucky recipient was would choose the hundred dollar bills. Barry especially liked to spend, much like her. His jaw drops when he reads the contents of the envelope. It reads, "This entitles the winner of the competition to a one percent share in Hope Farm." When the enormity of the prize dawns on him, he promptly faints. Everyone rushes to his aid. A few moments later he comes around, and for once in his life, he is totally lost for words.

CHAPTER 10

One evening, after supper, Nanny feels a sudden irrepressible urge to visit the Old Barn. Passing the mud splattered office window, she notices Grampy on his beloved computer as usual, only now he was sporting a set of large headphones. Just when I thought it could not possibly get any worse, she thinks.

Katherine the owl flies in, putting her wing around Nanny to keep her now frail frame warm. Nanny feels a warm glow engulf her entire body. As if by magic, all her pain evaporates. "I'm going to walk Jumper around the barn," she informs a surprised Katherine. In her wisdom, the owl decides to sprinkle a little magic dust from her feathers over Nanny.

Aitch nearly gives himself whiplash as he pops his head over the stall door, laughing loudly as Nanny had not been on horseback for around twenty years. He asks if she is absolutely sure about her intentions, using her real name, before continuing, "You know you vowed to Grampy that you would never ride again as long as you two were together?"

"That is true Aitch," is her quick response, "but if you cast your mind back, I promised never to canter or gallop. I carefully never promised not to walk or trot, although I have not done that either as it happens."

"Oh my goodness" comes his apologetic reply, "you are absolutely correct! I remember now. You are a very, very naughty old lady."

Nanny knows it is now time. She feels a little awkward and clumsy and is rather disappointed, as she does not feel as excited as she expected she would about her impending ride. It just felt right, like a pair of comfortable old slippers. Not a single word is spoken in the barn. Nanny remembers a friend saying to her many years ago, "Who needs words?" This is one of those moments. She gently mounts the old grey mare. Jumper whinnies gently back to her, encouraging her to continue. Nanny strokes Jumper's gorgeous ears, and then smoothens down the hair she has always wanted to cut above Jumper's right eye with her now painless fingers. They walk for probably ten minutes, drinking in the moment silently together. Nanny knows Grampy will have a fit if she passes the office windows and he sees her, so she decides to go in the opposite direction. At last, Nanny is the first to speak. "I've waited such a long time for these stolen moments." She continues in a contented voice, "We are a pair of old fools, but I feel it is now time to go and get Grampy."

Unexpectedly, Jumper brakes into a trot. Nanny is so tempted to press her once ample calves around the horse's tummy indicating for it to proceed to a canter. Nanny's common sense takes over. She pulls back gently on Jumpers soft mouth, having deliberately chosen the lightest bit to put between its teeth. She has also chosen the softest, lightest saddle to place on its back. Nanny remembers her vows at the last second and complies with the rules.

"Jumper," Nanny says as she dismounts rather ungracefully, "You will never know what this stolen half hour has meant to me." Jumper silently looks deeply into Nanny's misty eyes, nodding her head first to one side, then to the other. Nanny grabs the hose and washes her ride down to cool her now steaming coat.

"Nanny, can you rub my withers with a cold cloth please?" Jumper asks, "I am so hot after our ride."

"I certainly will, Jumper. It would be my pleasure. It is the least I can do for you." Nanny cannot believe how muscular and strong her ride is. "I'm hot too. I need to cool down. It's maybe for the best that we did not canter on this lovely evening."

"It is indeed," replies Jumper, "because I can see Grampy heading this way."

"What on earth do you think you are doing, Nanny?" he asks in a shocked tone as he enters the Old Barn. He leaves the door open and Katherine flies in, perching on Aitch's stall door, waiting for the show to begin. Nanny feels the room spin around her, so she lies down on a couple of blankets in the first stall. Lying down beside her Grampy asks if she is feeling okay. He notices she looks a bit grey and is sweating profusely. "Do you want me to call a doctor or an ambulance?" he asks, taking her frail hand in his.

"No," Nanny replies, "It's time for me to go."

"Go where?" he asks not really understanding what is happening around him.

"Now that, I'm not sure of," Nanny answers with a slightly worried expression crossing her fevered brow. Damn you Jumper, damn you, she thinks. I did not need or want to have my fire rekindled after all these years. I accepted that I had to give up horseback riding.

Grampy holds his wife tightly, stroking her impossible hair. He begins to pick out pieces of hay as she thanks him for always being there for her, even if she usually had to go via his office. "Look after the barn, as well as yourself. I will be waiting for you on the other side."

The last thing Nanny says to Grampy after telling him she loved him is, "I want you to know that surprisingly I have kept my promise to you after all these years. I so wanted to canter with Jumper this evening, but I didn't."

They both laugh through their tears, before she slips into a deep sleep. Grampy now realizes this sleep is one from which she will never wake up. She is pain-free for the first time in many years. She had achieved almost everything on her bucket list. Grampy raises his head looking upwards towards heaven. With sudden great clarity, he now realizes Nanny is not infallible. In the rafters, he sees a small tawny owl sitting next to Katherine. They are bathed in golden light cast by the setting sun and are both looking directly at him. The tawny has hazel eyes, he notices. "Just like Nanny's," he thinks aloud. They hold each other's gaze for some time. Grampy rubs his eyes as the owls turn to one another, then together they vanish into thin air. Tiny silver star-shaped pieces of dust fall from where the owls sat.

Grampy is proud about the many accomplishments they have achieved over the years. He begins to speak to her lifeless form, hoping that her spirit will hear him, "There is so much I am thankful for. The thing about you I am most proud of is . . ."

Out of the corner of his eye, Grampy notices that the horses all seem to be looking at him, listening intently. Turning to them he says, "Now, that is for me to know, and for you lot to find out about!" Grampy does not know that the horses understand every single word he was saying. He is blissfully unaware of the magic the wise old owl has spread prior to the demise of his wife. He is also unaware that she has become the tawny owl.

CHAPTER 11

The loud doorbell had remained silent since Nanny had passed. Everybody on the farm missed the shrill noise reverberating around the courtyard. Ring-a-ding-ding it echoed. A beautiful tawny owl with hazel eyes sits observing the farmyard from her perch high in the maple tree beside the Old Barn. Looking out of his office window, Barry sees a woman standing by the farmhouse door. He calls out, "Could someone please attend to this glamorous lady? I don't think Chris has heard the doorbell." The owl notices Jay-Jay and Kate exchanging puzzled glances.

On hearing Barry's request, Jay-Jay stands his pitchfork beside the open stable door then runs towards the rather striking looking tall woman. "Good morning," Jay-Jay politely greets her. "My colleague will be with you in a moment. How may we help you?" he asks. At that instant, Chris opens the heavy oak door with squeaky hinges. She is surprised by the presence of the lady standing in front of her.

"Hello, I'm so sorry to have kept you waiting," Chris apologizes. "I wasn't sure if I heard the doorbell ring or if it was a figment of my imagination. Thank you, Jay-Jay, I will attend to this lady. You can go back to your work now."

Jay-Jay, bursting with life, bids his farewell to the women.

"Do not give it a second thought," the tall woman replies, displaying the most perfect set of teeth that Chris had seen in a woman of her age, which she guessed to be somewhere

66

in her late forties. "I am Doctor Elizabeth McCormack," the woman introduces herself, extending a slender elegant hand towards Chris' outstretched wrinkled one. "I wonder if may speak with Grampy. I am sorry I do not know his real name." Hesitating slightly before continuing, "If that is not possible, I would like to make an appointment to speak with him as soon as possible," she firmly says making Chris feel slightly intimidated. "It was Alistair who recommended your stables to me," the doctor announces.

Chris finds herself inexplicably drawn to the doctor's green eyes. She holds her gaze for a few moments longer than intended. "I will escort you to the office and introduce you to Barry, the farm manager. Please follow me," Chris instructs. "He will be delighted to help you and is far more able to answer any questions you may have."

"Thank you," she says curtly, throwing her shoulders back.

"I tend to the house and staff. We are all one big happy family here," Chris informs her, hoping the doctor will get the picture. The owl watches intently, ruffling her feathers, as the pair cross the farmyard to enter Barry's office.

Chris introduces Doctor McCormack to him. He is getting ready to deposit the takings to the local bank. He notices that this prospective client cannot take her eyes off the open case sitting on his cluttered leather topped desk. A look of unusual curiosity spreads across her face. It appears as if she has never seen such a large amount of cash and checks in her entire life. He also observes she is twirling her diamond-encrusted wedding band around her slim finger, looking distinctly uncomfortable. Barry is now acutely aware he will have to postpone his planned trip to the bank. He firmly clicks the case shut before removing the handcuff from his wrist and locks the case in the safe. He places the key carefully in his jodhpurs' pocket, all the while smiling and remaining attentive towards the woman in front of him. "Sorry about that; you have my full attention, Dr. McCormack." Barry says gesturing for her to sit in the large leather chair opposite his own which Nanny had bequeathed him.

"Thank you, but please call me Beth. Please drop the doctor title, I seldom use it, although it can be useful at times, I must admit." Beth lets out a little chuckle, which momentarily makes her sound amusing and appear friendly, but Barry feels instinctively wary of her. He thinks she may be a prickly character.

"I am interested in boarding my two horses with you if you have any vacancies," she continues without hesitating. "I will require your best stable for each of them. They devour top of the range food and I need lots of love shown to them on a regular basis," she adds, flicking her long straight auburn hair over her left shoulder. Barry does not care for this woman's attitude but as she is a potentially valuable customer, he suppresses his gut feelings. He notes that she did not enquire about any costs during their conversation. Beth glances briefly at the leaflets on the desk but refrains from picking one up. Sitting back in the chair, she rubs her tongue over her perfect teeth, deep in thought prior to continuing her list of requirements, or demands depending on your point of view. "My horses are named Rupert and Nellie. Rupert is a twelve-year-old gelding and a loveable rogue. Nellie is a ten-year-old mare with major attitude." Much like you, Barry thinks. "I have had both of them since they were foals. I broke both of them in myself, and if I may say so, I am very proud of what I have achieved with them. It is a hobby of mine, not that I have much spare time." Barry holds her gaze, willing her to finish talking about herself. "My horses," she continues, "are my world since my dear husband passed away over two years ago."

He responds by saying, "I am very sorry to hear that," while trying his best to sound at least a little sincere.

"Thank you," she replies, her eyes welling up slightly. "He was in a coma for a couple of months before passing from pneumonia after a horrific riding accident in a show jumping competition."

"Oh that is awful. I do not need to know any more if it upsets you to talk about it," he replies with genuine concern.

"No, it does me good to talk about it," she continues with what Barry detects as a slight Irish lilt to her voice. Out of the corner of his eye, he notices Grampy returning home and waves to him as he passes the large mud-splattered window that he now wishes he had cleaned. He did not expect Grampy back so early in the day.

Entering the office, he is quickly followed by Kate who grabs a bucket and sponge to clean the mess from the window. "Excuse the interruption, I'm here to take Victoria to her hospital appointment," he explains. His eyes linger on Beth. He cannot help himself admiring her ample bosom for a few moments longer than he should have. Barry notices his gray moustache twitch for the first time in over a year. It is good to see some emotion other than grief coming from Grampy, he thinks, but I wish he would leave the office now and not pay any more attention to this phony.

At last, Grampy introduces himself to Beth. "Hello. I am Grampy," he says displaying unusual interest in the visitor.

"Beth McCormack. Nice to meet you, Grampy," she replies with a gleaming white smile.

Grampy appears lost for words for a moment then splutters, "Would either of you like a coffee?"

Barry nearly keels over in amazement as he cannot help but stare back at Grampy. In all the years he had worked at Hope Farm, he could only recall Grampy making two drinks for anyone. They had been tepid and had to be poured away. This was very out of character for him. The last thing the staff needed was for Grampy to fall for a woman who would be unsuitable in his golden years. Both say, "No thank you," so he leaves the office to collect his daughter and head back into town.

Following a long but productive discussion, Barry retrieves the briefcase from the safe leaving Beth with his newly appointed temporary assistant to view the premises. He gives the doctor his assurance that he will call first thing in the morning to get her verdict.

He rushes to the bank where Nigel is patiently waiting in the foyer beside two chairs with a bottle of juice in either hand. He personally deals with the deposit and he and Barry relax, chatting idly after the close of banking.

"What a day I've had," Barry sighs as Nigel listens intently knowing this will most likely be another story about a new client. Nigel thinks to himself, I'll bet this is Doctor Beth. Nigel has the misfortune of having had dealings with her and her late husband in the past but has no desire to disclose any information about either of them. He is acutely aware of her abrasive manner and hopes she has mellowed in recent times. When Barry confirms his suspicions, his immediate concern is that she will try to lure Grampy in. He knows that Grampy is still sad and vulnerable after his wife's demise. Nigel respects him very much as a person, and he does not want to see him get hurt in any way. Desperately trying to dismiss these thoughts, Nigel asks Barry if he would like to have a meal with him at the new Scottish pub in town.

"I sure would," Barry replies enthusiastically. "As it happens I was hoping to visit it this weekend. We could wash it down with a pint or two of Guinness. Do you think we need to make a reservation, Nigel?"

"I have taken the liberty of doing so already," Nigel laughs flashing his teeth and smiling his endearing smile as he always does.

Walking briskly up the steep hill from the bank, they both glance at their reflections in store windows, admiring themselves while checking that their hair is still in place. Both have naturally curly hair, which can only be controlled with scissors or with the use of copious amounts of products. Nigel and Barry are not the type of men to wear shorts with a dress shirt, or brown shoes with black laces. Neither would ever be seen unshaven while entertaining a woman. To them, the very thought of any of these scenarios is unthinkable. Nigel in particular liked his women to be fun loving, kind, and thoughtful, and he appreciated a smart appearance. Barry remembers him saying in a previous conversation "Any expensive jewelry would be an added bonus."

While looking at the menu by the door of the pub, Barry suggests, "I thoroughly recommend the local lobster, as I know it has been caught fresh this morning." He is looking hungrily across the road to where some fishermen are still unloading their day's catch opposite the harbor restaurant.

They admire the nautical décor as they enter the restaurant, appreciating the mood lighting providing a relaxing and welcoming atmosphere. The elegant slender server with a tartan apron shows them to their table beside a large aquarium which bubbles quietly. "I would like a bottle of your best white, chilled to perfection please," Nigel says seductively to her. Returning Nigel's gaze, she smiles and blushes slightly as she notices how handsome he is.

"Certainly, gents," she replies sweetly, "I will be straight back with your wine and some water."

Turning to Barry, Nigel asks, "Would you like to wear the bib they provide? I will if you will."

Barry, unsure if Nigel is serious retorts, "No I certainly would not! I would rather ruin my designer pants with melted butter and mayonnaise than wear one of those things. If you even think about donning one, even for fun, I will leave you sitting here by yourself. Bibs are for babies and tourists. Incidentally, you are beginning to sound like my mother." He laughs aloud as soon as the words leave his lips. Nigel admits defeat with a shrug. Enjoying their meal, Barry encourages him to talk about Doctor Beth McCormack, as he strongly suspects Nigel must know more about this woman than he is willing to divulge. A vague nagging suspicion about her grows stronger as he remembers hearing rumors regarding her husband's death circulating at the show-jumping competitions a couple of years ago.

Nigel is a master of discretion, a keeper of secrets. He is the type of man who takes great delight in throwing verbal bombs into conversation, then walking away with an expressionless face, leaving everyone wondering what is really going on, and what is behind what he has just said. Nigel hopes he has not said too much on this occasion but has said just enough to arouse Barry's suspicions about the doctor.

CHAPTER 12

The next morning, brilliant sunshine greets the farm. Barry remembers that his first job of the day is to phone Doctor McCormack to enquire if she has made her decision as to whether to board Rupert and Nellie at Hope Farm. He notices the message light on the phone flashing, indicating that business has started before he has. "Message number one," the phone says, "Good morning everyone, Beth here. I would like to confirm I have no hesitation in boarding both of my horses with you for the probationary period of six months as we discussed yesterday. From the onset, I would like them placed on either side of Sir Gareth's stall. I shall await your return call before setting up payments with Nigel Saunders at the bank. Have a good morning. Goodbye."

He stares at the phone for what seems like an eternity. He is delighted with her decision, but is acutely aware that she has already started demanding preferential treatment. Nanny had instilled in all of her staff training, that everyone is treated equally at Hope Farm. After taking a few deep breaths to calm down and collect his thoughts, he picks up the phone and calls Beth. As he expects, her phone goes straight to voicemail. He leaves a short but polite message acknowledging hers and asks for her to return his call at her convenience after surgery. I bet it isn't even her practice, he wickedly thinks before turning to his long list of chores. His first chore is a private lesson for a very rich local family.

Before leaving for work, Grampy pops his head around the office door, saying to Barry, "I think we need to employ a night watchman. What do you think? I am alone here at night now most of the time, and if anything were to happen to either myself or the animals, there is no way I could manage to get them to safety all by myself."

"That is a very good point, Grampy," he readily agrees. "The thought did cross my mind. I will advertise at the local job center and online later today. Will you want them to board in your house or how about including the unused trailer for them as part of the deal?"

"Yes, the trailer is a great idea. I do not want any strangers in my house. I will leave it in your very capable hands. I must rush as I don't want to be stuck in the heavy traffic on the bridge. Have a good day, Barry."

"Thanks. You too."

*   *   *

Arabella Farquhar has been a frequent visitor to the farm for several years. The frustrating thing for everybody is that she does not listen to instructions and takes umbrage when instructors try to help her. Arabella had been known to have hissy fits in the arena, much to the amusement of bystanders. On this particular morning Barry has no option but to correct her as she is pulling heavily on the bit and squeezing Pixie's tummy urging him to go faster, sending conflicting messages to the pony. As Barry corrects her for the wellbeing of the animal, which does not belong to her, she turns a shade of puce and screams at him, "You shut up! My father pays a lot of money so I can do whatever I like."

Just as he is about to correct Arabella, her father Charles enters the arena from the gallery, looking slightly embarrassed having heard his daughter's tirade. Trying to defuse the situation, and noting Barry's well controlled irritation, he asks Arabella to dismount and hands Pixie's reins over to Barry to hold. Barry cannot believe his ears when he hears

Charles ask his daughter if she would like a car or a pony of her own for her sweet sixteenth. "A horse, stupid!" she replies, "but not an old nag like this one."

Barry tries his best to remain silent, putting into practice the expression that Nanny taught all her staff to adopt when faced by clients being rude and disrespectful. "Good grief!" he mutters to the owls perched on the fence beside Aitch and Jumper. The horses are swishing their tails, swatting the copious amount of flies, which seem to have appeared this week out of nowhere. "I wonder what Nanny would have made of her attitude," he mutters. He holds onto that thought which he finds strangely comforting.

A disappointed Barry instructs Arabella to remount and indicates to Charles that this is neither the time nor the place for their conversation. She trots off around the arena without permission. Barry notices she only has one foot in the iron and that her mount's girth is loose. Barry shouts, "Arabella, stop and adjust your tack." His instruction for her safety goes unheeded. He shouts once more and again Arabella deliberately ignores him, thinking she knows better. He looks up in search of divine inspiration. The two owls sitting quietly in the rafters enjoying the show meet his gaze. After half-an-hour of lesson, which feels like two hours to him, he tells Arabella it is time to cool Pixie down. Still in a defiant mood, she uses her whip and taps Pixie heavily on the rear. Pixie, full of fear, sidesteps to the left and rears up throwing its rider into the air. Arabella crashes heavily into the wall. He runs quickly to her aid, picking up Pixies' dragging reins on the way.

Jay-Jay runs into the arena having heard the commotion while he was mucking out the adjacent stalls. He takes charge of Pixie, leading it back to the stall, quickly returning to assist Barry and Charles. A slightly embarrassed and bruised Arabella limps, with the boys' help, out of the Old Barn. She sinks heavily into the silver grey leather seats of her father's new Cadillac. Charles turns to Barry asking him, "Can we meet in the office, please, as we need to talk?"

"Step this way, Mister Farquhar," Barry says, escorting him out of the arena, "Would here be alright with you, though?" gesturing for him to sit on the comfortable sofa in the laundry adjacent to the arena. Barry sees no point in wasting his valuable time in going over to the office.

"Certainly," says Charles, "This will be fine."

Barry's begins to apologize but is quickly interrupted by Charles. "My daughter sometimes behaves like a complete and utter monster. I realize how much hard work she is for you and your fantastic staff; I greatly appreciate the time you endure with her. I have not been completely truthful with you. Arabella has certain difficulties which her mother and I find hard to acknowledge. We tend to bury our heads in the sand and make her behavior somebody else's problem. I now realize that we must get professional help for her."

A shocked and surprised Barry is unusually stuck for words at this unexpected statement and is unsure of what to say next. After careful consideration, he proceeds to say, "Arabella is making some progress. May I suggest that she take a break for a few weeks?"

Charles assures Barry, "I will speak to Arabella about her behavior," as he pulls out three hundred-dollar bills, folding them in half. He instructs Barry to buy pizza for the entire team as a treat. Barry begins to protest, saying, "We really appreciate your generosity, but we are only doing our job."

"Nonsense," replies Charles, "We are going on vacation for two weeks anyway. I will speak to my daughter while we are away. I will, of course, pay one month's fees to enable her place to be kept open, and I will call you on our return."

"No problem," a relieved Barry replies smiling, making sure he keeps eye contact. They shake hands firmly. Charles leaves the farm for home pleased that no argument or ill feeling has taken place.

The white owl amuses Barry for the remainder of the day, as it appears to him that she is showing the tawny how to catch mice and how to swoop and dive. He watches the two of them for a long time in between answering phone calls, riding lessons, and entertaining visitors from an out-of-town school.

He beckons to Kate, whom he recently promoted to head stable girl, to liaise with Lisa in showing the group of schoolchildren around the hydrotherapy pool. Their excitement and interest always encourages all the staff to give their best. "You only get one chance to make a first impression," is a phrase he remembers Nanny using frequently and, of course, she was infuriatingly correct most of the time.

"Jay-Jay," he shouts, "can you please assist Kate in taking Aitch, Perrah, Jumper, and Lady Jane to the pool for fifteen minutes? After that, take Sir Gareth, Rupert, The Jefster, and Nellie. If you wish, you can use any spare time you may have to take Flossie and Alfie. It will do them all the world of good."

"No problem, I will deal with them," replies Jay-Jay with a grin. "How I love to swim at the end of the day, it is so relaxing."

*　　*　　*

The following day, a rising sun shows the farm in its full glory. Ronnie the Rooster's call echoes for miles around in the still morning air. The crunch of gravel and the dust cloud indicates to Jay-Jay that Barry's Hummer is coming up the drive. The first job of the day is to enter Sir Gareth, Lady Jane, Perrah, and Jumper into the upcoming local agricultural show. On this occasion, Rupert will not be included. Paddy advised Barry to rest Rupert as he did not seem to be as calm and collected as he normally is whilst he was checked over the previous evening. Jay-Jay informs Barry, "He is still clearing the jumps, but something is bothering him. I can tell by his jerky movements."

"Okay, thanks for passing on the information, Jay-Jay. Now, take Aitch and Jumper to the hydrotherapy pool, please, before returning them to the field beside the duck pond afterwards."

Aitch has been retired from competitions due to an accident whilst out grazing. The cut on his leg has not healed as well as the vet has hoped, and his heart was just not in it any more since Nanny had passed. "Jumper is not firing on all cylinders either," Jay-Jay says to himself, observing the horses in the outdoor arena. He glances up into the sky where he sees a white owl circling the Old Barn with a tawny owl flying close by its side. Aitch looks up, following Jay-Jay's gaze.

Turning to Jumper that evening after observing Katherine fly alone into the Old Barn, Aitch turns to Jumper saying, "I wonder who the tawny owl might be? I don't know whether this is a good thing or not, but I think that the tawny owl is Katherine's trainee."

Jumper, deep in thought, shakes her head from side to side vigorously, then looks straight at Aitch, saying, "I am not sure that we are ready for the ramifications if indeed the tawny is Nanny, as I suspect."

CHAPTER 13

Katherine's regular magic enables the team to keep on top of their busy schedule. Each member of the farm's team simply thinks that someone else has completed the work. They never ever suspect that it is due to the magic spread around in the Old Barn.

At the next competition, Sir Gareth comes second, adding yet another gleaming trophy to Alistair Alexander's already impressive collection. The three thousand dollar prize brings a smile to his lined face. When the team returns to Hope Farm, he asks them all to gather in the staff changing room. Flicking his long grey hair, parted at the side, he smiles his crooked smile before giving a hesitant thank you. Reaching into his cream suede leather jacket, he pulls out a wad of notes. He kindly gives each of the staff a one-hundred-dollar bill as a personal thank you for their care given to his magnificent stallion.

Lisa immediately decides to bank hers. Every time she accumulates one thousand dollars, she gives it to Barry towards another "piece of Perrah" as she phrases it. He gently reminds her for the umpteenth time, "The phrase is 'a leg of Perrah', Lisa."

"Okay, okay. I will try to remember. Does it matter?" she asks, laughing as she packs her kit for the day. She shouts over her shoulder, "Do I own more than a hoof yet, Barry?" He simply smiles at her. "By the time I own her outright I will be too old and stiff to ride her."

79

Barry laughs, assuring her, "You will manage. If Nanny could do it in her old age, you can too."

With a spring in her step, together with this thought going round and around in her head, Lisa skips over towards the changing room, her mood visibly uplifted.

From the kitchen window, Chris Harrold, the farm's housekeeper, notices Lisa desperately requires new jodhpurs. She is aware that most of Lisa's money goes towards buying Perrah. Chris returns to thinking about the large clear bag of Nanny's old riding clothes she had spotted in the attic the previous week. Climbing the narrow wooden staircase, her wrinkled hands clutch the rail Grampy had made from a wooden oar. Carved into the blade is the name "Nibbs". The oar came from Nanny's old rowing boat. The memory stirs a deep feeling of sadness within Chris. I am so glad Nanny placed this rail here, she thinks gratefully. Oh, how I miss her. I wish I could meet up with her right now for a chat. It is exactly what I need.

Pushing the bags to the top of the staircase, she lets them tumble down the steep wooden steps, contents spilling onto the empty bedroom floor. Numerous pairs of jodhpurs, polo shirts, dress shirts, and tiepins scatter out onto the fringed woolen rug. Noticing a large black journal, she stares at it, realizing that it is private, but the temptation becomes too much for her. Kneeling beside the large pile of clothes, she reads the title, "My Years as a Single Parent". It has a sticker of a big smiley face on the top right hand corner of the cover. Chris flicks through the well-thumbed pages knowing she should not be reading it. Excitement and anticipation overwhelm her as she looks over her shoulder, checking that no one is around. She wonders if Grampy has ever read this little gem. After reading the first two pages, she decides most probably not! Tucking it into her large apron pocket, she tries to convince herself that she is protecting Grampy, all the while she cannot wait to get home and read it from cover to cover after her long day ends.

Carefully sorting the clothes into piles, she examines each article in turn before deciding what she will offer to Lisa. She takes three pairs of jodhpurs, a shirt and a tiepin. Deciding to take only a few items, she piles the remainder back into the bags before dragging them back up to their hiding place in a corner of the sunny attic.

On her way home, she decides to pick up a pizza for supper so as not to waste any valuable time before scrutinizing the diary.

The following morning, Chris returns Nanny's journal to where she found it. She has convinced herself that Nanny would not have minded. I had better get back to my daily duties, Chris thinks. Try as she might, she cannot erase the contents of the diary from her mind. She found herself bursting into fits of laughter periodically throughout the day. I had better come up with a good excuse as to why I am laughing so much in case anyone catches me, she thinks. Tears run into the deep wrinkles of her face from time to time as she recalls both the amusing and sad entries in the journal over the five-year period recorded by Nanny. Oh, how she missed her friend!

CHAPTER 14

This year, the competition season is very productive for Hope Farm, finishing in second place in the provincial standings. Nigel is both delighted and impressed with the balance of the farm accounts. He has a personal interest and takes great delight from the success in the last three meets of his horses The Jefster and Princess Pamela. He unexpectedly receives an offer for one of his racehorses. The caller had a German accent and was an acquaintance of Liz Smith's. A meeting was set up for the following month for the interested party to visit.

As Chris dusts Nanny's old room, she decides to pick up the journal to read it one last time. On doing so, she laughs and cries all over again. After careful consideration, she decides to take it home and burn it in her back yard. She feels extremely guilty but believes that it is for the best for everybody's sake. She sincerely hopes Nanny would have approved of her decision in the given circumstances. Chris knows she is going to join her friend very soon. She has suffered from a persistent cough, but after having visited her doctor for further tests, she made the difficult decision not to have any further treatment.

"It is my choice. I've had a good life," she informs Barry and Grampy as she hands over her letter of resignation to them, sad eyes welling up with tears. They stare at her in total shock as they were completely unaware her illness had returned. At that moment, all the stable hands burst into the office to collect their instructions for the remainder of the week, thankfully interrupting the somber mood. As Chris turns to leave the office, Grampy, not knowing what to say, clears his throat then issues the instructions to the team. Thankfully, they are oblivious to the sadness filling the room and carry on with their daily tasks.

Barry calls over to Jay-Jay who has come to collect the cart and pitchfork standing outside the office. "I'm sorry I forgot to return the cart to you. Do you fancy having a picnic supper with me in the paddock later?"

"That sounds like a fantastic idea; are you sure you have enough for two, as I am starving?" asks Jay-Jay.

"I have enough for three," is his quick reply, "I knew you would be hungry and I knew you would say yes!"

* * *

At suppertime, Jay-Jay meets Barry by the gate to the paddock. Barry has a small red cooler full of ice and drinks standing beside him. He is holding a picnic basket in his left hand, his iPhone in his right as he checks his messages for the umpteenth time that afternoon.

"I'll give you a hand with that if you like. You've got your hands full," Jay-Jay says.

"Oh, so what's new," he says, handing the picnic basket over.

They spread out their picnic neatly on the rug in the paddock, devouring the scrumptious food, washing it down with homemade lemonade. Suddenly they become aware that they are not alone. They peer through the white wooden railings to witness Grampy and Beth walking hand-in-hand along the path, flirting outrageously, completely unaware of spying company. Barry turns to Jay-Jay, saying with irritation rising in his voice, "We should move away from here." Just as they is about to stand up, they hear Beth say to Grampy, "I'm only trying to help so I hope you don't mind me saying, I think it is time you made a clean sweep with your staff. Life goes on you know, new broom and all that."

Barry looks at Jay-Jay in total shock and anger. "No way," he hears Grampy say, raising his voice higher than normal, "I have loyal, caring people working for me. I wouldn't dream of changing any of them, except for maybe just one of the laborers."

"No," Beth quips back, "You are in charge of them. They work for you, not the other way round," she snaps before continuing, "Come on, hurry up I'm running out of time rapidly here. I need to see Rupert and Nellie before I start my evening surgery at the practice." A stunned and angry Grampy trots behind her like a lap dog, admiring her slim silhouette in the fading light. I am so lucky to have someone like her pay me so much attention, he thinks. I must make sure she does not slip through my fingers so I will consider her opinion.

Barry and Jay-Jay pack up their picnic in an unsettled silence. They leave the paddock in total shock to complete their work for the day, neither uttering a single word as their minds race with worry.

CHAPTER 15

Grampy and Barry are working together in the farm office when the phone rings bringing sad news. Barry picks up the phone to hear that Chris had slipped away peacefully in her sleep. He sympathetically informs his boss of her passing.

Grampy is visibly upset as he recalls how much Nanny had loved her, probably more than Chris had realized. Feeling a little awkward at his selfish thoughts, he says to Barry, "Where am I going to get a housekeeper as good as she was? I only have Eldora, the temporary housekeeper, for another few weeks. She has to return to Riverhouse Hotel then and doesn't want the position permanently. I have already asked her."

"Well, today is your lucky day, Grampy. I took the liberty of looking around for available housekeepers, as I knew this would be the inevitable outcome. I bumped into Liz at the farmer's market yesterday. She mentioned her sister Annie is looking for a job. She is fifty and for the first time in her life is about to become unemployed. Annie had asked Liz if she knew of anybody looking for a housekeeper. Liz gave me her number, and I can call her later to set up an interview if you are interested."

"Yes, absolutely," replies a relieved looking Grampy, smiling as Beth glides elegantly into the office trailing a waft of expensive perfume.

"Come here, Grampy. I have something to show you." Beth beckons. They stand at the doorway looking out towards the car park. Grampy's square jaw opens slowly, his grey moustache twitching, as his eyes are drawn towards the gleaming new black Mercedes convertible parked in his parking spot. Flicking the remote, Beth opens the trunk, brushes her hair over her shoulder with an elegant wave of her hand and indicates to the contents. The trunk is loaded with plastic containers together with bags of fruit and vegetables. She smugly informs Grampy, "I've cooked lots of meals for you to put in your freezer. I know you haven't been eating properly since Chris left. Eldora's culinary skills have not been up to your standards, as you mentioned several times."

Witnessing this spectacle, Barry suspects Beth is trying to pull at Grampy's heartstrings through his stomach. Smart move, he thinks as he tries his best to shake the thought from his mind.

"What a fantastic car!" Grampy exclaims, his eyes widening. "You didn't mention you were getting a new car, Beth. You do have good taste." Gazing back at him lovingly, she nods her head in agreement. They empty the trunk and head towards the house with their arms heavily laden.

Barry turns to see Jay-Jay running across the yard towards the office wearing an extremely worried expression. "Oh no," he says almost running out of breath, "I forgot to leave a note for you yesterday, Barry. Alistair wanted me to enter Sir Gareth in the circuit's biggest competition at Willowvale. I told him I would do it, but I forgot. I am so sorry. I hope it isn't too late. If it is he will kill me!"

"Well, let's hope for your sake it isn't too late, you idiot. You'd think with age you would improve," Barry says with a broad grin on his heart shaped face.

"Oh, shut up, Mister Perfect!" Jay-Jay mutters under his breath.

"I heard that," Barry retorts. Out of the corner of his eye, he sees Beth crossing the courtyard heading straight towards them. Jay-Jay, not looking where he is going opens the door to rush out and bumps head on into Doctor McCormack. Breathing heavily and sweating profusely, he gestures for her to go ahead, while holding the door open. He apologies, "I'm sorry, Beth, I was in too much of a hurry, not looking where I was going as usual."

Beth looks directly at him as if he was a piece of dirt on her Italian leather court shoes, saying abruptly, "Get out of my way, boy. I am a very busy woman."

Jay-Jay turns round, desperately wanting to tell her to drop dead. Thankfully, he meets Barry's stern gaze, which stops him, just in the nick of time, from being rude to the customer. "Please excuse me, Doctor McCormack." Jay-Jay deliberately lifts his arm up high to hold the door open for her. Beth has no option but to inhale the aroma of sweat, stale horse muck, and hard work as she enters the office, wearing an expression as if she is sucking on a lemon. Barry is angry with Jay-Jay but equally finds the situation amusing. Keeping his smirk firmly under control he instructs the jovial Jay-Jay to go to the Old Barn and keep himself occupied. "I will speak to you after I've finished here," he tells him sternly.

"Good enough," he says, with a huge smile on his face. He swaggers over to the Old Barn, as only Jay-Jay can.

The two owls are sitting quiet and motionless on the farmhouse chimneys. Tawny watches as Katherine flies down and leaves a large present on the hood of Beth's new car before circling back to rejoin her trainee. "Oh Katherine," Tawny exclaims, "I can't believe you did that! I thought you were supposed to lead by example."

"I know," replies the white owl with slight embarrassment. "Let's go for a short flight. I need to drop off a martingale in the Old Barn for Jumper. She is entered in the downs cross-country tomorrow. I think I need to sprinkle some magic as I overheard a conversation between Barry and Jay-Jay. They are thinking of retiring her, but I know that she has a lot left to give. By leaving a martingale on the top of her tack box, her rider will try it, with a little bit of magical persuasion thrown in for good measure. Jumper will give a better performance, enabling her to be kept in the team, at least for the time being."

Tawny agrees with her mentor's decision, asking, "Do you intend to use just a tiny amount of magic dust?"

"Yes. Why do you ask, Tawny?"

"Well, much as I understand the reason behind it, I feel that my team may become dependent on it if it is used too liberally."

"Good point, Tawny. You are learning, but don't worry. I am only giving a little bit of help where I feel it is justified. As you grow as an owl, you will be able to judge better where and when to use your own magic powers."

*   *   *

Jumper is contentedly chewing through a net of juicy hay Kate had left for her. After oiling Jumper's hooves and bandaging her legs, Kate makes her as comfortable as possible after their long hack through the woods that afternoon.

The owls fly into the Old Barn once again. After spreading their veil of magic dust, they place the martingale in the tack box. The owls check all the remaining tack boxes lined up ready to be loaded into the horseboxes for the following morning. Everything is present and correct except for Rupert's sheepskin noseband, which they know is his rider's lucky charm. Tawny turns to Katherine and asks, "What would Hope Farm do without you?"

"They would do well, just not as well, without a little bit of magic here and there," is the wise reply. The owls begin to fly circuits around the indoor arena, inspecting the scene. Tawny watches Ruby canter Aitch around the edge, limber and nimble after a swim in the hydrotherapy pool.

After a thorough grooming, Lisa leads Jumper into the arena with Jay-Jay following close behind, checking for any signs of injury. Looking over to where the special needs horses, Sophie and Heidi, are standing, he says to her, "If I didn't know better, I would say those two horses are having a conversation."

Handing him the reigns, she replies, "You are crazy, Jay-Jay. Even I know animals and birds cannot speak." Lisa struggles to lift the saddle from Sophie's back. "Can you give me a hand with this large saddle, please? It is very heavy and wide."

"Wow, what size is it?" he asks as he lifts is down from the horse.

"I think it's a sixteen," she replies with amusement. "I hope my rear end never gets so big that I would need this." She affectionately pats the big brown mare on the neck.

Jay-Jay looks at Lisa, his squint teeth showing through his cheery smile. "I just want to say thank you for taking extra time with the special children in their class. It really does make a huge difference, you know. The horses mean so much to them. Their personalities shine through as they gain confidence with each lesson. When one of the parents came to pay, she mentioned how much more strength her son has in his legs now."

"Thanks, Jay-Jay. It is very kind of you to say so. I know from personal experience that it is true. Nanny encouraged me to do specific exercises to strengthen my grip, and I am passing on what she taught me to others who need the help."

"Good old Nanny," Jay-Jay says, "I should have listened to her more. She was a feisty dame."

Tawny looks down at them with pride in her heart. That's my boy, she thinks, that's my boy.

CHAPTER 16

A nip in the air accompanies the rising sun the following morning when Nigel calls into the farm to check on The Jefster and his new acquisition, Princess Pamela, before going to his work at the bank. Not wanting to get out of his Jaguar, he lowers the window and issues instructions to the stable hands. Humoring him, they reply with jest, "Good morning, Nigel. You do your job and we'll do ours, unless you would like to help us."

"Not a chance in these clothes. My pants alone cost more than your week's wages." Nigel raises his hand and roars away down the driveway shouting, "Eat my dust, Jay-Jay!" laughing all the way to the main road.

Both of Nigel's horses paw the ground in dismay on witnessing his departure. "I wish owners would either be of some help or keep out of the way. They don't seem to understand that horses are like children at times. It would serve Nigel right if both his horses failed to place," says Joe McGregor, the newest member of staff.

"Do not ever speak about a client like that in either Barry or Grampy's earshot, Joe. It is disrespectful even if you are correct," Jay-Jay informs him with a smirk on his tanned face. Joe nods and apologizes before walking slowly towards the main barn.

Barry is thankful to find anybody willing to do the thankless job of stable hand. It is a rewarding job but extremely hard work. On this occasion, he had regretted hiring Joe. Up until the end of his probationary period, his work had been meticulous. Now it appears he has lost interest. Looking out of his office window, he sees Joe ambling his way across the farmyard. Joe rhymes with slow, he thinks. "How can I get rid of Slow Joe, Grampy? Do you have any suggestions?"

"Not off the top of my head," Grampy replies sternly. "You must remember what Nanny used to say, 'Bide yer time' and more often than not she was right! We will get rid of him one way or another, you will see. Please be patient."

Barry watches Jay-Jay and Joe load the horses into the farm's large horsebox in preparation for the Willowvale competition. All load beautifully with the exception of Lady Jane, who has decided to be awkward this morning. "You had better pull your socks up, Lady," says Liz as she takes the reins from Jay-Jay to lead her horse around the yard before attempting to reload her into the horsebox. Her plan works, Barry notes.

* * *

The owls fly into the Old Barn after all the horses make a triumphant return. As Katherine had expected, Jumper takes first place at the downs cross-country, having had one of her good days thanks to Katherine's idea of using the martingale together with a little magic dust. Jumper kept her head up enabling her to focus and perform better than of late.

Tawny observes Jumper's rider slip the winning ribbon into her jacket pocket, so she sees to it that a duplicate ribbon appears on the winner's board above Jumper's stall. The white owl turns to her trainee, saying, "As it has been a long and troublesome day for the staff, we will spread a tiny bit more magic in the barn, Tawny. Just enough to ensure all the chores are completed before they load up the washing machines. The entire team looks exhausted."

Tawny is full of pride at Jumper's performance. "Okay Katherine," she agrees with her mentor, "you are a very wise old owl. They have all worked extremely hard." With that said, the owls take flight, trailing a thin veil of magic dust behind them as they fly around the Old Barn.

* * *

Paddy Lovett calls in for a coffee on his way home from work, reminding Barry to book Effy and Vic to come and shoe as many horses as possible for the following week. Paddy says to him, "I have a suggestion for you. I think I know how I can ease your work load."

"Oh really? I am all ears. Do tell!"

"Do you remember my saying that I thought I knew who owned Pixie?"

"Yes I do," replies Barry with an inquisitive look.

"A woman named Ethel owned her. This is where it gets a bit awkward, as Ethel is a very proud woman. I also happen to know she is an experienced equestrian. I knew her father and he insisted that she went to secretarial school. All Ethel ever wanted to do was ride horses. I happen to know that she is looking for a job, but to date has been unsuccessful. She told me this herself a couple of days ago when I met her in the Superstore. Looking very despondent, she remarked that if you are over thirty five, managers do not want you as their P.A."

With his curiosity piqued, Barry replies, "Well, I would be delighted to interview her. At the moment I am completely snowed under with work. Grampy is taking more to do with the farm now, but he still instructs part time at the college in town and he either cannot, or will not, do more here. It is his prerogative after all, but I could do with his help. I will work on him."

"Baby steps are the way to go," suggests Paddy, "with Grampy." He is relieved, as he knows Ethel desperately needs the money. "I can vouch that she is an excellent worker and has lots of experience in the equine fraternity. I will leave her number with you on two conditions."

"And what might they be?" an excited Barry asks.

"You must never let her know that I told you she needs the money, or mention that I know Pixie used to belong to her." "You have a deal. I can say I heard about her from the Job Bank. I am so glad you came by, Paddy. I will phone her shortly and hopefully set up an interview soon. I hope she is still available, I have a feeling that she is just what we need. I am sure Grampy will be happy to hear this news, and if he isn't I will persuade him otherwise."

"By the way," Paddy says hesitantly as he removes his glasses to clean them. "I just wondered if Effy and Vic are due any day soon. I heard Effy is thinking about retiring."

"I've got to call and book them for next week. Why do you ask?" Barry inquires.

"Just to give you the heads up, I think you should look for another blacksmith, as I heard a rumor that Vic only wants to do small businesses if he continues with his job at all, which I very much doubt."

"Oh, that's a surprise to me. I will put that on my to-do list. Gosh, can you imagine how long it would take Vic to do all the horses here by himself? He would have to live here permanently and work overtime!"

"Ha, ha," laughs Paddy. "You are wicked, Barry, but it's so true."

Paddy waves goodbye before jumping into his Land Rover closing the car door onto the flap of his waxed jacket and then driving away rather quickly. I'm so tired of telling him not to drive past the horses like Jay-Jay, Barry thinks, but I don't suppose he will ever listen.

Picking up the phone, he dials Annie's number, hoping that she will able to attend an interview within the next couple of days. Luckily, she is extremely interested in the vacant position and he schedules her interview for the following morning rearranging his very busy schedule. He then phones Ethel. As it turns out, she is in her car when he makes the call and is not far from Hope Farm. Ethel offers to come straight away if it is convenient. Barry thinks quickly and agrees to interview her immediately. He informs Grampy of the impending changes.

"That's what I pay you for, my man," Grampy says. "I trust your judgment implicitly. You do your job well. I'm off to look for a new computer tomorrow morning, as I don't start work until midday. One good thing about being single, Barry, is that you don't have to inform anyone if you are going to buy another computer," he chuckles before adding, "Neither do you have to justify it."

"How many do you actually need, Grampy?"

"I've always wanted an iMac and now I'm going to get one," he says as he leaves happily for work, waving enthusiastically to Liz Smith who is pulling up in the farmyard as he drives away.

"Hi Barry, how is my Lady Jane behaving?" she inquires.

"Beautifully," he replies confidently. "She is such a happy and contented horse. We treated her to a swim after being exercised in the woods and she is now about to be fed. Would you like to accompany me to the Old Barn to join the others?"

"Sure." They walk stride for stride towards the outbuilding. Turning towards Barry, Liz says in an odd but enquiring tone, "I hear Doctor Beth McCormack has joined us at the stables."

"She has indeed. News travels fast. She has brought both her horses, Rupert and Nellie, with her. Yesterday she indicated that she might be purchasing another horse, however, this might cause a problem as I am reliably informed that Nigel from the bank is also interested in the same one."

"Oh my goodness, if this is true it will be very interesting," Liz replies placing her hand over her mouth. "Which horse are they interested in?"

Before Barry can reply, an unfamiliar car pulls into the farmyard. He checks the Omega watch that Nanny had bequeathed him in her will. It is time for Ethel's interview. Trying his best to maintain his composure, he excuses himself, explaining, "I have an interview to conduct and this must be her arriving."

"No problem, I will speak to you later. Good luck with the interview," Liz says, waving a friendly goodbye before tending to her beloved horse.

The middle-aged, rather old-fashioned woman is wearing her hair scraped back in a bun. She smiles as she gets out of her ancient red Volkswagen beetle. She looks around the premises, unsure of where to go. On seeing Barry walking towards her, she asks, "Could you tell me where I can find Barry, please?"

"You have found him,' he says, thinking, Paddy must be having a laugh with me. I will get him back.

Ethel offers her hand. Barry notices how neat her short nails are and how firm her grasp is. "You must be Ethel. Please come into the office, make yourself comfortable, and I will get Kate to make me a coffee, I'm so thirsty. Would you like a drink, Ethel?"

Unsure of the correct response, Ethel hesitates before replying, "Water would be good, thank you."

He picks up the microphone on his desk and calls, "Kate to the office please, Kate to the office." Looking at Ethel he asks, "Would you like ice and a slice of lemon in your water, Ethel?"

"Oh, that sounds very grand. Yes, please," she replies, looking around at the exceptionally smart interior of the office. "It is unusual to see so many family photographs in a place of business," she observes.

"I suppose it is. Nanny always liked the place to be homely."

On hearing Barry's announcement, Kate throws her shovel to the ground aggressively. Folding her arms firmly in front of her, she points her left foot to the side and mutters to herself, "I'll bet he wants me to do something he could do perfectly well himself, then he'll expect me to have time to complete my long list of chores." Walking swiftly to the office, she soon finds out that her suspicions are quite correct.

Barry makes the introductions. "Kate, this is Ethel. Ethel, this is our head stable girl, Kate." The two women eye each other and smile politely. Barry continues, "Could you get water with ice and lemon for Ethel, and I would like a coffee with milk, please, Kate."

"I'll be right back," she replies politely. With a face like thunder, she reluctantly goes into the farmhouse to deal with the request. Spying a large glass bowl of fresh fruit on the table, she eats a banana while waiting for the kettle to boil and helps herself to an apple and a chocolate cookie which she places in her polo shirt pocket. After collecting the drinks, she carefully carries the tray back to the office.

On her return, noticing the two deep in conversation, she stands by the open door waiting for Barry to invite her in. Sadly, for Kate, she has forgotten about the chocolate cookie in her pocket. He beckons her to enter. "Thank you very much," Barry and Ethel say at exactly the same time. All three burst out laughing. Barry notices the spreading chocolate stain on Kate's chest and says, "You can go to our washroom if you like to clean yourself up," nodding in the direction of the spreading dark brown stain on her top.

"Caught in the act!" she says, turning on her heel to return to her chores.

After a surprisingly impressive interview, Barry has no hesitation in offering the position to Ethel on a three-month probationary period. She is elated, her lined face lights up. She immediately accepts the job offer together with all conditions, before asking, "Would you mind if I have a walk around the stables. I have my rubber boots with me."

"You can wander anywhere you like. Unfortunately, I cannot spare anyone to accompany you just at the moment, but if you are happy to wander on your own, it will help you to familiarize yourself with the surroundings in preparation for your start on Monday." Leaving the office, she cannot wait to go towards the field where Pixie is grazing happily. Tears of joy run down her face as she catches sight of the Welsh mountain pony. As she strides over to the field, Pixie recognizes her and trots happily towards the fence. Both are happy to be reunited.

*   *   *

The following morning, three applicants arrive for the position of housekeeper. The first one resembles Mrs. Doubtfire, Barry thinks as he leads them into the house. He asks two to wait in the drawing room, telling them to help themselves to the refreshments Eldora has prepared. He asks the Mrs. Doubtfire look-alike to come in first, knowing that he will not be able to concentrate on the others if he does not do so. The woman has a large bosom and several missing teeth. Way too distracting, he thinks, and she is too full of herself. The next applicant looks as though she would eat more than she would cook. He remembers Nanny instilling at staff meetings that "You should never judge a book by its cover," however, on this occasion he thinks he is most definitely correct. The final applicant, he is sad to find out, is not Annie. She is an inexperienced girl from Cuba. Uncertain of her immigration paperwork, he decides not to risk employing her. He feels guilty about this decision as he thanks all three for attending, promising to let them know his decision the following day. As he waves them off, he cannot believe his eyes as a motorcycle roars up the driveway. He stares in disbelief as the rotund driver removes her helmet and shouts, "Hi, I'm Annie. Sorry I'm late."

Just as the words leave her mouth, she switches off the bike's engine and it splutters to a halt. "No problem at all," Barry replies trying not to laugh at the unexpected vision before him. "Do come in."

Annie follows Barry and collapses onto the soft comfortable chair, grateful for its width and high back. He allows her a few moments to compose herself before starting the interview. He uses the pretense of excusing himself to get a drink of water, knowing that Annie would benefit from a drink also. After he gives her sufficient time to cool down, Annie gives the interview of her life and Barry knows within two minutes of starting it that he has found the correct person to fill Chris's shoes. Annie is unable to stop herself throwing her arms around Barry's neck when he offers her the position of housekeeper. She can hardly contain her excitement as she waves goodbye before roaring away on her motorcycle at a great rate of knots, nearly knocking Liz into the fence in her excitement as she zooms past.

The toot-toot of Grampy's jeep is heard as he returns home early. "Hello everybody, how are we all today?" he asks sporting a huge grin before enquiring, "Has Beth come over to see her horses yet?"

"No, not yet but no doubt she will be within the hour," Barry answers slightly irritated. "Why do you ask?"

"Oh no particular reason," he lies. His chocolate brown eyes twinkle in the twilight as he informs Liz and Barry, "I am going to spruce myself up before supper. Can you phone Henry and ask if Elliot can come over to give me an estimate to redecorate the drawing room and the lounge in the farmhouse, please?" Without waiting for a reply, he heads towards the house as both Barry and Liz look up towards heaven, praying that they are both wrong in their thinking that Grampy is trying to get the attention of Beth. "He is trying to obliterate Nanny, bit by bit," Barry mutters to nobody in particular.

"Are you thinking what I'm thinking?" Liz asks him.

"Yes, sadly I think we are both on the same page. I find her aggressive, rude, and abrupt."

"Me too," Liz agrees. "I find her quite frightening to talk to and rumor has it she is a recovering alcoholic."

"Oh my goodness," Barry exclaims. They both stare at each other as he shrugs his shoulders, "This is all I need, on top of everything else."

CHAPTER 17

At the end of the following day, everybody was exhausted. Barry makes an announcement over the PA to ask for as many staff as possible to assemble in the farmhouse kitchen. In the huge kitchen, a large plate of freshly baked cookies sits in the middle of the century old farmhouse table. Two large pots of freshly brewed coffee fill the room with a wonderful aroma. As the staff members enter in dribs and drabs, the coffee and cookies are shared around. Barry, wearing a serious expression, is the last team member to arrive.

"I apologize for the short notice," he begins, "but it has been brought to my attention that we need to employ yet another trainer and stable hand. My concern is that the stables are becoming bigger than we can manage ourselves." He pauses for a moment as a murmur of agreement passes around the room. "Much as I recognize that this is a good complaint to have as we appreciate all the business, I feel we cannot give the required time to all the horses as some require more time than others. Can everybody please put on their thinking caps and get back to me with your suggestions of how we can improve our service, bearing in mind that this is a business. I do not want to hear that we must hire more people. It is not as simple as that; contrary to belief, money does not grow on trees around here." An array of heads nodding in agreement meets his gaze. "My second and final point, and I will try to keep this brief, is the recent poor performance of Jumper in competitions. As most of you are aware, it costs a great deal of money, not to mention our time, to keep a horse in top form. I would also like to remind everyone that the entry fees at this level are very expensive. I would like to give you this opportunity to voice your opinions about Jumper's inconsistency and your suggestions as to what we can do about it."

Kate responds immediately, "Jumper did win last time out, but I do realize she has recently stopped taking chances at fences. She has become so cautious that she is picking up three points for refusals on a regular basis. It defies comprehension at times. Using a martingale last time did help, I must admit. I will see to it that it will always be used from now on."

"Thanks for your input, Kate. Jay-Jay, you look like you want to say something."

Turning to Kate, he says, "I might have known you would stick up for her. In my opinion she's a lost cause and takes up way too much of our time and energy these days."

Barry quickly interrupts before the situation escalates, saying, "I do not want to take up any more of your valuable time this evening. Personally, I think she is a sweet old girl, but then again, we may be better off retiring her and putting her with the donkeys. They would blend in well together."

"That is an awful thing to say," Lisa interjects, with a hurt look on her face.

"Meeting is adjourned," proclaims Barry, not wanting the conversation to continue any further. "You may all go. Thanks for your time."

*   *   *

A new day of competition begins at the Willowvale showground. The team is relieved when all horses board well and arrive without incident. The atmosphere is electric as the riders in full regalia walk the course in their red jackets. In the outfield, every single horse looks magnificent. Without exception, their pricked up ears show they are ready to go.

Lady Jane's mane looks gorgeous in a newly crimped style. Her tail is in a tight bun with ribbons woven through it. "Where on earth did you find the time to do that?" Jay-Jay asks Liz.

She replies smugly, "I didn't. I dared Seamus to do it for fun, but as it turns out, she looks fantastic. I am grateful to him as I have just been informed we won one hundred bucks for the best turned out horse. It is so sad that he is socially inept as he is such a kind-hearted young man."

Liz notices Seamus running towards her with a huge grin on his face, waving the prize money. "This is crazy," he says. Liz immediately informs him, "You can put that in your pocket, on the condition that you put it towards your wedding, Seamus." He stares at her in disbelief before shaking her hand vigorously and does as Liz suggests. He grins from ear to ear and appears to float as he runs to tell Lisa about his stroke of luck.

Lady Jane continues to have a successful day. She gallops with pride, every muscle rippling as she glides over the last double oxer at the end of a very grueling course. She shaves almost three seconds from Sir Gareth's impressive time, knocking him into second place, much to Alistair's displeasure. Liz accepts Alistair's congratulations with a gracious smile as they receive their prizes at the presentation ceremony.

Barry has to leave the showground before the final event of the day, as he is interviewing two candidates for the position of night watchman. "Awesome job, everybody. I will see you all back at the ranch!" he teases before climbing into his Hummer.

Seconds later, Perrah breaks loose after a bucking and rearing horse from another stable startles her. Perrah charges straight into a cotton candy wagon. Jay-Jay and a terrified Lisa run to her assistance, grateful that nobody was in Perrah's path. After checking the spooked horse over, Lisa walks her around the show ring twice while the duty vet follows inspecting the animal for any signs of injury. Loud neighing and whinnying aside, no damage is apparent. The team gives out a huge sigh of relief as Kate phones Barry to inform him of the incident. She has to leave a voicemail message, as his phone is off while he is driving. This is a great relief as she knows she would be peppered with questions had he been able to answer his phone.

* * *

Back at the farm, the interviews for the night watchman go well. Barry makes the difficult decision to hire a man with dark wavy hair and a slight stoop. His name is Ian Mitchell, but most people call him "Flash" he informs Barry. He is thankful for the offer to live in the trailer located behind the new stable block. Barry and Grampy are relieved to have someone occupy it, as it had been vacant for several months. Flash leaves the farm to pack up his possessions in his lodgings at the old sawmill where he worked previously.

It suddenly dawns on Barry that he has not totaled up the "treat money" since Nanny had passed. This was something she had started over twenty years ago. She would treat her staff periodically to a cinema ticket, a meal, or sometimes a day off with full pay if she felt they required it. On opening the large blue cash box, he is amazed at the amount of large denomination bills filling it. Confused, he tips it all out onto the top of the filling cabinet. A pink envelope addressed to "The Farm Manager" sits on top of the notes. The letter inside reads as follows.

> *"Dear Barry or his successor. I have left some money for you to distribute at your discretion, or to use for a staff party if any occasion arises for celebration. I have just the one exclusion that I hope you will respect. It is not to be used for any celebration that involves Grampy with any other woman! I trust that you will carry out my wishes*

implicitly. If you are Barry, then I have another surprise for you that you will receive at a later date. If you are not Barry, then I wish you good luck in your position, you have big boots to fill. Thank you and enjoy the celebration. Nanny, xx."

Barry remembers that of late, more than one member of staff has lost their sparkle and many are looking fatigued. A night out might be exactly what they need. Nanny had always been acutely aware that people had different needs. He remembered during his second week of training her exact words, "Always be discreet and never let the person know that you are aware that they may be struggling for whatever reason. Use your initiative and experience. If you cannot think of a valid reason to give them a rest without making them feel inferior, then use yourself as the reason they need to stop and talk with you. This will enable them to catch their breath without embarrassment."

Suddenly, Grampy appears at the window, breaking Barry's daydream, smiling a weak and weary smile. "Hi Barry, how's it going?" he asks trying to sound and appear interested.

"Busy as always," Barry replies, "only one problem today that I can't solve myself. Effy is sick and he left a message to inform us that he is now running two days behind schedule."

"You mean you can't shoe horses as well, Barry?"

"Thankfully not or you would have me doing that too!" he says in jest. He notices Grampy cannot even muster up a chuckle at his remark. He watches him walk towards the locked glass cabinet. Carefully unlocking the door, he removes the silver casket containing his beloved wife's ashes. Barry stares silently at his boss as Grampy whispers, "I'm taking Nanny to the cottage. It is the right time for me. She will be in pole position for the first time in her life as I scatter her ashes by her headstone. It sits in front of the one that will someday be mine." Few people knew where their hideaway was located. That was how they had wanted it and that was how it would stay.

As Grampy leaves, Barry struggles with the vision in front of him, made even worse when he imagines Beth zooming into the picture. He tries desperately hard not to imagine Nanny wrapped in a blanket on the veranda. After a few minutes deep in thought, the shrill ring of the office phone brings him back to reality. He picks it up.

The caller is Henry McCulloch, a trusted painter and decorator, and an old friend of the family. He is calling to confirm that his son, Elliot, and his new assistant Pedro will call in on their way to another job the following morning. They will measure up for the decorating and leave sample books. He asks Barry optimistically, "Have you been given carte blanche?"

"Gosh no! That raises a good question. Who on earth is going to choose the materials?" Barry's immediate thoughts turn to Beth as his heart sinks to the pit of his stomach. "I will need to discuss this with Grampy. Let's hope it's a day where he will listen to what's being said. I'll speak to him when he comes home and let you know what is decided. On second thoughts, I have a better idea. I will phone him. We will have a better chance of him being focused on the phone, rather than trying to speak to him face-to-face."

"I'll leave it in your capable hands. Bye, Barry," says Henry.

Hanging up the phone, Barry is reluctant to think of the idea of new decor, as losing both Nanny and Chris within a relatively short space of time has been hard for him to deal with. With everybody being so busy with the daily business, he has not really given himself enough time to grieve properly. He thinks back to a conversation that has taken place shortly before Nanny died. He had popped in to have a coffee and a cheese sandwich with them. They were discussing that there were no real short cuts to the grieving process. Disbelief, numbness, anger, and the rollercoaster ride of emotions all have to be worked through. "The passage of time alters the pain," he remembers Chris saying to Nanny, who had broken down at that point. Now he himself realized what both women meant. He turns back to the treat tin as if in a trance, still stunned by Nanny's generosity, to put the money away.

Jay-Jay, Kate, and some of the owners enter the office just as Barry scoops the money back into the tin before locking it securely away. They all start to talk at once about the successful day they have all had. A visibly shaken Lisa starts to tell him about Perrah.

"Whoa, whoa," he interrupts. "What are you talking about?" Barry has not checked his iPhone, still switched off in his jacket pocket, so he is unaware of what happened after he left the showground. Henry was the only person he had spoken to since leaving.

"Perrah broke loose and clattered into a wagon," Lisa starts to explain. "It is all right though. Doctor David Whillis, the duty vet, checked her over and declared her fit to travel, as there were no obvious signs of injury. However, he recommended someone be with her for at least the next twenty-four hours at all times." Lisa shoots her hand up into the air, "I will be delighted to be that person of course. It goes without saying."

"Okay, that's great Lisa," he tells her, "The cot is in the laundry. You might want to take a comforter from the house to lie on. I think there are only blankets in the stables."

"Thanks, Barry. I will do that."

Barry's eyes drift towards Seamus who is staring out of the window wearing an exasperated expression. "What's up with you?" Lisa asks her fiancé, noticing the sour look on his face.

"Oh, nothing," Seamus replies with a downtrodden look, his shoulders hunched. "You have obviously forgotten," he continues sadly, "that you are supposed to meet my Aunt and Uncle Stevens this evening to have a meal with them.

I do understand though, I might as well get used to it as I know Perrah will always take first place in your heart." Seamus hugs her and swings both her hands from left to right before placing a kiss on her cheek.

"Good night, Seamus. I will still be here in the morning. You know where to find me. Can you bring me a coffee from Tim's please?"

"Would you like a breakfast sandwich too? We could eat together."

"Oh yes! What would I do without you?"

Barry watches a tearful Lisa wave goodbye to her fiancé. Blowing her nose noisily she walks silently, with hunched shoulders, towards the Old Barn.

* * *

Tawny and Katherine decide to take a night flight around Hope Farm. Noticing that the light is shining more brightly than normal under the barn door, Katherine gives the order to investigate. The owls soundlessly fly in, landing on Sir Gareth's stall. He softly whinnies to them tossing his magnificent head in the direction of Perrah. "Stay here and stay perfectly still until I tell you otherwise," Katherine instructs Tawny.

"Okay," Tawny responds reluctantly. She wants to be included in the action. Katherine flies up to the rafters looking down on a sleeping Lisa and an uncomfortable-looking Perrah who is tossing her head back and forth wildly. The wise old owl, having assessed the situation flies back to Sir Gareth's stall and asks Tawny to accompany her. "Only a small amount of your weakest veil of magic dust, Tawny, distributed in and around the stall. This will ensure both Lisa and her horse are rested and well. A very important point you must remember is that any magic dust used around the witching hour of midnight is twice as potent as a normal measure. You must never ever forget that Tawny. Too much, if you do forget, can do more harm than good.

At the midnight hour you must always keep your wits about you."

"Thanks for the advice," Tawny replies. "I had no idea about that. Can I talk to Perrah?"

"No, I want us to fly away from here, as we really should not have come in tonight. It isn't strictly necessary, just helpful. I think I'm getting soft in my old age," Katherine says with a laugh.

"Twit-to-woo," Tawny cries as they fly over Perrah's stall. They then fly out in a leisurely manner through the gap in the Old Barn door into the dark night, lit up by the twinkling stars and the almost full moon.

CHAPTER 18

Dawn breaks, and Seamus is the first to arrive at Hope Farm, carrying a brown paper bag containing two breakfasts. Just as he is about to enter the Old Barn, out of the corner of his eye he sees Grampy heading towards Perrah's stall. "Good morning," they both say to each other in unison, followed by fits of laughter. Grampy exclaims, "Oh boy, this is too early for this nonsense! I'll be exhausted by lunchtime as I know this is going to be a long and possibly a sad day."

Both men stare at one another in disbelief as they enter Perrah's stall. They see Lisa curled up in a ball on the cot with her left leg sticking out from under her purple comforter. The horse is munching on the dampened hay and blows bubbles mischievously in the water trough. "I take it all is well then," declares Grampy, "I will leave you and your fiancée to do whatever you need to do in peace. Barry phoned me half an hour ago to enquire about Perrah. Tell Lisa he called when she wakes. I will call him with the good news on my way to work. Have a great morning."

"Thanks Grampy. It looks like I just might have a good one now. I'm going to let Lisa sleep a little longer if that's okay with you."

With a wide grin, Grampy replies, "Let her sleep as long as she needs. It's fine with me."

"Thanks very much. I will. You have a great morning too. It looks like it's going to be a gorgeous day."

Grampy struts happily across the farmyard, climbs into his pumpkin colored Jeep and heads off down the drive only to meet Barry coming towards him. Both vehicles stop side by side and their windows simultaneously buzz as they are lowered, inviting the crisp morning air in. An anxious looking Barry asks, "What sort of night did Perrah have?"

"Absolutely fantastic by all accounts," Grampy assures him. "Go and see for yourself. Lisa is fast asleep and I have given Seamus my permission to let her sleep as long as she needs. I think you should get Kate to assist him with the special needs class today. The apprentices can deal with all the feeds. I'm sure you can deal with whatever else requires attention," he laughs before speeding away. Barry shakes his head and mutters to himself, "He'll never change."

Barry checks his reflection in the office window before unlocking the heavy door. The phone starts to ring before he can remove his leather jacket. "Here we go," he says to himself. As if by magic, Ethel breezes in behind him, bringing an overpowering waft of lavender perfume, and picks up the phone. He turns on his heels and heads towards the farmhouse, preferring the aroma of Annie's bacon to Ethel's perfume.

"Morning Annie," he shouts as he pushes open the oak kitchen door. "I'm here with the breakfast order. Jay-Jay will be here soon with the order for the stables. Six bacon rolls with HP sauce, two sausage with ketchup, four fried egg rolls, two over easy and two hard, please and thank you, Annie."

"Yup, I've got it," she chirps as she writes the order down on her notepad. "I hope Jay-Jay won't be long as today I have a lot of shopping to do to restock the pantry. I am also expecting the decorators. I can't leave until they arrive, which is a pain in the neck actually, but I didn't like to mention this to Grampy with me being new to the job. He doesn't seem to realize how much goes in to running this house. Other than that, I find him to be a very good boss so far! Did you know that Grampy asked me for my opinion on color schemes?"

"No, I didn't. I'm glad someone else is involved in that decision," Barry says, filling a travel mug with freshly brewed coffee. "I was hoping to have some input, but I haven't been asked. I hope he doesn't involve too many people in helping him out, especially in an area he knows absolutely nothing about. He should stick to his electronics and computers and let everyone else get on with what they do best."

"Well, he is paying for it!" she retorts as she quickly makes up the order. "We will have to let him have his say. Then we can convince him otherwise, if my previous discussion regarding color schemes was anything to go by! I thought he was pulling my leg when he gave me his suggestion for the drawing room. I don't know what the old girl was like but her impeccable taste shows throughout. I absolutely love the house the way it is, but I do understand he wants new decor. It does need a bit of freshening up I suppose."

Retying the bow on her apron for her, Barry reluctantly replies, "I guess you're right, Annie. Time waits for no man. A word of advice, please don't refer to Nanny as the old girl." He leaves the warm and organized kitchen carrying his coffee in one hand and the huge oval wicker basket containing all the breakfast orders over his other arm. Annie had thoughtfully covered the basket in a red gingham towel to keep the food warm. He meets Flash the night watchman on his way over to the barn and hands him his breakfast sandwich.

"Thank you so much," Flash says gratefully, his salt-and-pepper wavy hair sticking out from underneath his black baseball cap, "I am ready for this. This morning at four thirty, I would have given you twenty bucks for a bacon sandwich. I only had two pieces of chewing gum and a candy bar to keep me going through the night. After I have had a sleep, I must go to the store to stock up on groceries. Do you need anything while I'm there?" he asks Barry politely.

"No thanks, Flash. Annie will get the stock required for the office when she goes later, but I appreciate you asking. Boulderstone Construction is coming today to start widening the gallops. I hope the backhoes and machinery won't keep you awake."

"Don't worry about the noise. Thanks for the heads up, I will put my earplugs in."

"Oh incidentally, Flash, Kate won the equestrian voucher for nicknaming the gallops 'The Racing Snake'. I think it is a very good name don't you?"

"I'm not surprised she won with that name. I love it." Flash heads off in the direction of his trailer with his head hanging low with fatigue.

"Have a good sleep. See you later."

Barry delivers the basket of food to Ethel who distributes it to the waiting staff seated on the old wooden bench in the vestibule at the side of the office. Through the window, a movement catches Barry's eye. He thinks he sees Beth's slender figure slipping into the house, but the arrival of a battered old white Mini Cooper grabs his immediate attention. From the car steps ten-year-old twin girls, Carole and Fiona, accompanied by their exhausted Aunt Jean. They are very excited at the prospect of their first riding lesson at Hope Farm. Barry has a keen interest in cars like hers, as his uncle had owned a blue one a long time ago. His uncle had frequently taken him out for drives in years gone by, much to his delight. Aunt Jean slams the car door shut, calling out, "Where's Barry Gordon? Are you Barry Gordon?" Jean asks in a demanding tone, her forehead creased as she speaks in a gruff voice.

"I am indeed, Ma'am." He offers her his hand. As luck would have it, he has their paperwork with him in preparation for their arrival.

"No need for sarcasm," Aunt Jean replies, "I need to sign the papers for the girls and pay somebody responsible for their tuition." Desperately trying not to laugh, he thinks, she is worse than my mother was. He assures Aunt Jean, "I am the farm manager, and I will also be the girls' instructor for today. I can take your money, or if you would rather, you can pay my assistant Ethel." He gestures towards his assistant who is brushing the office entrance with a corn broom.

Aunt Jean glances over his shoulder and scrutinizes Ethel from head to toe as she stands in the office doorway. Ethel leans her broom against the wall and steps forward expecting to receive the prepared check. Aunt Jean decides that Barry looks more responsible than Ethel does so after careful deliberation she hands him the fee. Ethel and Barry exchange glances, both intrigued by this character. Lifting her left leg, Jean rests the consent forms on her thigh, taking the top off the pen with her teeth before proceeding to sign them. There are two benches and numerous cars around which she could have leaned on, but nobody dared to suggest it. She then proceeds to wave the papers directly under Barry's nose.

Carole and Fiona giggle in the background whilst trying to tie their brand new black velour riding hats. "Carole, tie yours tighter!" Aunt Jean demands. Fiona smiles and shyly follows Barry towards the indoor arena.

"Okay girls, your Aunt Jean has informed me that you have ridden many times in the last two years, so I would like you to look at the horses in front of you and choose whichever one you would like to ride today. Let's see what you can do."

"I would like the piebald, please," Carole immediately informs him.

"No problem," he replies. "She's all yours."

Fiona looks up and down the animals but cannot decide which one she would like to ride. Carole starts to tack up after Barry introduces her to Domino, her ride for today's lesson. Fiona is still undecided, so Barry chooses a skewbald called Morag for her, as he is acutely aware of the time passing rapidly. "She can be a bit feisty but keep her head up at all times and you will soon get used to each other," he advises Fiona.

She quickly tacks up trying to catch up with Carole who is already at the door of the arena shouting, "Heads up," as she enters confidently. "Hurry up, Fiona, Morag is eager to start, and so am I."

"I'm coming as quickly as I can," Fiona says, scuttling along behind her sister.

A voice from the end of the corridor calls, "Where can I get some coffee around here?"

Kate, who is working in the adjoining tack room soaping up all the leather, hears the commotion. Dropping the sponge into her bucket, she rises and puts her head around the corner of the room and shouts, "Sorry, we don't have a coffee machine here. It would be too dangerous for the animals. You are welcome to bring in your own flask of coffee in the future if you wish."

"Humph," Aunt Jean snorts, "If I were to bring a flask, it wouldn't have coffee in it." Kate returns to her work unable to hear whatever tumbled out of Jean's mouth next.

Surprisingly, the girls' lesson goes exceptionally well. Aunt Jean had been accurate in her statement about the abilities of the twins as they were both competent riders. Barry assures them that they will have a lot more time in the saddle on their next lesson, as they now know the ropes in getting their mounts prepared. "Any time wasted means less time in the arena," he gently reminds them.

"Can I have the same horse next time?" Carole asks.

"That depends on how often Domino has been ridden on that particular day. We will decide when I see you next week." Both girls thoroughly enjoy grooming their horses before thanking Barry. They clamber back into the little old car driven by their little old aunt who is now wearing a yellow turban with a huge sparkly pin attached to the front. A huge bang comes from the car's muffler as it backfires when Aunt Jean turns the ignition on. Whinnying and neighing echoes around the farm and the thunder of hooves from the paddocks add to the hilarity as Aunt Jean and her nieces depart, allowing the farm to return to daily business.

CHAPTER 19

The decorator's white van pulls into the car park. Elliot McCulloch knocks before entering the office. "I like the new image," Barry remarks greeting his friend.

"Thanks," Elliot says, "I felt it was time for a more mature look as I was getting tired of my long hair."

"The short brown spiky cut suits you. It complements your hazel eyes."

"You are too kind," he says laughing, "Let me introduce you to Pedro, my new assistant."

Barry extends his hand shaking Pedro's hand firmly. What a foxy looking face you have, Barry thinks. Feeling slightly guilty at that inexcusably rude thought, he offers both men a cold drink.

"No thanks," they reply in unison, before Elliot adds, "We won't be here long. We are just here today to measure up and provide an estimate for the job. I will leave the books and swatches here for Grampy to peruse. Now while I remember, Henry passes on his good wishes to you."

"Oh, Henry, yes thank you. Are he and his wife both well? Still making a fortune with his artwork?"

"They are very well, thank you. I don't know about making a fortune, but he and his wife still have lots of fun in their golden years. Both enjoy playing golf in various parts of the world. I believe he met up with his sister who was on vacation in Australia last month. So, I guess you could say they are enjoying life to the full."

"I'm very pleased to hear that. Pass on my best. I will let you and Pedro get on with your work. Annie will let you in and show you what needs doing. You will have to excuse me, I have to go and confirm all the entries for tomorrow's show. I must see to it that the riders have all the equipment they require. I also need to confirm all travel arrangements before I can go home tonight, so you will have to manage without me, which is probably a good thing."

Elliot and Pedro thank Barry and walk towards the farmhouse where Annie is standing in the doorway waiting to greet them. She smiles her toothy grin and waves her arm gesturing for them to enter the imposing hallway. Annie takes out the list of instructions Grampy had left her to give them from her large torn apron pocket. Opening it with a flick of her finger, she begins to relay the instructions to the decorators who are standing in awe at the size of the job before them. Elliot is the first to speak, "Gosh, I don't remember this house being so big. Has a wall been taken down in here?" he asks Annie indicating to the massive expanse on his left.

"I don't know," she replies, "I haven't worked here long. My predecessor worked here for many years but sadly is no longer with us. It does look like the property has had some alterations done at some point. My note says the drawing room requires top quality wallpaper on the top half and the oak wainscot needs stripping and staining," she reads from the instructions.

Before Annie can continue with Grampy's list, a voice booms out, "It would be a much better idea if the wainscot was removed all together. Classic pale wallpaper should be hung throughout the entire room and hallway." Elliot and Pedro look at one another silently in confusion, unsure who the interrupting woman is. Annie's mouth is wide open as if in preparation to catch flies before she retaliates by saying, "Excuse me, did Grampy forget to inform me that you have some say in this? This house is not for the public; I am in

117

charge here at present until Grampy returns or Barry tells me otherwise. How did you get in anyway?"

"Who on earth do you think you are talking to?" Beth asks the shocked housekeeper.

"As far as I'm aware, I'm talking to a rude horse owner who should not be in here."

"Well, we'll see about that," a slightly embarrassed Beth replies as she glares at the three stunned faces staring back at her in astonishment.

"We can come back later when Grampy gets home," Pedro suggests.

"Absolutely not," Elliot says in disagreement. "I will phone him right now and get this sorted out." He takes out his cell phone and relays the incident to a patient Grampy on the other end of the line.

After a short pause, he hears Grampy reply, "Although I did not ask Beth to supervise, I think it is a fantastic idea to get her input, she has impeccable taste. My knowledge of interior design, as you know, is dire at best, so the opinion from a classy lady like Beth would be of great help to me, don't you think?"

A pregnant pause ensues. Knowing this was not the reply he expected or wanted, Elliot's stomach starts to churn. "This is very awkward," he says to Annie, "I don't know how to say this." Trying to avoid the smug expression on Beth's face, he relays Grampy's wishes. In disgust, Annie throws the written request from Grampy into Elliot's outstretched hand, turns on her heels, deliberately brushing Beth's elbow as she storms back to her kitchen in fury.

Beth continues to bombard Elliot and Pedro with orders, which Elliot dutifully writes down on the expensive notepaper taken from the hall table. The sound of Annie banging pots and pans with force on the granite worktops echoes around the building as she tries, unsuccessfully, to alleviate her pent-up frustration.

Snatching the phone from its cradle Annie dials Grampy's number. It immediately goes to voicemail. Slamming the receiver down, she then grabs it again, this time she presses the speed dial for Barry's iPhone. He answers her tirade by saying, "Whoa, whoa, slow down, Annie. Take a deep breath and tell me slowly exactly what has happened to upset you."

After Annie recites the entire story, Barry assures her that he will sort it out this evening before going home, on condition that she bakes him a chicken pot pie. "It's a done deal," she readily agrees. Before putting the phone down, he reassures Annie that he will meet up with her at the house for a chat and a coffee as soon as he possibly can fit her into his busy schedule. Knowing that he will keep his promise, and that he is on the side of Hope Farm staff, she feels reassured enough to focus on her daily tasks and she returns to her chores.

After spectacularly upsetting the apple cart, Barry witnesses Beth slip out the same door she had entered as if nothing has happened. He phones Grampy leaving an urgent message for him to call him back as soon as possible.

On checking his voicemail, Grampy realizes this request is out of the ordinary. He gingerly dials home expecting the worst.

Barry's phone rings four times as he takes a deep breath before answering. "Hello Grampy, bit of a problem here I'm afraid. Doctor McCormack has taken it upon herself to take control of the home improvements, overruling the suggestions you left with Annie who is now extremely upset."

"I don't see what the problem is," Grampy quips, "She only means to help. Besides, I think Doctor McCormack is an asset to the business."

Shocked and disappointed by Grampy's response, Barry thinks it best to keep the conversation short finishing with,

"I will see you later, or I will come in early tomorrow to speak with you."

"Okay, fine. I really don't know what all the fuss is about," Grampy exclaims.

This is going to be trickier than I thought, Barry thinks. Just because Grampy believes that Beth isn't vindictive, he appears to think it makes everything okay. He doesn't notice the things that other people see. Barry decides to let sleeping dogs lie as far as this episode is concerned but takes a mental note of the trouble ahead for them all. Beth's card is marked in his mind, and he makes the decision that he will never work for her, not even for Grampy's sake. He would rather be unemployed.

CHAPTER 20

The following day Liz has an unexpected success with Lady Jane in a show jumping competition. They had not expected to place at this particular event. She is so excited by her win that she decides right there and then whilst still on horseback to phone her husband in Dubai to inform him of the news. Liz quickly takes her feet out of the irons, dismounts, and jumps three times in the air with joy as she tosses the reigns to her stable lad. "Hurrah!" she exclaims loudly, "My husband is coming home for a month in two weeks' time. He told me to look around for another horse to add to our string as an early birthday present. He has suggested purchasing a racehorse this time."

All the entrants from the farm had produced their best efforts with Sir Gareth and Lady Jane bringing home firsts in their respective classes. Perrah scooped a third place from her closest rival from the next town, much to Lisa's delight.

A phone call to the office from the duty vet at the show, Doctor David Whillis, brings bad news for Barry and Hope Farm. Kate and Jumper have given their best performance, when Jumper clips the top rail of the triple oxer awkwardly. Jumper stumbles, throwing Kate over her head to the ground with a loud thud. Thankfully, Kate is unhurt, just a little bruised. Her fall looks worse than it actually is. She grabs the dangling reins and immediately witnesses Jumper's distress. Initially Kate tries to pretend she has not heard the loud crack of the horses' leg breaking, even though deep down she knows that Jumper will have to be destroyed if she is correct with her diagnosis. Try as she might, she is unable to ignore her beloved ride as it limps and finally comes to a complete and utter halt. Jumper is completely unwilling and unable to move.

Recognizing the horrific inevitability of the situation, Doctor Whillis immediately indicates to the team seated on the bottom row of the bleachers to enter the arena with the screen required for privacy in the event of an animal having to be put out of its misery. A single shot rings out, causing Jumper's relatively short career as a show jumper to come to an abrupt end.

"Oh my goodness," a stunned Barry replies, "I can't believe it. What a freak accident! Is Kate okay?"

"Yes, she is fine but still in shock," Doctor Whillis replies.

"Okay, thanks for letting us know. You make the necessary arrangements. I will attend to the rest."

"I will do, Barry. I really am truly sorry for the farm's loss. Jumper was a good horse, much loved by everyone," he said with genuine sadness in his voice.

"Thanks," is Barry's sad reply as he slowly puts the phone down. He stares in shock out of the windows looking across the farmyard. He watches Dom the Dude and Forget-Me-Not, the farm cats, as they sit on the tree roots grooming themselves. They clean each other's ears attentively, as Barry observes the first of the returning horses being unloaded.

Understandably, a somber mood hovers over the Old Barn on the team's return. Katherine, the wise old owl, sensing something is wrong, instructs Tawny to accompany her to witness the unloading of the horses. The owls perch on the large branch of the oak tree watching the scene. Katherine notices that the riders are all wearing sad expressions. She observes that everyone seems to be carrying out his or her tasks in a mechanical fashion without the usual banter being present. Katherine silently counts the horses as they enter the Old Barn, immediately noticing that Jumper is missing. Unsure of whether to mention her observations to Tawny, she decides to fly in circles around the farmyard in the hope that there is a good explanation for Jumper's absence, but suspecting all the while that a tragedy has indeed occurred.

Tawny notices her mentor's avoidance, while observing the team's return. Unwilling to wait for Katherine's return and instruction, she takes it upon herself to check out the Old Barn. The trainee owl flies through the gap in the wall, landing on Sir Gareth's stall door. She looks into Sir Gareth's now-glazed eyes. A very worried tawny owl spreads a thin veil of magic without her boss's permission, realizing that this is an emergency. "Where is Jumper?" she asks, all the while suspecting what the answer will be.

"She didn't make it," Sir Gareth says quietly, lowering his head. "At the triple she should have lifted her inside leg much higher than she did. She fell heavily, snapping her leg in two places. If it is any consolation to you, she was in pain for only a very short while until the vet dealt with her. He and his team were very close to the incident, so they were able to deal with the situation very quickly."

At that very moment, Katherine flies in and realizes Tawny has already learned of Jumper's demise. The wise old owl is displeased with her trainee for leaving the tree and using up some of her magic. However, on this occasion she decides to let it slip. The owls look into each other's eyes. Katherine extends her large wing placing it around Tawny's now slumped shoulders and gently pulling her closer. "Who needs words?" she asks Tawny.

Tawny gazes into Katherine's eyes, unable to move her beak. The shock and feelings of grief seem to ricochet around the stables. Tawny hugs her understanding boss. Sadness ensues around the entire farm. When Tawny was Nanny in her previous life, she had always instilled in her staff, "It is the way that you deal with difficulties that counts. You dust yourself off and carry on to the best of your ability with a brave face and positive outlook. Everybody has to understand that disasters can and do happen, especially with so many animals."

CHAPTER 21

Nigel arrives full of the joys of spring as today is the start of a long weekend. He greets everyone with his flashy smile as he strides towards the new stable block, now affectionately known as Miggles' Retreat. He had requested that his horses, The Jefster and Princess Pamela, be stabled there. Surprisingly, he had no hesitation in paying the large inevitable difference in fees for their relocation. He meets Liz en route, "Hi, Nigel," she says enthusiastically. "I haven't seen you for a while. Have you heard my news?"

"Well, that rather depends on what it is," he replies. A naughty look spreads across his face and his pale blue eyes twinkle with impish fun.

"My generous husband is looking for a new racehorse. He is coming back soon but I am starting to look now if you would like to assist me."

Nigel, unable to believe his luck, launches in with, "I would absolutely love to. It would be my pleasure. I wonder if you would like to walk your dogs with me later. We could go for a swim in the lake after we have tended to our horses if you'd like."

"That sounds like a great idea," she replies handing Lady Jane's reins to Kate.

Kate asks, "Would you like me to take her to the Racing Snake, or do you want to gallop her yourself, Liz?"

"Just warm her up for me, please, and I will race her against The Jefster presently."

"Oh, yes?" says Nigel enthusiastically. "I will wager dinner if you fancy."

"You are on, and what's more, I will beat you, hands down," she teases.

Nigel tends to his two horses before tacking up and meeting Liz at the start of the Racing Snake. The race is on. Nigel takes an early lead, The Jefster foaming at the mouth as they thunder along. Lady Jane almost catches up at the four furlong mark. One crack of Nigel's whip sends The Jefster into overdrive. Thinking she has lost the race, Liz presses her slim calves into her mount's tummy, giving her the encouragement she needs. They race neck and neck until the final furlong. The Jefster seems to run out of steam and Liz wins by a head. She suspects Nigel allowed this to be the outcome, but her suspicions cannot be proven.

Both riders dismount gracefully and take their horses back to Miggles' Retreat before turning their tired but happy horses over to the stable hands. Having thought Nigel's invitation through, she decides not to take her dogs to the lake, but arranges to meet him at the picnic bench by the water at 6:30pm.

Nigel glosses his white hair with oil before collecting his designer trunks together with a brand new Egyptian cotton bath sheet. At the lake, they greet each other with huge smiles and a friendly hug. Nigel leads the way as Liz follows behind, admiring his long legs. She seductively bobs up and down waist deep in the warm clear water creating ripples and bubbles. She feels angry at her own excitement at being in Nigel's company. Trying to appear calm and collected on the outside, she is incredibly aware of her heart pounding uncontrollably in her chest.

Nigel is also trying his best to appear cool and in control. He tries to keep his eyes from wandering over her impressive figure. They swim together in the warm water until their skins resemble prunes. He strides confidently ashore, leaving her alone in the water. He lifts Liz's velour towel from the lakeside bench, holding it open for her, inviting her to walk into his arms as he drapes it around her shoulders. He places a small towel over his head, taking his time to rub his own hair dry, so she has time to admire the toned, taut muscles of his smooth body. Liz is acutely aware of what he is doing, but cannot help admiring the view in front of her. They both smile widely at one another, before playfully sticking their tongues out at each other resembling children. Neither of them knows what the next move, if any, will be.

CHAPTER 22

Another morning comes around all too soon, only on this morning the decorators arrive in force. Annie dons her frilly apron with the now repaired pocket, asking what the men would like for lunch. "Could you possibly make a pepperoni pizza for me?" Elliot asks.

"I most certainly could, young man, and for you, Pedro?" She looks thoughtfully at his fox-like features.

"I would like fajitas, chicken if you have it."

"Great idea," says Annie, "I will make those two dishes for everyone with a large garden salad. That should keep everyone happy."

The two men work extremely well together and by lunchtime, they are both amazed at how much they have achieved. They now realize just how big a task decorating this house is going to be. Elliot in particular loves a challenge. Pedro goes outside to pet Flossie and Alfie, slipping them a mint from his deep pocket. After a few minutes, he returns to the house with his tummy rumbling hoping that Annie will have their lunch ready soon. All of a sudden he remembers he must ask Elliot if he could have the following Thursday off as his mother is having an operation on her foot. As he breezes into the kitchen the aroma of freshly baked pizza greets him, but he cannot find Elliot anywhere. Not wanting to disturb Annie, he wanders aimlessly from room to room without success. "Elliot, Elliot, where are you?" he shouts at the top of his screechy voice.

A voice from the floor above replies musically, "I'm painting."

Standing still with his mouth gaping open, a voice booming from the kitchen interrupts Pedro's thoughts, "Pepperoni slice is ready." Annie is standing with her large arms outstretched holding a huge tray laden with pizza and fajitas. As Kate passes, Annie asks her to announce lunch over the PA for all available staff before going to the cold room to fill up the pitchers with fresh lemonade and ginger ale.

*   *   *

On his journey home Grampy makes a massive decision. Just as he indicates to turn right at the farm entrance, he notices the love of his life on the opposite side of the road who is also indicating to turn into the farm driveway. "Good timing," he says to himself. They wave to one another and Grampy leads the way up the tree-lined driveway with his car windows firmly closed because of the enormous amount of pollen in the air.

Katherine and Tawny survey the land from high above. Noticing Beth and Grampy's arrival, Katherine gestures for Tawny to take a breather on their wide perch in the tree beside the office, oblivious of what is about to happen.

Barry watches the owls land from his open office window. How content the two owls look together, he thinks. Staring in panic, he watches Grampy stepping out of his car, saying hello to Beth then dropping on one knee. His jaw drops in horror as he hears Grampy ask, "Doctor Elizabeth Jane McCormack, will you marry me?"

"Oh yes, I would be delighted," a beaming Beth replies, throwing her slim, tanned arms around Grampy's neck, affectionately kissing his bald patch. Grampy slowly opens the lid of the bottle green velvet box in his left hand, revealing an exquisite diamond solitaire which sparkles in the afternoon sunshine. Looking into Grampy's eyes, Beth offers her manicured hand to him as he slips the perfectly sized ring onto her slim finger. He stands up and the couple head towards the office, hand in hand, smiling broadly. Grampy swings the office door open and enters with a newfound spring in his step. "I have fantastic news," he proclaims. "Beth has graciously accepted my proposal of marriage and we are now engaged!"

Barry suddenly feels a tremor in his hands that he cannot hide, as he extends his right hand towards Grampy. "Congratulations," he offers, addressing the happy couple.

"Gosh, you are shaking with excitement just as I am," Grampy observes as he feels Barry's hand tremble in his own. Barry politely turns to shake Beth's hand, observing the impressive rock on her slender finger. She deliberately flashes it right under his nose, wearing a pompous smirk. This is even more irritating to Barry than her normal smug grin. Knowing at this point, he should make a comment about the ring, he feels he simply cannot. He makes an excuse and leaves the room before he says something that he may later regret.

Ethel offers her good wishes and enquires, "When is the big day going to happen? I have a beautiful hat I would love to wear."

Beth and Grampy look at one another. Grampy stands silently resembling the Sphinx. Beth for once in her life is also dumbstruck. "Oh I don't know," she answers after a long pause. "This was a complete surprise to me. We haven't discussed it yet, but sooner rather than later if I get my way," she laughs as Barry re-enters the office with a face like thunder.

Here we go, this is the start, Barry thinks. "You will have to excuse me folks, I have a tremendous amount of work to do," he states, picking up his schedule from his desk.

"Absolutely no problem," Beth replies, "We will get out of your way and let you both get on. We have a celebration to organize, my man." Turning to Grampy, she commands,

"Follow me and take some notes as I dictate them to you." She marches out of the office.

Following behind and slightly surprised by her changed tone, Grampy, not wanting to have any type of confrontation, tries to diffuse his irritation by answering, "Yes my lady," hoping his sarcasm will make Beth laugh.

It does not. Annoyed by the stupidity of his reply, Beth glares back at him but thinks it better on this occasion to say nothing about it. For the first time she makes a mental note that, perhaps, he is not as quiet and reserved as he appears to most people.

Barry sits tapping the end of his pen against his teeth, deep in thought. He had known Grampy for a very long time so he knew him well. He appreciates that his boss needs to move on in his life, but is gravely concerned with Grampy's choice of partner. Not that I am any expert, he smiles to himself. From day one, he suspected there were many hidden agendas associated with Beth, and in his opinion, she is a phony. His mind flashes back to the day the check for Beth's fees bounced. He remembers witnessing her being in a major panic on her cell when he had informed her of the problem. He found it odd when two minutes later Nigel phoned the farm to say that the bank had made an error and that Doctor McCormack's payment should clear by the end of the day. It was entirely the bank's mistake. Barry suspected otherwise.

*   *   *

The newly engaged pair stroll hand in hand into the large entrance hall of the farmhouse. Annie, unaware of the latest development shouts, "Goodnight folks," as she grabs her old grey raincoat from the cupboard under the stairs.

"Annie, before you go I have something important to tell you," Grampy announces. "The doctor and I are engaged to be married. Beth will be making some changes around here." A stunned Annie drops her coat on the floor. He rushes to pick it up for her and they bump heads. Annie laughs while rubbing her forehead, mumbles her congratulations and staggers out, pulling the door just a little too hard for his liking, behind her.

* * *

Barry hears the slam of the front door and looks out of the office window to see what is going on now. Annie is marching towards him with her elbows pumping. It looks like she might take off any second, Barry laughs to himself. "Well, what do you make of that?" Annie proclaims. "I take it you've heard the news!"

"Yes, I have, and not a lot," he replies solemnly. "I feel it would be wrong to discuss our employer behind his back. Suffice to say I am going home to have a large drink and a long soak in the hot tub."

"Good idea," she says, "I wish I could do the same, but as I don't drink and I do not have a hot tub either, I will have to think of some other distraction. Goodnight, Barry. Tomorrow is another day."

"Goodnight, Annie. Thank you for the lovely meals today. Did you leave something in the fridge for Flash?"

"I did," she replies chirpily, "And a sardine for his cat, Slippers."

"You are a good soul. We will see you tomorrow. Try not to have nightmares. I have put fifty dollars into a box to start a collection for an engagement gift. Please inform all the staff whom you see tomorrow and I will deal with the remainder down at the stables. I will ask Ethel to type up a poster to put on the office door. I would like everyone to make a contribution, no matter how small."

* * *

At the farmhouse, Beth spins around gracefully in the hallway. She notices the huge painting of Nanny above the inglenook fireplace. That will be gone by this time next week, she decides. She grabs Grampy by the hands and waltzes him around for a couple of minutes. "Stop, stop," he cries, "I'm getting dizzy and my hip is hurting."

"Well I'm just the person to sort that out, am I not?" she asks playfully, before her gaze rests on yet another painting of Nanny tending to the some unknown farmhand's children. "What a beautiful painting," she says. "Who is the artist and who are the children?"

"That was painted by Henry, an old friend of ours. The children are a few of many over the years who were always around Nanny's apron strings. She was wonderful with children for many years before they became too much for her later on in her life." As he looks wistfully at the painting, Grampy momentarily questions himself as to why he is standing here with another woman.

Beth notices his sorrowful expression, so decides that this painting must go too. Handing him an embossed leather-bound notebook and a fountain pen, she begins to list the names of people she wants to invite to their engagement party.

"Why don't we light the log fire Annie has set for us, have a drink and relax? Surely tomorrow is soon enough to start making the arrangements," he suggests.

Beth gazes lovingly into his eyes and grudgingly says, "I suppose you are right. I'll have a mineral water, please. Let's have supper, I'm starving." Suspecting he may be procrastinating about the celebration, she goes into a huff, pouts her lips and bats her long eyelashes at him. This expression reminded Grampy of his sixteen-year-old daughter Victoria when he relayed to her the story of his proposal to Nanny. He had not planned that event either, and therefore he had no ring, far less a diamond solitaire. How Victoria laughed when she asked, "Did you not even have a ring pull from a can of pop?"

"No," was his wistful reply, "We only had a single bed, a sleeping bag, and a Chinese take-out!" How times had changed for him. He had felt huge pangs of guilt when he ordered the ring for Beth. He felt even worse when he had to ask for a slim fitting size six. For one horrible fleeting moment, he wondered if he had done the right thing but quickly managed to dismiss these thoughts. "I have an engagement present for you, Beth," Grampy informs her with his hand outstretched, indicating for her to follow him, which she does eagerly.

"What is it? What is it?" she asks excitedly, as they climb the wide spiral staircase.

"If I told you it wouldn't be a surprise," he says with his moustache twitching. His top lip rises slightly on the left hand side in a half smile. He opens the bedroom door with a flourish to reveal an enormous new sleigh style bed draped elegantly with a deep purple velvet comforter. Elaborate matching shams complete the luxurious look. Beth is understandably delighted with this gift as she realizes he must have gone to a great deal of trouble and expense to get the custom-made bedding. She glances around the room and is delighted to see both of the arched windows have new velvet window treatments in her favorite shade of muted pink, complementing the decor beautifully. She also notices that he had also taken down the large photograph of Nanny holding Aitch, stroking his mane which had hung above the headboard for many years. It had been Nanny and Grampy's favorite photograph.

Beth turns to kiss him and for once, she is truly grateful for the effort he has made for her. "How thoughtful you are, Grampy," she says, seductively stroking his neck. "I really appreciate the trouble you have gone to for me." Slight panic overcomes the doctor, as she does not have any gift to exchange. She has a flash of inspiration and excuses herself, using the excuse of needing some fresh air to get over the shock. Grampy is very glad of a few moments to gather his own thoughts. He is feeling incredibly unsettled.

Beth grabs her cell phone, looking up the home phone number for her surgery receptionist, Tina. Beth apologizes profusely for the intrusion as Tina answers. Tina is completely astounded, as she has never heard her boss apologize to anybody for anything, even when proven blatantly wrong. "Could you do me a massive favor, Tina, please? This is an emergency. Unexpectedly, Grampy has proposed to me. We are now engaged to be married."

"Congratulations," offers Tina hesitantly, "You have done very well for yourself." She quickly covers her mouth with her own hand, realizing she should not have made a comment like this to her boss, but she cannot retract it.

"Thanks," answers Beth quickly. "Can you go and buy a winch for his ATV? I am going to stay here tonight, otherwise I would go and get it myself. I would really like to surprise him with it tomorrow if possible. I have no idea how much it will cost, nor do I care. It will be money well spent."

"Don't worry, Doctor McCormack," Tina replies cheerfully, wondering what she meant by her last remark. "I will use my credit card, as long as it is not up to the limit, as my horses have cost me a fortune this month," she laughs.

"Call me back if there is any problem. I really appreciate this Tina, I won't forget it. I will see you at the surgery tomorrow morning." Beth flips her phone shut as Tina replaces her phone in its stand, noting that the doctor had not said even said thank you. She knew that Doctor McCormack seems to think she is above using basic good manners. Unbeknown to Beth, her rudeness is one of the many reasons why Tina is looking for a new job.

Neither Beth nor Grampy sleep well that night. The sound of hooting owls seemed to disturb their sleep on the hour, every hour. The farm cats are fighting and howling loudly at various times throughout the night. Beth thinks she hears the sound of a shotgun in the distance. She is unsure if she has been dreaming or if it has actually happened.

CHAPTER 23

Dawn breaks all too soon, with Ronnie the Rooster crowing at the top of his lungs. "Morning, Grampy," a disheveled Beth greets her betrothed. "Did you sleep well?"

He stretches and yawns before replying sharply, "No, I did not. Those owls need shooting as far as I'm concerned."

"You know as well as I do that they are a protected species," she replies with a tiny chuckle.

"I know," he replies reluctantly. "I must get a move on or I will get stuck in the traffic on the bridge."

"I must get a crack on too," Beth replies. Grampy notices her Irish lilt is more pronounced this morning. "I know I have a full case load of patients today. See to it that Kate and Joe exercise Rupert and Nellie first," Beth orders.

Grampy is shocked at her assumption in expecting preferential treatment already, but decides not to make any comment. He is fully aware that neither Kate or Joe, or anyone else in for that matter, will deviate from their assigned schedule, except in an emergency. That is how a business like his must operate in order for it to run smoothly. He heads towards the washroom to take a shower, feeling rather disgruntled.

Much refreshed after his shower, Grampy glances out of the bedroom window overlooking the stable block. To his horror, he notices some workers that he does not recognize using a backhoe. Slightly concerned, he picks up the old people's phone from his nightstand. He quickly calls Barry, aware that his heart rate is beginning to rise. "Good morning, Barry," he says courteously, "Do you know who these people are by the stable block? There are lots of workmen digging up the ground."

"No, I heard some noise when I arrived. I assumed you had hired the local firm we had used last time, and that you had forgotten to inform me. I intended to call you after I have dealt with the phone messages to find out what is going on."

"Well, unless I am losing my mind, I did not give permission for any construction to be carried out. I'll find out what's going on in a few minutes and get back to you."

"Erm, that would be very helpful, thanks."

As Grampy replaces the phone, a voice calls out, "Cooee," The echo of Beth's dulcet tones reverberates around the hall. "Oh my!" she suddenly exclaims, "I only spoke to them yesterday." She shouts up the stairs to Grampy who is standing at the open bedroom doorway looking angry, "I asked them to come round and build a new stable for my horses."

"You did what?" Grampy asks angrily. "What on earth do you think you are up to? For a start, you know full well that it would require planning permission."

"Well, you will automatically get that," she interrupts.

"Not necessarily," he disagrees, following up his statement with, "Who is going to pay for that, eh?"

"Well I am, of course," Beth retorts. He can tell by her expression that she is not telling the truth. She fully expected that the farm would pick up the tab. Panic begins to set in.

"This is my farm, Beth. We did not discuss any of this. As it turns out, planning permission shouldn't be a major issue." He decides to try to defuse the situation yet again. "I do agree the lady of the manor should have her own domain, but I would be obliged if you would discuss any future matters with me first. I am the farm owner and main wage earner."

"Now you just hold on a minute," Beth continues, her temper visibly rising, "Who do you think earns more money, you or I?" Without waiting for him to respond, she turns on her heel and storms away to see her horses before starting work, leaving her fiancé baffled, angry, and confused.

Feeling that his fiancée is manipulating him, he begins to feel despondent about the predicament he now finds himself in. Grampy knows he requires his partner to have a strong character. He feels grateful to have met a person who apparently cares for him and who is also academic. It made a pleasant change for him to have intelligent conversation at home, as well as at his workplace. Nothing delights him more than to be able to discuss politics, modern technology, and math with a partner who can follow the subject at hand. At this moment in time, Grampy realizes how much he misses the simplicity of Nanny. He misses the constant laughter, the spontaneity as he recalls the adventures they had at the drop of a hat for less than fifty dollars. They frequently had a great time without spending any money whatsoever. He greatly misses her ability to laugh at herself. What he misses the most of all was the drivel she used to discuss on a daily basis. The memory of the impressions she sometimes performed to highlight a story make him laugh even now. After a busy day in town, he would look forward to coming home to hear her humorous account of her day's events. The only thing he does not miss about his beloved wife was the deliberate and constant interruptions she made when he wanted to watch a Sci-Fi program. He is so relieved to learn Beth adored many of his favorite shows that he successfully convinces himself that they have a lot in common.

Sadly, he already realizes that Beth will never provide the fun Nanny did. He knows she is simply not capable of doing so. Already this is a concern to him. He also notices that every single member of staff, with the exception of Flash, politely refrains from comment regarding his new fiancée. Everybody is polite and they pass on their congratulations;

however, he is acutely aware that Beth is an unwelcome addition to the family. Needing to clear his head, he decides to take his three Welsh Springer spaniels for a walk beside the gallops.

He feels guilty after phoning his workplace to tell them he is feeling ill. However, not as guilty as when he asks himself some serious questions, being brutally honest with his answers. Am I really in love with Beth or am I just after her status and in need of companionship? Would I love her if she were penniless? Would I love her if she did not have her own business and income? Would I love her if she were uneducated? To compensate for his thoughts of doubt, he smirks wryly to himself as he thinks how beautiful Beth is visually. Knowing the answer to this one for sure, his guilt only deepens. He is not normally a shallow person.

Continuing his walk, he watches the dogs run freely, nipping each other's tails in fun in the morning sunshine. The thunder of hooves interrupts Grampy's deep contemplation. He whistles to the dogs who all come back immediately to his side. After firmly securing their leashes, he waits for the dozen or so horses to pass them by.

Major Dann is surprised when he sees Grampy leaning over the rails at the gallops, so he pulls up his mount, Pauline's Pride, to speak with him. The Major is Grampy's head trainer for the racehorses. He is an ex-army cavalry officer with many years' experience in training horses for the military. He has fitted in exceptionally well at Hope Farm after retiring from the forces. Much hilarity always seems to surround the Major, even more so if Jay-Jay was working beside him in any capacity. They made a great team. The Major has not seen Grampy for quite some time. "Hello, boss, I believe congratulations are in order," he says, screwing up his deeply lined tanned face.

Grampy removes his baseball cap to swat a longhorn beetle sunning itself on the rail beside him. The dogs jump up wondering what he is doing. "Thank you very much indeed, Major, I am ready to take the plunge again," he says with a chuckle. "Pauline's Pride is looking extremely well. What a beautiful sheen she has to her coat. Do you have anybody in particular looking after her?"

"Ah, no one specifically, but Kate does tend to favor her. She certainly does beautiful braiding and grooming prior to races. I am particularly grateful to her for the good job she did last week in creating a maple leaf on Pauline's hindquarters for the Windy Oaks show. She told me she got the idea from the Mounties' display team. She certainly seems to spend a lot of her spare time with them."

"Yes, she does," replies Grampy. "But I often wonder in what capacity?"

"Do you think she may want to join the RCMP as a horsewoman?" the Major asks with genuine interest.

Grampy nearly chokes with laughter at the thought of Kate in an RCMP Uniform. "I don't think she would get passed the second day of boot camp, but you are right, Major, she would be wonderful with their animals. I will pass on your comments and suggestion to her although I do think it will fall on deaf ears."

Major Dann pulls on the left reign, waving goodbye as he gallops away down the track to rejoin the other horses. Grampy looks down. Lucy, Flick, and Flack are wagging their tails vigorously in anticipation of a swim. Observing their excitement, Grampy decides to take them through the woods to the lake where he can amuse himself by throwing sticks and skipping stones across the still water. Lucy, the liver-colored puppy, particularly loves to swim chasing the stones that Grampy skims. Her latest trick is to submerge her head trying to retrieve the stones. The twins, Flick and Flack, work as a team, bringing the sticks back to their master, usually one at either end of the branch.

Not only did Grampy have arthritis in his hip, it has now spread to his fingers. He gets tired more easily than in previous years. How he wishes he had not laughed at Nanny as much as he did in the past. Looking upwards to the sky after checking his watch, he observes some oddly shaped clouds in the distance. One of them looks like the Statue of Liberty. It reminds him of a special day he and Nanny had shared whilst on vacation in New York.

Their eldest son, Gordon, had been looking after their daughter Victoria, enabling them to leave the farm for a few days. They had tried for years to get away, but the responsibility of looking after all the horses always seemed to prevent them from getting a much-needed break. New York had been on their bucket list for a very long time. On the day in question, the sun shone beautifully as they approached Ellis Island. They had chosen their spot on the ferryboat to enable them to get the best photographs possible. Just as the Statue of Liberty came into view, Nanny's cell phone chirped showing an incoming text from Victoria. Thinking this would be her texting to tell them to enjoy their day they were horrified at its content. It read as follows. "Gordon won't let me smoke. He is telling me what to do all the time. He won't even let me chose which horse I can ride. Can I stay with someone else until you get back?"

Grampy remembers with fondness the look of disbelief on Nanny's face. She just felt like throwing the phone into the Hudson River. She had waited patiently for so many years to be in New York. It was farcical that the text arrived at that precise moment in time. Nanny had to control her volatile temper as she was in a very public place, much to her frustration and his good fortune. I am glad it didn't completely ruin our day, Grampy thinks. He was so proud of the way she had contained her disappointment and saw the funny side of it later, as she nearly always did.

"Let's go girls," Grampy calls to his dogs as he feels his tummy rumble with hunger. He checks his watch again and realizes that two hours have passed since he started his walk. Quickening their step, they all head back towards the farmhouse. The aroma of Annie's cooking greets them as they near the Old Barn. It must be steak and onions today, if the smell is anything to go by, Grampy thinks hopefully. The three dogs rush into the mudroom, and Grampy opens their treat tin. They immediately sit without being told, looking lovingly at him as he hands them each a small dog biscuit. He plumps up their cushions for them to rest on before removing his muddy boots and jacket.

On hearing their return, Annie opens the glass door. With a big smile, she informs Grampy, "I've cooked your favorite meal, sir. Steak, onions, mushrooms, and pepper sauce. How will that do for you?"

"Annie, you are an absolute treasure," he replies, his mood lifting considerably. "I am ravenous. I cannot remember when I last had steak. I must go and get cleaned up first."

Just as he starts to climb the stairs, the front door bell jingles. It appears to be in competition with the wooden wind chimes that Beth installed the previous week. "Hi, Grampy," Beth calls as she barges through the door, "I thought I would join you for lunch as I saw your car parked outside. Why are you not at work?"

"I had a migraine earlier," he lies.

"Oh! Are you feeling better now? I just popped in to lunge Rupert and Nellie but I will get Jay-Jay to do it for me now," she says without hesitation or any consideration to the farm's schedule.

"I am feeling much better, thanks. Annie has cooked me steak for lunch. I'm quite sure she can make it stretch to two. You don't eat much," he says patting her taut tummy affectionately.

"That would be super, but I don't want to impose," she remarks.

Grampy ignores her protest. He goes through to the kitchen to ask Annie, "Can you make a small steak for Beth, please?"

"Small and rare," Beth's voice bellows from the hallway.

Grampy cannot help but notice the slightly disgruntled look on Annie's face as she replies, "Certainly, Grampy, I will do that for you right away. Can you both be seated in the dining room in ten minutes time, please?"

"We will thank you very much," they reply, almost in unison.

After cleaning himself up, Grampy heads towards the open dining room door where he recognizes a designer purse sitting on the table. He fidgets uncomfortably as he asks Beth, "Is that your purse?"

Looking apprehensive, she replies, "Of course it is. Who else would it belong to?"

"Oh I'm just being scatterbrained today. Just ignore me," he says trying to dispel his suspicious thoughts.

Annie enters carrying two scrumptious meals, which Beth and Grampy devour, without much conversation, Annie notes. Beth excuses herself, throws her linen napkin on the dirty plate, and leaves the room. Grampy seizes the opportunity to inspect the purse more closely, which is now sitting beside the leg of her chair. Noticing an ink stain just above the inside zip pocket, his heart sinks to his boots. He suspected that this purse had belonged to Nanny when he saw Beth using it the previous week. He knows the purse is not of a unique design, so he did not mention anything to her at that time, but his suspicions had been aroused. He knew Beth had the opportunity to access Nanny's closets, as he had not yet completely cleared them. He had intended to but could not face it. Now he finds himself in an awkward position.

Grampy is the type of person who tries to avoid confrontation at all costs. This, however, more often than not, led to miscommunication with people. He had learned over the years to deal with what was happening at the time, rather than brushing things under the carpet. He found this to be advantageous avoiding resentment building up. He was improving with age.

As Beth re-enters the room, she observes the serious look on his face. "What's up with you?" she asks, "You look like you've seen a ghost."

"I feel as if I have," he says quietly, looking down at the dining table.

"And just what do you mean by that?" she retorts.

"Where did you get that beautiful purse from?" he asks pointing at the offending item.

As quick as a flash, she replies, "I got it as a gift. Why do you ask?"

"Please don't insult my intelligence, Beth. That purse belonged to Nanny and we both know it. I bought it for her as a gift when we were on vacation in Greece many years ago. I was only able to purchase it as it was in the end-of-season sale. My heart sank when I picked it up when you left the room and my suspicions where confirmed when I saw the ink stains on the inside zip pocket." A tear runs down his lined face as he remembers the large outer zip had been stiff also.

Realizing she has been caught red handed, thankfully Beth does not attempt to deliver her prepared untrue response. Resembling a scolded child, she has no choice but to admit defeat. She exits the room in disgrace, leaving Grampy sitting alone in the dining room, fuming silently, his lips pressed firmly together.

CHAPTER 24

Katherine and her trainee loiter a great deal around the farm. Tawny decides she feels ready to revisit the Old Barn under Katherine's supervision. The young owl is horrified at the show Grampy is making of himself with Beth as she knows only too well that he is just fooling himself. The owls watch as Ruby Weaver leads Aitch into the indoor arena to be lunged. Perrah, Rupert, Nellie, and Sir Gareth closely follow them. The stable hands line the horses up ready for exercising before being led back to their freshly prepared stalls. Aitch does not need a lot of exercise these days, but the farmhands like to include him whenever possible. This has been his routine for many years. All the stable hands agree it is beneficial to the animals to stick to a routine whenever possible. He is an old favorite and will continue to be so until the end of his days. Nobody wanted him to feel excluded.

The owls exchange glances, Tawny is the first to speak. "Can I talk to the horses after you spread your veil of magic, please?"

Katherine tells Tawny, "You may have a short time with each horse in turn, but you must promise me you will leave without question when I decide it is time to go to the training school, as you refer to it!"

"Yes Katherine. I promise to obey the rules," Tawny eagerly replies.

"Fine," Katherine hoots. Not wanting to scare the horses, Tawny gives a little hoot from the rafters as a warning prior to her descent. Aitch looks upwards as does Sir Gareth who tries his best to ignore her. Both horses are afraid of what might come out of her beak as both strongly suspect that the trainee owl is indeed Nanny in a new form. All the horses appear nervous in the stillness of the evening air. Aitch paws the ground several times with his front right hoof. He tosses his mane vigorously as he blows hard through his nostrils displaying his large grey teeth. Katherine flies around the barn trailing a thin veil of magic dust behind her. Her words of wisdom echo around the building. "Just a reminder, Tawny, you must do exactly as I tell you."

Tawny flies down toward Aitch in his stall, landing on the cantle of his saddle, which sits on the door. "Hello," he says in a welcoming tone. As Aitch has the password to Nanny's real Christian name, he takes great delight in taking this opportunity to use it. "Is that really you?" he asks.

"Yes, it is," replies Tawny with great excitement. Aitch detects a hint of a Canadian twang in with her normal voice. "It is really good to see you. You look well, old friend. I'm glad you are taking some time to yourself. You worked long and hard for so many years. You deserve your retirement."

"It is good to see your leg has healed well," Tawny observes. Aitch begins to ask a question, but Tawny interrupts, assuring him she will return as soon as she can some other time. "I only have a short time to spend with each of you right now. I promise to revisit the farm regularly and I will perch on the fence beside the Old Barn when I have permission to do so. You must remember, though, I do not have the power of speech outside of this building, but I can still observe," she says laughing loudly.

"Very good, I will look forward to that," Aitch replies. Tawny flits from stall to stall having a brief conversation with every horse. Only a few suspect that this trainee owl is no ordinary bird. Tawny swoops over Sir Gareth's stall, delighting in the opportunity of being able to converse. "Hi, handsome," Tawny jests.

"Hello, Granny," he replies as fast as lightning.

"Err, two things, right off the bat. How did you know it was me and what have I told you before about using the G word?"

"Firstly, I am just so clever. Secondly, I do apologize. I didn't mean for the G word to slip out in your presence."

Tawny turns her back so as Sir Gareth cannot see the huge smile spreading across her face. Two of her feathers come loose, so she pecks them both out, tickling the horse on his muzzle with them, which in turn makes him sneeze uncontrollably. "Serves you right for calling me Granny," she says with great satisfaction. Feeling she has taught him a lesson, she continues her journey through the barn. Lady Jane is the last in line to chat with the owl. Out of the corner of her sharp eyes, Tawny notices Katherine scrutinizing her every move.

"Hi, Lady Jane, your mane and tail look magnificent, as always," Tawny compliments her old friend.

"Well, thank you very much. Your eyes look familiar. Do I know you?"

Desperate to say yes and sit down for a chat, Tawny knows better than to give in to her desires on this occasion, so she replies, "No, I don't think so," before flying back to report to the wise old owl watching from above. With both wings spread out wide, Katherine embraces Tawny before congratulating her on her restraint. The old owl is acutely aware that this exercise must have been very difficult for her trainee to abide by the rules. She will see to it that Tawny is richly rewarded for her performance.

As a reward, Katherine decides to give her an extra five minutes to do whatever she would like to do in the barn. After a brief discussion, Tawny chooses to have a general chat with the horses. "Twit-to-woo," she hoots to attract the attention of all the animals. "I just want to say," she starts with great confidence, "that I am so proud of each and every one of you, together with your stable hands, for your achievements at all the competitions this year. Most of you have done extraordinarily well. It is also of great personal delight for me to see the progress Lisa is making and I am delighted she has found such love in Seamus. Keep up the good work everybody. We will see you again soon. Thank you for your time and remember, always have fun and be kind to each other."

CHAPTER 25

At suppertime, Beth joins Grampy. She leans over to nuzzle his ear, trying to worm her way back into his good books. Licking her soft full lips, he watches with interest as she slowly pours a chilled beer for him. The lingering stare she gives the crystal decanter containing Nanny's vodka raises curiosity in his mind. Beth quickly avoids temptation and proceeds to slice a lemon and a lime before placing a slice of each, together with crushed ice, into her sparkling mineral water. She hands the beer mug to him. "Sláinte," they say, as they raise their glasses in a toast to one another.

Grampy presses the button to recline his soft leather chair to ease his aching hip. "I have a little surprise for you," Beth informs him. "As you are a master of procrastination, I have taken the liberty, and I hope you don't mind, of setting up a joint account for us at the bank." With a flourish, Beth produces the prepared documents from her Chanel purse. "All I need is your signature on line two," she informs him. She passes him her fountain pen, along with the papers, fully expecting him to sign them right there and then before adding, "I have deposited ten thousand dollars in the account."

An astounded Grampy stares at her in total disbelief. A deafening silence fills the room. His lips smack together, but no sound comes out of his mouth. Placing his beer mug on the marble-topped table, he screams out, "You have done what? Who do you think you are?" The lines on his large forehead grow deeper as a frown forms on his tanned face his eyebrows almost meet. He stammers slightly in his rage, "I am going to bed. Alone!" Grampy stands up and throws the phone, which had been lying on the wide arm of his chair. Unfortunately, the phone hits a chandelier sitting in a corner of the room. Annie had removed it for cleaning earlier that day. Both look suitably shocked as Annie knocks on the door alarmed by the commotion.

In a loud clear voice, full of panic, she calls, "Is everything all right, sir?"

Shaking with rage, with beads of perspiration on his brow, he gently replies, "Yes, thank you Annie. Do not worry about the mess. Beth will clean it up. She knows where the broom cupboard is."

"You have got to be kidding!" Beth exclaims a look of shock spreading across her beautifully painted face. "This is your mess and your own doing. You can clean it up yourself." She grabs her bag with one hand and her pashmina with the other. The front door of the farmhouse slams behind as she storms out. Undecided whether to go home or to visit Miggles' Retreat to ride Rupert or Nellie, Beth suddenly decides to go to the office to check on her accounts. Her conscience is beginning to prick her.

Through the office window, Ethel notices Beth striding towards her with a pompous look on her face. As Ethel always feels intimidated by Beth, she shouts for Barry, in the hope that he will be able to deal with her instead. Unfortunately, for her, Barry is substituting for Lisa with the special needs children and does not hear her call. Ethel has no option but to deal with Beth herself, so she greets Beth, saying, "Hello, Doctor McCormack." Forcing a smile, Ethel removes her glasses from her face, adding, "How may I help you today?"

"I would like you to check my account, just in case I have any extras to pay for as I have just remembered I requested a new diet for Rupert a few weeks ago. I have not checked my livery statements. I have been unbelievably busy recently. Being in love doesn't help my memory either."

Picking up her glasses, Ethel taps on the keyboard of her computer. Her jaw drops and eyes widen as she looks at the screen in front of her. There must be some mistake, she thinks. For a split second she wonders, do we have two doctors McCormack, as if one isn't enough? Thinking she must have looked up the wrong account, Ethel checks the computer again as Beth taps her manicured fingers repeatedly on the desktop. The sound of drumming nails makes Ethel increasingly nervous. Ethel knew both Barry and Grampy were meticulous about people paying their fees on time, so she is very confused by what is on the computer screen in front of her.

Nanny and Grampy had devised a system long ago which had always worked well in the past. This system is simple. If anybody was unable to pay their livery fees for three consecutive months, the farm invited them to come in for a private discussion to see if alternative arrangements could be made. If, after a further agreed period, a satisfactory solution had not been found, but the owner still hopes to pay, Hope Farm would allow the horse to stay. If the owner was still in arrears after the agreed period, the farm would purchase a percentage of the animal in question against the outstanding debt. This system worked very well, always giving owners options. After exhausting all other avenues, occasionally some owners did have to hand their beloved animals over. The blow was made softer for them as they were still able to ride and care for their horses. The few owners who had fallen into difficulties were happy in the knowledge that their horses would live out their years in wonderful caring surroundings. It was a great comfort to all concerned.

"Do you know how to operate a computer, Ethel?" an impatient Beth asks. "What is taking you so long?" Ethel looks over the top of her glasses, staring her squarely in the eye. Slightly taken aback by the expression on Ethel's face, she steps back two paces from the desk, panic rising in her throat.

"One moment please," Ethel says slowly but deliberately, a small smirk creeps across her face as she picks up the phone to call Barry. As she expected, his phone immediately goes to voicemail. A disappointed Ethel does not leave a message, realizing he is unavailable. Scratching her head with her pen, she wonders what to do next for the best. Deciding she must say something to Beth to break the silence, she blurts out, "I am sorry, but I am not at liberty to discuss your account. There must be a simple explanation for the amount of arrears showing. I am sure Barry will be able to give you an answer when he becomes available."

"He always has lots to do, I need this sorting now," Beth demands thumping her left hand down on the filing cabinet. The sunlight shines on the Beth's engagement ring, creating a majestic rainbow of colors across the office walls.

Taking a deep breath, Ethel continues, "I can assure you I will make it top priority on his return. If you would like to come back later, or go for a hack perhaps, Barry will have an explanation ready for you on your return."

"Humph!" she retorts. Now feeling rather uneasy, Beth leaves the office deciding to get her riding apparel from the trunk of her Mercedes and to take Nellie for a trial run over the cross-country course adjacent to the gatehouse. Panic begins to rise in her chest. Her throat becomes dry at the realization of when she had last paid her account in full.

* * *

Seamus' head appears through an open window in the arena. He asks Barry, "Do you have a few minutes to speak to a parent from the 'healing horses' class?"

"I always have a couple of minutes to speak to clients, Seamus," he replies happily. Turning towards the striking looking grandmother on the other side of the glass, he enquires. "What can I do for you?"

"I just wanted to thank you and your staff for all your hard work. Every time my grandson comes here horseback riding, we can tell the difference the horses make to him when we do his physiotherapy the following day." Barry nods and a grateful smile spreads across his face. "An added bonus is that the riding triggers more smiles than frowns from him, as you know he is not one to show his feelings! That is what we, as a family, appreciate the most. It makes it so worthwhile for all of us."

"Well that is great to hear," Barry smiles and assures her, "I will pass your kind comments on to all concerned."

She nods back at him gratefully, adding, "His balance has improved enormously in the short time he has been coming here to this class. I assume his leg muscles have become much stronger because of gripping the animal's sides?"

"That is correct," Barry confirms. "The muscle groups that are required mimic walking. I also noticed that your grandson's confidence is improving with each lesson. I'm sorry but you will have to excuse me now as Lisa was unable to come in today and I'm even busier than usual."

"I understand. Thanks again," the delighted and grateful grandmother replies.

*   *   *

Ethel cannot resist looking at the doctor's account again after she had left the office. Looking furtively over her left shoulder, she scrutinizes Beth's account in its entirety. With total disbelief, she laughs aloud just as Barry returns after taking Lisa's class. "Oh, man! My back is killing me. Could you make us a coffee, Ethel, please?" he asks.

"Certainly; we do need to talk straight away, though. I tried to phone you earlier while I had Beth in here drumming her nails on the desk spitting orders at me."

"Oh no! In future, if this ever happens again, and you feel intimidated, or you require immediate assistance, all you need to do is announce on the PA, Michele, bring your broomstick to the office, please."

Ethel looks up from making the coffee, spilling the grains over the counter top asking, "What did you just say?"

"What do you think I just said?" he asks, grinning from ear to ear.

"Why would I say that?"

"Whoever is available will come straight away to help you out. I apologize profusely for not informing you of this phrase before now. I don't think I have ever forgotten to inform new staff members of the procedure we use. I must be getting old, as my mother used to say."

"No problem at all, I will know what to do if this ever happens again." Ethel replies, laughing before asking, "Who's Michele?"

"You really don't want to know," Barry assures her. "She was famous for riding her broom around here a long time ago. Just ask Inspector Whipton the next time he drops by. On second thoughts, don't! I'm only joking. Just forget I ever told you anything about her. I am getting myself into trouble here!"

"Aw, come on Barry, you can't just leave me with half a story. Was she magical? Was she some type of witch?"

Smiling to himself at this thought, Barry uses the excuse of needing the washroom as his exit strategy, leaving Ethel dumfounded and intrigued.

CHAPTER 26

As a new day dawns out on the downs, the racehorses are running as fast as their jockeys and trainers will allow. The trainers lean heavily on the white rails with binoculars draped around their necks, their stopwatches at the ready. If a horse shaves as much as two seconds off their best time, great whoops of joy echo for miles around. Trainers frequently throw their caps into the air if one of the horses produces a spectacular time. The sight of hands clapping and high-fives elevate the euphoria for everyone involved.

Tawny and Katherine fly around the farm after enjoying a brief spell of flying low over the waves at the beach. They had visited their friend Stella the buzzard, who lives in the tall pine trees above the cliffs. They all happily ate brunch together while catching up on local news. This was one of their favorite things to do which they did on a regular basis. Today's meal had consisted of mice and mealworms washed down with spring water.

Annie is feeling frazzled and overwhelmed by the enormity of her job. She had not realized how busy the farm was when she readily accepted the post. She did not regret accepting it for a moment, but she knew it was getting the better of her. She notices Grampy's reflection in the garden doors, so she seizes the opportunity to speak with him. "Grampy," she shouts loudly so that he can hear her. "May I have a word with you, please, if you can spare a moment?"

"I always have time for you, dear Annie. How can I help?" he asks quizzically.

"I love working here," Annie begins, tears welling up in her eyes as she reaches into the pocket of her apron for her blue lace handkerchief. She carefully dabs her eyes before continuing, "I am finding this job harder than I had anticipated. I am not as young as I used to be."

"None of us are," Grampy interjects before allowing her to continue.

"I wondered if I could get some help in the house as there are so many people to cater for. I could do with someone to help with the meals in particular, but if I could get a little help with the housework as well, that would be really good."

"Sounds like a good plan to me, Annie. Do you have anybody in mind, or will I ask Barry to advertise in the local newspaper?"

"I do know of someone I think you will approve of, sir."

"Oh, drop the 'sir'," Grampy laughs. "I have already decided you can have your way. You don't need to grovel anymore."

A relieved Annie laughs gratefully before continuing, "I think my friend Yvonne Ashgrove would be suitable for the post. I can personally vouch for her. She is trustworthy, reliable, and has an enormous heart, together with a wicked sense of humor."

Grampy lifts his index finger and places it over his mouth. He brushes his moustache (which Annie wishes he would trim) before replying, "Ask her to pop round this evening if possible. I will chat to her myself as Barry has more than enough on his plate without my adding to his heavy load."

"Oh, thank you, I am most grateful. I will see you later then."

"Very good," he says, "I'm looking forward to meeting her."

As Grampy takes his leave from Annie, Seamus runs across the yard, his arms flailing resembling a bird in flight. "Annie, Annie!" he shouts, "Did you remember to get the brochure from Betty's Bridals for Lisa?"

"Aw, dash it! I completely forgot; however, I promise I will stop on my way home and get one for you today."

"Thanks, it will keep her happy as this is her weekend off. It will give her something to do."

"While you are here, Seamus, can you take the nectar and fill up the feeders for me please? Ella and her brood will be thinking we are neglecting them."

"No problem, I will do it. It is my pleasure, ma'am." Seamus takes the two enormous bottles and heads back to his work.

"Don't spill any," she cries, "as we are very low on sugar. If Yvonne gets a start soon I will be free to go and get some desperately needed supplies. Grampy has no clue as to how a house needs to be run."

"I know," Seamus shouts back over his right shoulder, "but I think he is trying his best. See you later, Annie. Fingers crossed it all works out for you."

"Thanks," she replies, heading back to the kitchen. Annie picks up the kitchen phone to call Yvonne and give her the good news. Annie feels slightly guilty, as she did not inform Grampy that she had already spoken to her friend and told her all about Hope Farm. "Hey Yvonne, I've spoken with Grampy,"

"And he doesn't need anyone," a despondent voice at the other end of the line interrupts.

"Stop interrupting and let me finish. He wants to see you tonight if you are free."

"Fantastic," Yvonne replies chirpily, "what time?"

"He didn't say, but I know around seven will be a good time for him. I will pick you up at six thirty."

"Sounds great; I will be ready. Thank you, Annie, you are a star."

"Be sure you are ready, Yvonne. You are usually running late," Annie quips.

*   *   *

Yvonne immediately goes into panic mode. She shouts aloud, "I have nothing to wear. Nothing fits me. I wish I had done some ironing and not thrown everything into the closet in a heap now."

"Stop panicking, mom. Just do what you usually do."

"And what's that, son?" she asks, knowing what the reply will be.

"Buy more," her eldest son quips. He throws a cushion at her from the sofa where he is sitting.

"Less of your lip," she smiles in jest as she tries to scold her six-feet-tall first-born.

"Good luck, mom. You can charm the monkeys out of the trees. Don't worry about a thing. You will be a knock out. Incidentally, where is that brother of mine?" he asks as he fastens the vest of his uniform. Picking up his truncheon in his right hand, he taps it slowly into the palm of his left hand patiently awaiting her answer.

"Dad has just left to take him to the railway station as he got a call to return off-shore two days early due to someone being sick."

"He didn't even say goodbye. Brothers! Who'd have them?" he asks looking around what is now an empty room.

Yvonne has grabbed her car keys without his noticing. She is already on the other side of the hump-back bridge, indicating to turn right to go to the store for a new outfit. Glancing at her watch, she notices it reads four-thirty. "Oh hell! I must get a move on."

Flicking through the rails of clothing on offer at her local store, she is completely uninspired by what she sees before her.

"Hi!" a voice from behind her cries out, "How are you?"

"Hello," Yvonne replies, slightly shocked and irritated by the intrusion.

"I haven't seen you in about two years," her long-lost work colleague says. "Let's have a coffee and catch up." Desperately wanting to decline the kind offer, Yvonne is dragged by her left elbow to the store café acutely aware that time is marching steadily on. They spend the next half-hour exchanging idle chitchat. By now, it is after five o'clock. Yvonne has no new outfit, no supper prepared for her husband's return, and she has not done a stroke of housework all day. "Oh, bother," she says aloud, "I will just have to go to the farm as I am. I must remember to apply some lipstick. That will have to do." Crestfallen, she heads for home after saying goodbye to her former colleague.

Her mounting panic is momentarily stopped by the ringing of her cell. She is relieved to see Annie's name on the display. "Are you ready?" Annie enquires.

"As ready as I ever will be," is her immediate response.

"Super, I will be for you soon."

Yvonne rushes upstairs to apply her lipstick, stumbling over a pile of clothing at the top of the stairs, which has been lying there all week. She kicks them out of her path whilst trying to reach the toothbrush lying on the washroom floor. After quickly brushing her teeth, she grabs her lipstick from the cabinet. Speaking to her reflection in the mirror, "At least nobody moves my makeup," she says gratefully. After carefully applying a coat of lipstick, she throws it, along with a hairbrush, into a large purse, muttering to herself, "I will never find these items again. I don't know why I'm bothering." Yvonne runs to meet Annie who has parked her car beside the shed at the end of the yard. The tall hedgerow obscures the vehicle.

Annie is unaware that Yvonne is almost at the car and blasts her horn, hoping that she is ready. If she is not, the horn will make her laugh, Annie hopes. Grabbing the door

handle, Yvonne opens the car door and promptly tells her friend, "Oh be quiet, I'm going as fast as I can."

Before Annie can reply, the hem of Yvonne's skirt rips as it catches on a piece of metal sticking out from the hedgerow. They burst into fits of laughter. "Oh no! What do I do now?" Yvonne asks with a worried look on her flushed face, beads of perspiration appearing on her upper lip.

"Rip the other side to match," advises Annie.

"Are you serious?" a now frustrated Yvonne replies.

"Deadly. Now calm down," she instructs as she opens her car window to let the overpowering aroma of expensive perfume escape, coughing slightly. "Grampy knows nothing about fashion. He won't even notice what you are wearing."

"Sorry," apologizes Yvonne, "is the perfume too strong? I got it as a present from my mother."

"Just a little bit," Annie says tactfully.

"I want to accompany Dave for his check-up next week, but he is so independent I'm not sure he will want me there," Yvonne informs Annie, who turns to her with a sympathetic expression.

"I think it is fantastic that you are of enormous support to one another. I wish I had a partner like you have."

"One day, Annie, maybe one day. Your time will come."

The two women idly chat for the rest of the short journey. They are both laughing heartily as they arrive at the farmhouse.

*   *   *

On hearing the crunch of gravel, Grampy opens the front door with a big welcoming smile across his face. He gestures for the women to come in, and escorts them to the lounge where he offers Yvonne a seat. "Annie, could you put the coffee pot on for us, please? I will call when I am ready for you to come back to the room." Annie nods to her boss and scuttles off towards the kitchen.

With authority in his deep voice, he orders his three dogs, Lucy, Flick, and Flack to go to their room. The spaniels run wagging their tails as they head towards their private domain. "Peace at last. Let me introduce myself properly. I am Grampy." He offers Yvonne his tanned hand.

Yvonne offers him her hand, which he grips firmly, observing that she is trembling. "I'm not an ogre despite what they might tell you," he says with a warm smile. "Just relax and have a seat wherever you would like. Nobody needs to stand at attention here."

"Thank you," Yvonne replies, "I will take a seat beside this very inviting log fire. It is so welcoming," she adds as she crosses the room with increasing confidence. Grampy notices that she has blistered her heels as she walks unsteadily towards the brown velvet chair. He hopes she has not gone to the trouble of buying new shoes just for the interview. After quick consideration, he refrains from making any comment, remembering what Nanny had always asked him to do. The advice was to be acutely aware of people's imperfections or any disability they may suffer from. Do not draw attention to them, she used to advise him. Grampy had learned over the years to become more subtle, allowing him to become the sympathetic person he is today.

He slowly looks Yvonne up and down. He could not help but think how much she reminded him of Nanny. He is confused as Yvonne has blue eyes, not at all like Nanny's hazel ones. She also has beautiful straight hair, nothing whatsoever like Nanny's crazy curls! However, Yvonne wears the exact same smile and has a similar button nose and little chin. Perhaps this is a good omen, he thinks before quickly making conversation, as he is acutely aware he has been staring at this poor woman looking back at him. She is now wondering if she has a piece of spinach stuck between her teeth. He breaks the silence, trying his best to keep his mind on the task in hand. "Okay, Yvonne, just relax," he starts with authority once again, raising his voice as is if he were addressing a class full of children.

Is this man deaf? Yvonne wonders. Just as Grampy takes a deep breath to continue, his daughter, Victoria, barges into the lounge unannounced. "Oh, please excuse me," she offers, stepping backwards in the doorway, leaving mud and pieces of straw on the blue wool carpet, which had been steam cleaned earlier that day. "I didn't realize you had company, Dad. Hello," she adds laughing, in an attempt to cover her embarrassment. Victoria does a double take on seeing Yvonne, thinking, that woman reminds me very much of mom when she used to straighten her hair for fun. How odd!

"It's not a problem; however, I do need half an hour of privacy, please, Victoria. I will owe you two candies if you attend to Flossie and Alfie for me."

"Deal!" she readily replies. Leaving the room, she grabs a bunch of carrots and two apples from the pantry adjacent to the mudroom. Victoria heads towards the duck pond to tend to the donkeys for her father, trying to dismiss the turmoil which is now foremost in her mind.

The informal interview goes extremely well and an agreement between Grampy and Yvonne is struck within fifteen minutes, to each other's satisfaction. At the end of the interview, Grampy lifts the silver bell from the table. On hearing the bell ring, Annie assumes it is time for her to return. She knocks politely on the door before entering with a tray of cups and a coffee pot. "Perhaps, you would prefer tea, Yvonne."

"No thank you. I drink black coffee, but thanks for the offer."

Annie brings in a mint cake she had baked especially for the occasion that afternoon, unbeknown to Grampy. She slices the cake and places it on the willow patterned side plates before handing one to each of them. Grampy and Yvonne bite into the delicious cake. "Mmmm!" they say in unison, they then proceed to lick their lips at exactly the same time. The vision in front of Annie makes her rock with laughter. Her laughter is infectious. Grampy realizes he has not laughed like this in a very long time.

It becomes abundantly clear to Grampy that Yvonne possesses a terrific sense of humor. Their conversation flows well. Yvonne decides to recite one of Annie's favorite stories about an evening when she drank too much pop. Thinking it was a good idea at the time, she had also consumed an entire bag of luminous green candies. During the night, she awoke with the most horrendous stomach pains she had ever encountered, including childbirth. Acutely aware that she was going to vomit, she ran to the washroom. Unfortunately for her, after sweating profusely she did indeed vomit. When she saw the lime green mess in front of her, she panicked. She had forgotten about having eaten the candies earlier that evening. Thinking she was about to be abducted by aliens, she had screamed out for her family. It took a few minutes before they could compose themselves enough to remind her of what she had eaten. "From that day to this, they will not let me forget it," Yvonne recounts.

"That is exactly the sort of thing my wife used to do," Grampy told the women with tears of laughter in his eyes as he reminisced. "Don't feel embarrassed. Remind me to tell you both the story about the time Nanny got locked in the back of a hearse."

"Oh please tell us now, Grampy," Annie pleads with a look of wonder and amusement in her eyes.

"I don't think Reverend Trisha, or her husband Dave, would thank me for spilling the beans. Some other time, maybe," he replies, firmly dismissing the subject, much to the women's disappointment. The shrill ringer of the phone interrupts their conversation. "Please excuse me, I must get this. Hope Farm, Grampy speaking," he says with authority, all the while hoping that it is not his fiancée on the line. Unfortunately, it is Beth. "Not now," he says gently before replacing the phone firmly back in its cradle. Striding purposefully across the room, he looks in Yvonne's direction and asks, "How does the day after tomorrow suit you to start assisting Annie?"

"That would be absolutely perfect," is Yvonne's prompt reply. "Thank you very much. I would be delighted. What time would you like me to be here?"

"Six thirty in the morning," he informs her without batting an eyelid.

She concentrates on keeping her mouth firmly closed, as she was unaware that she would have to start work so early in the morning, not having given it any thought whatsoever. "No problem. I will look forward to it," Yvonne says, lying through her teeth.

Annie sniggers quietly, avoiding Yvonne's shocked expression. After finishing their drinks and cake, Grampy escorts the women to Annie's car, opening the car doors for them as they climb in. Yvonne trips on the running board and falls head first into the cab. That is just the type of thing that would have happened to Nanny at an interview, Grampy thinks as he assists Yvonne who now has tears of laughter streaming down her face.

"Pull yourself together Yvonne," Annie instructs, while trying desperately not to laugh. A moment later, they manage to settle into their seats. They fasten their seatbelts before driving away looking much happier than when they arrived.

As the car pulls away, Yvonne turns to Annie saying, "Oh my goodness. I hadn't given a second thought to the starting time at the stables. I should have known it would be like a night shift!"

A shrewd Annie replies, "I'm glad you forgot to ask me," adding, "I would have lied anyway! I know we will work well together. You will soon get used to the early start. Dawn is the best part of the day."

"I don't believe you!" Yvonne shrieks back at her friend before they both start giggling again like schoolchildren.

CHAPTER 27

Jay-Jay delivers a hand written note in a sealed envelope to the office, asking Ethel to make sure Barry reads it at his convenience. He emphasizes, "It is not at all urgent, but I would like it to be given consideration before the meeting at end of the week, if that's possible."

"No problem, Jay-Jay, I will that see he gets it."

"Cheers," he says before clicking his heels together giving her a cheeky grin.

I wonder what is in this envelope, Ethel ponders, before returning to her long list of duties for the day.

* * *

Tawny and Katherine perch on a fencepost watching the staff enter the office for their weekly staff meeting. Barry and Grampy usually take half an hour to discuss any private business matters prior to the others joining them. This gives them time to discuss any personal matters that may have arisen. On this occasion, neither party wants to discuss the latter. The unexpected arrival of Beth interrupts their private meeting with a "Cooee,"

"Good morning, my dear," Grampy beams at his beloved. Barry tries not to show his rising anger at her presence. He walks away in the opposite direction on the pretense of getting himself a drink before starting the meeting formally. Unbeknown to him, Grampy believes this is the perfect opportunity to introduce Beth as an addition to the team.

Her arrival means that the men do not have time to discuss any business prior to the staff arriving.

As usual, Barry opens the meeting, trying desperately hard to hide his irritation at Beth's attendance. He informs the group that Jay-Jay and Kate have requested to learn to train racehorses. "They have offered to work free of charge at weekends, schedule allowing, in exchange for a three-month trial period." As his gaze wanders around the room, he sees shocked glances being exchanged. It appears that no one had a clue about Jay-Jay and Kate's intentions. They had never mentioned anything to the others.

Barry asks Grampy for his opinion and he readily agrees with the request. He authorizes Barry to set it up with the trainers as soon as it is practical to do so. "I'm quite sure Major Dann will be delighted to help you in any area as he is such an experienced and informative trainer. He told me he is impressed with Kate's enthusiasm, and I know he has many laughs with Jay-Jay, so they should make a good team." Grampy turns to face Jay-Jay and Kate, smiling warmly at them. His nose twitches slightly as he continues, "I am encouraged by your devotion and dedication to Hope Farm. I hope you enjoy your new venture. I will be following your progress with great interest."

Jay-Jay and Kate are absolutely thrilled as neither truly thought it would be possible. Kate pipes up, "Sorry guys, you will have even more muck to shovel now." On observing the reactions of the group from that comment, Jay-Jay decides that on this occasion it is best to keep quiet, letting Kate bear the brunt of the discontented glares. Seamus and Lisa glance at each other in panic as to lose both Jay-Jay and Kate from the same team will be catastrophic for them.

Much to his disgust, Barry hears Beth blurt out, "I also think that's a great idea." Trying his best to hide his anger, he looks at her, thinking, who asked for your opinion? "I would like to offer my vast experience in helping both of them if I may," Beth continues.

Grampy's face flushes slightly. He appears embarrassed by Beth's boldness and is unsure of what to say next. He turns to Beth, stammering slightly, "Thanks for your kind offer, but I think we will leave that to Major Dann and Barry to organize. Ethel, please make a note that Beth has offered her services, but on this occasion we will decline her generous offer."

Ethel deliberately avoids eye contact and duly continues to take the minutes of the meeting. Turning back to Beth, Grampy continues, "Beth, we will call you to attend the next trainers' meeting and we will take it from there as we do realize you have a wealth of knowledge and experience in all equestrian fields."

"Okay, thanks," she agrees, flashing Barry an irritating smirk which inwardly sends him into orbit.

Do that again, he thinks, and I will personally see to it that you will not get another opportunity to repeat this performance. Taking a deep breath, he swiftly turns the conversation to the recent competition results.

"Truly amazing," Grampy quips upon reading the impressive list of achievements and awards. "I trust you will all agree that nobody expected us to accomplish as many victories as we have this year."

"Absolutely," several voices call out in agreement.

Seamus asks, "Would it be possible to purchase two more horses for the special class?"

"I have been thinking about that," Grampy replies. "I will speak to you after the meeting in private if you can spare me the time. I was thinking more along the lines of one horse, not two. Not to worry, Seamus. Aim high," he says with a chuckle.

Beth interrupts again, "I can help with that too." Wearing an even bigger smirk, she informs the group, "A colleague of mine is putting her horse up for sale in about a months' time. I believe it would be very suitable for the special class."

"As I said, we will talk about this after the meeting," an increasingly agitated Grampy says firmly. "Moving on,

I suggest we close the livery waiting list as we are, for the foreseeable future, able to pick and choose the horses we now stable, thanks to Alistair and Liz having given out so many fabulous recommendations." Turning towards Beth, he says, "We should invite them out for dinner and drinks as a token of our appreciation."

"Wow," Beth says, nodding her head. "I am going to be a very busy lady. I will have to buy a new outfit." Silence fills the room. The hairs on Grampy's neck prickle uncomfortably. He cannot wait to get out of the room and the dreadful atmosphere in there.

Turning back to the group, Grampy continues, "We have built this business up to a level where our reputation speaks for itself. However, this does not mean that there is any room for complacency. Thankfully, we do not have to scratch about as we did in years gone by. Well done everybody. Your hard work and dedication do not go unnoticed. If there is nothing further, we will see you all again next week. Have a good evening."

The scuffle of chairs scraping the floor fills the room as the farm team prepares to leave the meeting. Grampy holds his hand up. He apologizes saying, "I forgot to say, I am thinking of leaving my job in town." Barry keeps his eyes focused on the table. "I would like to be here full time to assist you Barry. At my stage in life, I don't need to work anywhere else other than here. The farm's income is more than sufficient to keep me in the style to which I have become accustomed." He laughs quietly to himself.

A stunned Barry looks up from the table. He then glances at Beth who is sitting back in her chair gloating. The talon like nails of her fingers drum gently on her laptop as she closes the lid. "That would be an enormous help to me, Grampy," Barry says with hidden horror. "Thanks. I hope you come to the correct decision soon." On hearing this, Beth shoots an evil look at Barry wondering what he is inferring.

The meeting is adjourned and the farm workforce rushes out to continue with their duties. Barry's legs go weak at the thought of what could happen now under these new circumstances. *Perhaps it is time I looked for a different job. I will never work with that woman. That much I know for sure,* he tells himself.

Ethel meets his gaze and stares back in horror at his ashen face. She decides to remain silent, with butterflies in her stomach. She knows she has no alternative but to go with the flow until she finds other employment which she knows full well at her age will be very difficult. Truth be told, Ethel cannot bear to be parted from her beloved Pixie again, so she will just have to adapt.

*   *   *

Grampy and Beth walk towards Miggles' Retreat to visit Rupert and Nellie. Checking over his shoulder twice to check that they are alone, Grampy takes Beth by her right elbow, pulling her towards him. He looks her straight in the eye, telling her, "If you ever show me up in public like you did in that meeting again, I will have no alternative but to ask you to leave the room."

"In front of the staff?" she quips. "Are you crazy? You would be undermining yourself, not making a fool of me," Beth retorts.

"I am absolutely sick of you trying to take control of everything." Putting his hand up with his fingers open wide, he continues, "I do understand that you are trying to please me and be helpful, but I will only take so much. Whether you realize it or not, you are trying to fill Nanny's position. Take it from me lady. That will never happen. Not in this life or the next."

Completely stunned by his unexpected outburst, she blurts out, "That half-wit?" before covering her mouth. It is too late. The words are out and they cannot be retracted.

Grampy stares at her in absolute horror as the reality of what she has said sinks in. He knows he had not misheard her. "Don't you dare you talk about my ex-wife in that manner! She may not have been educated like yourself, but you will never be half the person she was. I already know that," Grampy fumes.

Even Beth knew not to vocalize her true thoughts on this matter. Weight wise, I am half the person, thank goodness, she thinks.

Grampy turns on his heels and strides back towards the farmhouse. "I have nothing more to say to you today," he shouts over the sound of the tractor in the adjoining field. Beth strides confidently towards the stable block, oblivious of the pain she has inflicted.

*   *   *

Kate comes out of an empty stall carrying two heavy buckets of pony nuts. Oh no! There is no escape this time, she thinks seeing Beth stride towards her with a face like thunder. Unsure of how to react for the best, Kate places one bucket in front of the tack room. She then scuttles into the nearest stall, pouring the contents of the other bucket into the feed trough. "Hey!" Beth's voice booms from behind her. "Why are you not attending to Nellie?" she asks in a harsh tone.

Trying her best to remain calm, while keeping her gestures to a minimum, Kate replies, "I have already dealt with your horses, Doctor McCormack. I have many others to attend to, which I am trying to get on with."

"Don't you dare take that tone with me, young lady! I am a valued customer. Don't try to be clever with me. I have more degrees than a thermometer. Whom do you think is the smarter, you or I?" Beth shouts arrogantly, resting her right hand on her boney hip.

With hackles raised to their peak, Kate manages to bite her tongue, replying in an even voice, "We treat all customers the same here, regardless of titles, social status, or wealth."

Beth's jaw drops at the audacity of the stable girl. It has been a long time since anyone had the nerve to stand up to her in this manner. "To think I have just stuck up for you and that other imbecile in the meeting to help you both out. You have got another thing coming if you think I am going to bother giving up my free time now," she spits angrily at Kate waving a skinny arm in front of her face, almost touching her freckled nose.

Stepping back, Kate shouts, "Get out of my space. You only offered to do that to make yourself look good in front of Grampy. Jay-Jay and I are both well aware of that. Don't try to pretend it's any different."

"You are a disrespectful, rude brat. I am going to put in an official complaint to Barry, and I will of course be telling Grampy," she retorts snootily.

Kate decides her best plan of action at that moment is to ignore Beth and continue with her chores. Feeling tears welling up in her deep brown eyes, she carries on regardless with her duties, hoping nobody can detect her frustration. Kate knows she is probably in big trouble and fears that she may have messed up her chances of becoming a trainer. I wish I could keep my big mouth shut in such situations, she thinks.

Kate completes her duties and decides to take Pixie out to the woods for a leisurely hack. They both enjoy their ride and she returns to the stables a little less stressed than when she left. She hoses down her mount, something the old pony loves. She then grabs a pitchfork to fluff up Pixies' bedding even though she had done it earlier. Still upset by Beth's rudeness, she decides there and then that she must speak with Barry. On checking her cell, which she had left in her jacket pocket, she notices she has received a text message from him asking her to call into the office before leaving for home today.

* * *

Beth tacks Nellie up, taking her to the Racing Snake for their daily exercise. Galloping along, Beth has time to reflect on her impulsive outburst. *Perhaps I was too hard on the girl*, she ponders. *I do need to build some bridges with a few people here already. I must make a conscious effort to be more tolerant towards others. I have to remember that the people here are not as intelligent as I am.* On her return, she decides to try to make amends with Kate, not because she would ever admit to being in the wrong, but she realizes this is not going to go down well with the management.

After her ride, she spies Seamus tidying up his tools by the shed. "Have you seen Kate?" she shouts over to him.

"No ma'am. The last time I saw her she was on her way to exercise Pixie. I haven't seen her since. Sorry I can't be of more help," he replies politely feeling intimidated by her presence.

Walking towards him, a packet of cigarettes falls from her riding jacket pocket. "Okay, thank you. If you do see her in the next hour, ask her to give me a call on this number, please." Beth hands him her business card which he places in the pocket of his jodhpurs.

"I will do that," he says. As she leaves the stable block, he picks up the cigarette packet and places it in his pocket. *I didn't know she smoked*, he thinks.

Beth's cell rings. It is Grampy calling to ask her to meet him at the farmhouse. She replies, "I will be there in fifteen minutes. I have to see to Nellie as no stable hands are available to assist me here," she wickedly points out.

"That will be fine," he says, before he quickly hangs up.

True to her word, exactly fifteen minutes later, Beth arrives at the farmhouse wearing an indignant expression, immediately putting Grampy on the defensive. "Sit down over there and listen carefully to what I have to say to you," he instructs. "I will not put up with your constant interference, no matter how well-meaning you think you are being."

Unable to reply due to this unexpected dressing down from her fiancé, she has no option but to allow him to continue. "Barry has reliably informed me that you owe a great deal of money to Hope Farm for the stabling of your horses. I was unaware that your account was outstanding when they were relocated there from the Old Barn. It now appears that on top of the other arrears, you owe for the entire time they have been in Miggles' Retreat." He pauses for a moment to let the enormity of the situation sink in before continuing. "I'm interested in hearing your explanation. It had better be good." He hands her a sheet of paper detailing her account.

Beth studies the statement of her account. "I didn't realize I owed for the Old Barn, nobody informed me of that. Are you seriously asking me to pay stabling fees? I am now your fiancée," she reminds him, as if he didn't know.

"Of course you have to pay. This is a business, not a charity. It is a very costly business at that, may I add. If I had wanted your horses to stay here free of charge, do you not think I would have mentioned it? How dare you make that assumption! That is the same as if I were expecting you to get one of your colleagues to operate on me privately without paying."

"Oh don't be so dramatic!" she spits back. "That is not the same thing at all," she says, trying to justify her actions. Beth is unsure whether to laugh or cry as she feels the anger and panic welling up inside her.

Grampy stands, straightening his back, before yelling at her, "People warned me about your attitude a long time ago. I chose to ignore what they said. I thought they were just jealous. You are a cold, heartless, callous, selfish woman. Because of your position as a doctor, you are used to calling all the shots and getting your own way. I don't think you know how to behave any differently. I cannot, and will not, take any more. I have had enough of this. Get out of my house!"

"Your house?" she retaliates, her voice rising to a screech. "This will soon be my house too." Her eyes widen as she realizes, yet again, she has spoken aloud in temper. In a wild fit of rage, he throws a large textbook that he had only purchased the previous week. The book catches a horse brass hanging next to the fireplace, enraging him even more. Beth is shocked by his outburst and backs out of the room. She never, ever imagined he was capable of behaving like this. She thought he was a quiet-spoken, mild-mannered person. She also thought he was shy and reserved. Doctor Elizabeth Jane McCormack has now seen the other side of Grampy as she has pushed him too far. For the first time in her life, she is afraid that the tables may have turned on her. She also fears he may strike her. Fleetingly she thinks, if I back down now and say I'm sorry, I wonder if it will calm him down.

Grampy's face is turning a pale shade of puce, his eyes bulging under his deeply furrowed brow. He is beside himself with rage. He would never hit a woman, but Beth does not know this. She is afraid for her own safety. "I have not finished with you yet," he shouts, finding himself talking to her back as she tries to leave the house. He is so angry at her apparent indifference to him that he punches the closet door, hurting his arthritic fingers. "I don't think I can go through with this," he says aloud to the now empty room, "It is too high a price to pay. We are just making each other unhappy. I think it best if I break off the engagement."

Grampy recognizes his need to calm down and to clear his head. However, he has made his decision. Calling for his dogs, he opens the back door and strides purposefully towards the back of the farm, forgetting to take their leashes with him. They head in the direction of Roseisle Wood. He realizes on approaching it that it has been over two years since he last visited. That visit had been with Nanny. Unable to cope with the turmoil in his mind he turns back towards the gallops. One of the farm hands is heading towards him together with Flash, the night watchman. They are distributing apples for the deer which are plentiful in Roseisle Wood. The men wave to him. Grampy waves back dismissively keeping his head bowed down, indicating to his employees that he does not want to chat at this particular moment in time. On his return to the farm, he grooms all of his dogs taking delight at their affection. He fluffs up their beds and calls them one at a time, slipping each of them a little treat before settling them for the night. He decides to have a long soak in the bath before retiring to bed, hoping it will relax him. He hopes he will be in a better frame of mind the next day.

The bubbles are almost to the top of the roll-top bath when his cell phone rings. He answers the phone with one hand as he turns the flowing water off with the other. "Hello," the caller says, "You don't know me, my name is Grant. I am a friend of Beth's. My wife Marilyn and I have a horse which I have reason to believe you may be interested in purchasing. It may be suitable for use as one of your healing horses."

"Thank you for calling," a puzzled Grampy replies, "that could very well be the case. I am looking for a horse as it happens. How did you get my number?"

"Doctor McCormack phoned me half an hour ago,"

"Oh I see," Grampy replies trying his best to keep his voice level, suppressing the anger rising in his chest once again. I cannot believe the audacity of that woman, he thinks before asking, "Where do you live so that I can visit and assess the horse's temperament?" Grant gives him their address and they arrange to meet the following evening. "What is the horse's name?"

"Miss Capers," Grant replies. "She is a wonderful old mare. I feel confident that you will find her suitable for the wonderful service you provide."

"Many thanks. I am looking forward to meeting yourself, Marilyn, and Miss Capers tomorrow evening. Goodbye." Grampy shakes his head trying to switch off from the day's stresses. Sadly, the only thing he can switch off is his phone.

CHAPTER 28

Tawny and Katherine sense trouble is brewing. They look at each another and without saying a single word, they fly towards the sound of raised voices. Katherine turns her head towards Tawny informing her, "This may be an occasion where we have to intervene. You stay perched on the fencepost unless I tell you otherwise. I am going to sit on the roof as I can see from here that the office window is still open. I will assess the situation and then decide what will be the best plan of action." Tawny nods her head in reluctant agreement. Following her leader's orders, she digs her claws into the large post beside the gate awaiting her next instruction. She ruffles her feathers aggressively before settling, ready to spread some magic if required.

Kate comes to the office, her cheeks ablaze and with tears in her eyes. "That ghastly woman has been throwing her weight around again," she says with a tremor in her voice.

"I assume we are talking about Doctor McCormack, Kate?" Barry knowingly enquires.

"Who else?" she snaps before continuing, "She treats me like her personal slave. You know how many horses I have to look after. I didn't want to mention it before, but that witch gave me a list of orders the other day demanding that I attend to her horses before anybody else's."

Barry raises his hand for her to stop. "Regardless of what we feel about a client, and on this occasion I do understand how you feel, you must not speak about them in this manner as you may be overheard by an existing or potential customer, Miss Nelson."

"Whatever," Kate says, shaking her head from side to side resembling a nodding dog on the parcel shelf of a car. "She expected me to have Rupert ready by eight a.m. for her. How can I possibly exercise, groom, and have everything done by that time of day?"

"I know, Kate, it is unrealistic of her. I don't think she needs more than four hours sleep, so therefore she expects everyone else to be on the go like herself. I have heard through the grapevine that she does work long hours at the practice. You know how much time she spends here, so she must have extraordinary stamina."

"I don't give two hoots about her stamina," Kate replies defiantly, waving her arms about vigorously. She folds her arms in an unsuccessful attempt to calm herself down. "I wish that woman would find somewhere else to go and other people to antagonize." Waving her arms about again, the sleeve of Kate's sweater catches in her braces. Barry is desperate to laugh, but under the circumstances, he turns away, afraid that Kate will go ballistic if pushed any further. Thankfully, for everybody's sake, she sees the funny side of the incident which defuses her anger.

Ethel looks up from her computer and removes her glasses. "Let me help you, Kate. I used to wear braces when I was young," she says sympathetically.

"Thanks, that would be good," laughs Kate, thinking, you were young? I can't imagine it. As Ethel carefully starts to remove the wool from the metal encased smile, Barry takes the opportunity to inform Kate, "I have spoken at length to Major Dann as well as the senior trainers, Bob Stillwater and Cathy Brooks. They are all prepared to work together with you and Jay-Jay. Now, about your kind offer to work without payment while learning to become trainers: much as we appreciate your very generous offer, Grampy will not take advantage of either of you in that way. We feel that you would be working far too many hours."

Ethel interrupts, announcing, "I'm almost finished, Kate. I'm unpicking the last stitch now."

"So, what we are suggesting," Barry continues, "is that you finish two hours earlier each day. We will find cover for those hours during the three-month period. You will both meet up at the Racing Snake at the end of your workday. Bob and Cathy will take it from there."

"Wow, thanks Barry. That would be fantastic," she says, "Does Jay-Jay know?"

"No, not yet. I was just about to ask you if you could pass on the good news to him on your way back to work."

"I certainly will," she assures him, gratefully. "I might as well warn you now that the witch has threatened to put in an official complaint about me. She gave me such a mouthful of verbal abuse that I could not help myself giving her back as good as she gave me. I know I was out of order, and I apologize in advance."

On hearing this admission, Katherine quickly fires a thin veil of magic in the direction of the ceiling fan in the office. Barry turns towards Kate and surprisingly says, "Don't worry about it in the slightest, dear. I will deal with it, but promise me that you will not do it again." Barry and Kate look at each another as if in a trance, their eyes glazed for a moment.

"Thanks, Barry. Thanks, Ethel," Kate chirps, nodding her head with appreciation. "I will get on with what's left of my day now."

"Don't work too hard," he jests, watching her skipping away happily.

Tawny observes Katherine as she descends from the roof. "That was much easier to sort out than I had anticipated," Katherine exclaims with glee.

"You really are a wise old owl," Tawny says as she gives Katherine a big hug. The owls decide to go and hunt for their supper.

*   *   *

After a night interrupted by constant rumbles of thunder, the rain is lashing hard against the farmhouse windows. Grampy's three dogs bark in annoyance at the noise. Lucy runs from room to room, trying to find the source of the thunder. Annie chases the twin dogs around the kitchen table, trying to herd them towards the mudroom. She and Yvonne need to make a start on the breakfast orders before Yvonne leaves for the wholesalers to stock up on much-needed produce. The dogs have to be out of everybody's way.

Annie speaks through gritted teeth, "These damn dogs shouldn't be here anyway, they should stay in the mudroom. I will speak to Grampy about it when I feel it is an appropriate time."

Yvonne looks up from her ever-growing shopping list. "Now would not be a good time!"

Jay-Jay arrives ten minutes late on his neighbor's bicycle, as his car would not start this morning, soaked through to the skin. "Sorry I'm late, Barry," he says.

Trying not to laugh, Barry shakes his head in disbelief at the apparition in front of him. "It's no problem. Why didn't you phone me? I could have come to collect you."

"I didn't think of that. I was in such a hurry to get here as I have some information regarding Beth you may be interested in."

"I am a bit busy right now, but I always have time for that sort of information. Do come in," he says handing Jay-Jay a large fluffy towel. "What kind of information do you have?" Barry asks with growing interest.

Jay-Jay gratefully takes the towel and rubs his arms and head vigorously. A glint of mischief sparkles in his eye as he begins his tale. "I was getting ready to leave yesterday when I remembered I had left my jacket on top of the washing machine in the laundry. I had gone there to speak to Joe before my shift started and simply forgot to pick it up. I was just about to leave when I overheard Beth talking quietly on her cell."

"Do you have any idea who she was talking to?" Barry asks hopefully.

"No, but I hid behind the door beside the drier and listened to her conversation. I just knew by the tone of her voice that she was up to no good. I clearly overheard her say, 'I fear that my plan is beginning to backfire. I'm pretty sure I have pushed him too far, not once, but twice that I am aware of, perhaps even more. I suspect he may be beginning to see through me. He is much smarter than I anticipated.' What does 'anticipated' mean, Barry?" Jay-Jay enquires with a puzzled expression.

"It means 'expected', Jay-Jay. Goodness me, give me a break! Do go on," he urges.

"I assumed that's what it meant," he says with a straight face, fibbing through his teeth.

"Okay, did she say anything else?"

"Only 'I think I have blown it. I will try to speak to him tomorrow,' was all she said before she marched off towards her Mercedes. I watched her speed away before I dared to leave the laundry. I didn't want to give her the opportunity to complain about my exhaust being noisy again."

"Will you please get that wreck of a car of yours roadworthy? It causes us almost as much trouble as Beth does," Barry jokes.

"You couldn't lend me a couple of hundred bucks, could you, Barry?" Jay-Jay smiles hopefully at him.

Taking a slow intake of breath, Barry shakes his head saying, "I will give you the benefit of the doubt and assume that you are having a laugh. Please go now, and have yourself a good day."

Jay-Jay responds with a huge grin, "It was worth a try. Kate told me about the trainers. Thanks for arranging that with them." He picks up his work schedule and whistles

'Always look on the bright side of life' as he leaves Barry to get on with his day in peace.

Barry throws his arms up in mock exasperation. "No problem," he shouts as the door swings shut. "That boy will be the death of me," he says to Ethel before continuing, "he is extremely likeable though, don't you agree?"

"He sure is, and he means well."

The office phone rings and Ethel answers it. "Hi, Grampy, I'm fine, how are you?" Barry hears her say, before wondering why his boss is calling at this time of day. Ethel nods her head silently several times leaving him even more intrigued. Removing the top of her pen with her teeth, she jots down the message before handing it over to an anxious Barry. He shakes his head as he reads from the pad.

"Oh, for crying out loud! How long is this going to go on for?" he asks rhetorically. Ethel shrugs her shoulders as she hangs up the phone. "Yet another meeting after work for as many staff as possible! I wonder what Grampy has in mind this time," he exclaims. "It doesn't bear thinking about after the last performance."

*   *   *

That afternoon, Barry's iPhone rings. It is Nigel calling from the bank. "Good afternoon, young man. How are you?" he enquires politely.

"I'm great, how are you? What can we do for you?" is Barry's reply, trying to keep his curiosity in check.

"I feel we need to meet to discuss something of great importance. I don't wish to discuss it over the phone, and I don't have the time to go into details right now. How does nine a.m. in three days' time suit you?" Barry checks his schedule and confirms the appointment with Nigel. When Barry presses him further, Nigel replies, "It concerns Hope Farm and Beth. I've been battling with my conscience for some time now, and I hoped I would never have to divulge the information I have for you, but recent events have forced my hand. Say absolutely nothing to Grampy for the time being. I must make that absolutely clear."

"I understand, Nigel. Thank you for your concern. I will see you in three days' time then." Barry gently taps his mouth with the phone several times before placing it back in its cradle. He shuffles his papers aimlessly before carefully placing his engraved gold pen back in its holder on the desk.

* * *

After an exceptionally busy day, Grampy arrives at the meeting carrying an enormous box of cakes and donuts. Placing them carefully at the end of the desk, he asks Ethel to pour some hot chocolate for those who might like it. Clearing his throat, he takes a handkerchief from his pants pocket and wipes his sweating brow. "Whoever is whistling, could you please stop? It is very distracting," Grampy demands. Waves of laughter fill the office as Jay-Jay finishes his rendition of 'Happy days are here again.' "If only," Grampy laughs, looking at Jay-Jay with half a smile. The tension in the room seems to ease.

"Nice one, Jay-Jay," Kate whispers, elbowing him sharply in the ribs. "Now keep quiet."

Noticing how uncomfortable Grampy looks, Ethel's heart goes out to him. He starts, stammering slightly before saying, "Okay everybody, I promise I will not keep you longer than ten minutes. Thank you all for coming today. It has been brought to my attention that my fiancée Doctor McCormack has ruffled quite a few peoples' feathers around here. Let me make this perfectly clear: I am not here to defend her behavior. However, I would like to explain her circumstances. Beth is under a great deal of pressure at her practice right now. As you are aware, she has a very demanding job. In addition, you will also be aware of how much time she spends personally with her horses. Now, on top of everything else, the poor woman has to put up with my quirks and foibles." Grampy's gaze wanders around the room hoping everyone would laugh at this point. He feels slightly embarrassed as a stunned and awkward silence fills the room. Each and every member of staff stares back at him with expressionless faces. Holding his head up he continues, "I can assure you Doctor McCormack does not mean to take any of you for granted, however, I must admit she doesn't always treat people in the correct manner." A murmur of agreement circulates around the room. He continues with his speech, "I will be speaking to Beth tonight regarding her abrasive demeanor. I feel it is my duty to all of you to make her aware of how she has upset so many of you over the last few weeks." He cannot help but notice the mood starting to lift amongst his team after the conclusion of his speech. This reaction creates personal sadness for him. "That's all I have to say on this matter. I would like to take this opportunity to thank you all for your time and keep up the good work. I truly appreciate your loyal service."

"Thanks, Grampy," they all reply as Ethel hands the box of treats around the room.

"Barry, can I have a word with you outside, please?"

"I'll be right there," Barry replies wondering what could possibly be coming next. Grampy informs his manager he is going to the store to purchase lottery tickets. "As a token of my appreciation I would like to purchase an extra ticket for both you and Ethel. Do you have any preference to the numbers?"

A very puzzled Barry replies, "No, not at all. Don't feel you have to do anything special as you pay us all very well."

"No, I insist. It is the least I can do. I think Jay-Jay and Kate deserve extra also, especially after offering to work without pay during their training period with Bob and Cathy."

"Okay, thanks, if you insist," Barry laughs. "I won't try to persuade you otherwise." He turns to go back to the office and, as he opens the door, he hears Grampy say to him, "I realize myself that it is not working out with Beth, either on a personal or on a business level." Unsure of the appropriate response, Barry walks back towards him as Grampy continues, "There is no way that woman, or any other come to that, can fill Nanny's shoes. I realize that now. It is still too soon for me."

A sympathetic Barry assures him, "Life goes on. You must do what you feel is right for yourself. We are, after all, only your employees. However, if I may be so bold, I know you will be looking for many replacement staff if Beth has anything more to do with this business. She should stick with the medical profession and leave us to run the stables."

"I know, my boy, I know," a reluctant Grampy admits. "I will go and get the lottery tickets tomorrow morning on my way into work. Thanks for your time and understanding."

"Goodnight, Grampy," a tired and relieved Barry says, suspecting and hoping Grampy intends to buy a substantial amount of tickets. If he intended to spend twenty bucks he would have just given them to us as he has done several times in the past, Barry thinks. He begins to daydream of buying a racehorse of his own. After tidying his desk, he heads for home. Driving down the highway, he cannot dismiss the thought of becoming a racehorse owner. He tries exceptionally hard to dismiss these thoughts and concentrate on the traffic. The road is surprisingly quiet for the time of day which does not help at this particular moment. His mind continues to wander.

*   *   *

That night, after a heavy supper, Barry decides to have an early night. He falls quickly into a deep sleep. Before long, he has a wonderful dream. He meets up with Alistair and Liz. The dream brings him to Windy Oaks Farm where two racehorses are up for sale. He opens the barn door and reads the brass plaque above the stall. It reads, 'Golden

Fiddlehead'. "Hi, can I help you?" a friendly voice calls from behind. "I'm Lynn."

Turning to face the owner of the voice, he says, "Hello, I'm Barry the manager at Hope Farm."

"Yes, I thought I recognized you," Lynn replies with an infectious smile. Barry glances at her pink rose print cane. He tells her, "My boss's wife would have loved your cane. She used a bronze cougar print one."

"Oh!" exclaims Lynn, her eyes lighting up, "You must be referring to Nanny. Her reputation went before her. What a wicked sense of humor she had. We shared many a story before she passed away."

"I'll bet you did," Barry replies, chuckling to himself. "I am interested in finding out some details about this magnificent beauty in front of us."

"For the farm, Barry, or is it for one of your clients?"

"Actually, it is for me. I am interested in becoming a racehorse owner."

"Oh, I am sorry. I just assumed," she begins to say, her face flushing slightly with embarrassment.

"Not a problem at all," Barry assures her. "Ordinarily, I would be looking at horses for other people, but not on this particular occasion," he says laughing loudly.

"Come this way," says Lynn, gesturing for him to follow her. "I apologize for walking so slowly."

"Don't give it a second thought, I was used to Nanny," he reminds her.

Lynn smiles at that thought. Twisting her chunky turquoise necklace around her fingers she informs him, "I will call for Stacey or Tanya to lunge Golden Fiddlehead in the arena for you, so that you can see what a beautiful gait it has."

"I'd really appreciate that," he replies with mounting interest. He notices a tawny owl with hazel eyes perched on the gate at the end of the enormous arena. It is watching intensely as the horse enters through the double doors in the center wall, eager to show off its graceful power. Barry turns his attention to the horse as he scrutinizes every single movement that Golden Fiddlehead makes. He notices out of the corner of his eye, that the owl is sitting virtually motionless, watching every rippling muscle of the horse's body as Stacey puts it through its paces. Barry feels his eyes drawn back to the owl, wondering why it is so engrossed in the animal.

He wakes up with a start, feeling extremely deflated, realizing that the fabulous dream he had just had, was not real. "Oh, well," he says to himself with much disappointment. On checking his alarm clock, he decides he might as well get up, taking the opportunity to go into work early. Despite his initial disappointment, he feels optimistic today. After a long power-shower, he grabs a breakfast bar along with a carton of fruit juice from his refrigerator, and heads out towards his waiting Hummer. He begins to feel anxious as he approaches the entrance to the farm, worrying what surprises the day may bring.

CHAPTER 29

Barry arrives to the sound of Katherine and Tawny exercising their vocal chords in unison from the branches of the maple tree. "Morning ladies," he calls out to them in jest. He is most surprised when the owls turn to him and hoot, seemingly in reply. He sees Grampy striding across the gravel towards his jeep. Barry calls out, "Morning Boss. Are you still intending to get lotto tickets?"

"Of course I am. If nothing else, I always keep my promises—when I remember," he laughs. "I have decided to give every staff member a ticket as a small token of my appreciation."

"Thank you very much. Would you mind getting me some extra tickets as well? I'm feeling lucky today."

"No not at all. How many would you like?"

Reaching into his breeches pocket, Barry produces three one hundred dollar bills. "Wow," Grampy exclaims, rubbing his wrinkled brow, "I must be paying you too much!"

The laughter is reciprocated before Barry explains, "Jay-Jay and Kate each gave me a hundred bucks, I have an extra hundred also to put into the pot," he says as he hands over the money to Grampy's outstretched hand. "Somebody has to win the mega-jackpot this week. Do you know anyone who has won on the lotto?"

"I do, as it turns out," replies Grampy. "A distant relative of Nanny's who lived in Australia turned up on her mother's doorstep one evening." Barry stares in amazement, urging him to continue, which he now feels obliged to do. "They had bought an RV and decided to visit as many relatives scattered around the world as possible. They were in their golden years and it had always been a pipe dream of theirs. They never thought for a split second that it would ever come to fruition."

"Wow!" Barry exclaims enthusiastically. "What a lovely story."

"What would you do if you won?" enquires Grampy, out of politeness but with building curiosity.

Without any hesitation, Barry replies, "I would buy you out." A wide smile spreads across his face. "And I have always wanted to own a racehorse."

"Oh really? I had no idea you had a desire to have your own horse. I thought you would see more than enough of them at work."

"Not the same as having your own private interest," is the quick reply.

"No, I suppose not," agrees Grampy. He delves into his jacket pocket searching for the remote for his Jeep.

"Don't tell me you've misplaced the keys again, Grampy?" Barry says with a wry smile.

"Oh be quiet! Do you ever get tired of always being right? Between you and Nanny harping on about always hanging keys up on the peg, I don't know how I ever managed on my own. She used to remind me about getting my work things ready for the next day the night before also, so as not to be rushing about like a headless chicken in the morning."

"And did that work?" Barry inquires.

"Sometimes it did. I've had enough of this conversation, I'm off. I'll see you later."

"Before you go, just out of interest, what would you do if you scooped the jackpot, Grampy?"

After a few seconds of deep thought, Grampy simply replies, "The way I feel right now, I would sell up and go home." Before Barry can say anything more, he continues,

"You're right. I think I will treat myself to three hundred dollars' worth also, to match your syndicate with Jay-Jay and Kate. How does that sound to you?"

"Do you mean that we split any winnings?"

"That is exactly what I mean. Gosh, just think, you lot could buy me out and I really could go home and retire altogether." Both men laugh and dwell on that thought for the rest of the day.

Barry's iPhone rings. He checks the display which shows Beth's name. He then shows it to a puzzled looking Grampy who asks, "Why on earth would she be phoning your personal number at this time of day?"

"There's only one way to find out," he says, "Good morning, Doctor McCormack, what can I do for you at this hour?"

Barry puts her on speakerphone so that Grampy can also hear the conversation. "I'm sorry to call you so early, are you driving?" she enquires politely.

"No, I'm at work, actually. I came in early this morning."

"Well, in that case, I hope you can tell me why I was not informed that an eight-year-old bay belonging to Windy Oaks Farm is up for sale? I have just heard from a reliable source that this horse is the bargain of the year." Grampy notices the pitch of her voice is climbing steadily. "Can you hear me?" she demands before Barry has a chance to reply.

Looking at him with wide eyes, interjects Grampy, "May I?" Barry nods, handing him the phone. "Just who do you think you are speaking to like that, Beth?" roars Grampy. "Don't you dare speak to my staff in such a rude and abrupt manner!"

"What are you doing there?" she asks in surprise. "You should be on your way to work by now."

"This is neither the time, nor the place. You are right. I should be on my way to work. Do not bother my staff any more today. I will phone you at midday, if that is a convenient time for you. We have a great deal to discuss."

"I suppose so," she says grudgingly, lowering her voice and changing her tone substantially. Grampy clicks the off button as quickly as possible and hands the phone back to Barry. He finds his keys in his other jacket pocket, jumps into his Jeep and leaves with the sound of squealing tires.

"Oh no! What a start to the day!" exclaims Barry as he enters the office to begin his real job. He waves to Kate as she leads Aitch towards the hydrotherapy pool for his morning exercise. Aitch whinnies at the top of his voice, flaring his nostrils wildly in anticipation of the pool relieving the aches in his old bones. Spooked by the owls flying too close for comfort, he stops to paw the dusty ground with his cracked and untidy hooves. Kate waves her left arm in the air. "Go away birds," she shouts as if they could understand her.

"Twit-to-woo," Tawny replies loudly, hovering above Kate and Aitch before flying into the Old Barn through the gap in the wall.

Inside, Katherine is waiting for her. "Come on, Tawny, spread your magic," she says invitingly. "Today I would like you to demonstrate everything I have taught you. Use your magic wisely and constructively. You have ten minutes, which includes your assessment time, starting from now." Katherine starts counting silently, looking at her startled and stunned trainee. "You have wasted twenty seconds already," she informs Tawny.

Realizing she must make up for valuable lost time, the trainee owl flies as quickly as she can up to the rafters. Looking downwards, she quickly assesses the situation. Taking a deep breath, she spreads her veil of magic around the tack room, which she quickly observed needed tidying. She proceeds to the stalls to assist there. Next on the list, she thinks help is required in the feed store. As she does this, she takes a mental note never again to waste time prior to starting to spread her magic. She realizes she could have accomplished much more in the way of lifting if she had not hesitated initially. Tawny is fully aware that she is in a very privileged position and never takes the special powers Katherine chose to give her for granted. Lifting her right wing Tawny slaps herself on the leg out of sheer frustration and disappointment at her own actions. She is acutely aware she could have dealt with all the water troughs and the hundred or so pellet bags if she had started when told to do so. "I now know the real meaning of 'time is precious'," she tells Katherine, wiping away a tear of frustration with her ruffled feathers.

"Overall, you have done very well," Katherine assures her. "Do you really want to be my replacement, Tawny, as I am now ready to retire? I have had a good life and I feel I have done my time, as they say."

"You certainly have; you deserve a well-earned rest, Katherine. However, I don't think I am the one you are looking for." Tawny has never truly been comfortable with the position bestowed on her by Katherine. The younger owl looks over her right shoulder as if somebody else has spoken. Little does Katherine know how powerful Tawny's magic has become. A plan begins to form in Tawny's mind. Without further hesitation, she tells Katherine, "I don't want to take your place, not that anyone could. I truly appreciate your giving me this opportunity. I have thoroughly enjoyed learning magic from a wise old owl like you. I never realized I could do magic until now. You enabled me to spend extra time on the farm with my friends."

A very surprised but disappointed Katherine opens her wings widely, beckoning for Tawny to embrace her. As they move towards each other, Katherine replies, "You are very welcome. I cannot pretend that I am not disappointed. However, I do understand that you do not want this extra responsibility and burden placed upon your broad shoulders. I am feeling ill right now, so I think we should retire for the night. You have my permission if you wish to do a night flight on your own. I will credit you with five minutes of magic time."

"No, Katherine, but thank you for your kind offer, but I would like to keep you company tonight if you would like me to."

"I was hoping you would say that," she says gratefully. "Let's go home. I have prepared mouse sandwiches and some blueberry crumble for supper."

"Say no more, Katherine, let's go." The pair of owls fly gracefully over the Old Barn before retiring, enjoying every moment of one another's company.

CHAPTER 30

Ethel is looking particularly lovely today in her floral print dress. Her hair is in a velvet snood tied with gold braid. She looks pleased with herself as she runs to meet Barry waving a large paper in her hand as if her life depends on it. "I wish everyone was as pleased to see me, Ethel. What is all the excitement about?"

"A very posh sounding gentleman has called to make an appointment with you tomorrow afternoon." Ethel pauses for breath before continuing, "He owns a racehorse. I have all the details here for you." Her face is getting rosier by the minute as she gushes, "He wants to board his mare here. Liz recommended Miggles' Retreat to him. Isn't that fantastic news, Barry?" she asks like a child waiting to be rewarded with a candy.

"I'll let you know tomorrow, Ethel," Barry laughs as he puts his riding boots down at the side of his desk. "What did you say his name was?" he shouts as Ethel attempts to leave the office to deliver the breakfast order to Annie.

"I didn't, but his name is Captain Huntington-Church and his horse's name is 'My Little Muffin'," she calls back.

"Oh well, we will see what tomorrow brings," Barry remarks.

Later that afternoon, the door bursts open and a distraught Lisa stands before him with tears streaming down her face. She is covered from head to toe in horse muck and the smell is so strong that Barry feels like asking her to step outside.

He reluctantly invites her to sit down, gesturing towards the wooden chair. At least it can be cleaned easily after she leaves, he thinks. "What on earth happened to you?" he inquires, a little afraid that there is a distinct possibility that her reply may take some time. She stares at Barry, trying very hard to control her tears, gratefully accepting the handkerchief he takes out of his designer vest before he tells her, "Please keep it. I have plenty more."

Lisa is taking deep breaths and is trying her very best to regain control. She starts to explain, "Seamus came to my condo last night after I had tended to the horses in the Old Barn."

She is now shaking so violently that Barry interrupts her by saying, "Sorry, Lisa, but I think you should be checked over by a doctor. Did you fall from a horse?"

"No, I know it looks like it," she replies sheepishly, "I don't need any doctor, thank you, a lawyer perhaps, but not a doctor."

"Okay," he replies sympathetically. Ethel returns and is visibly shocked at Lisa's condition. "Ethel, please take all calls until I am free," her boss instructs, grabbing the 'DO NOT DISTURB' sign as he hangs it on the boardroom door. He beckons Lisa to follow him. Once inside, he invites her to sit down and pulls the ribbons on the turquoise Austrian blind, lowering it down over the window to give them some extra privacy. Having given Lisa a few minutes to compose herself, he urges her to continue with her story.

"Last night Seamus had a face like thunder when he demanded I give him my heavy duty pain killers which I had left over after falling off Sir Gareth a couple of months ago. I told him I did not have any left, but he did not believe me. He grabbed both of my arms tightly, shaking me back and forth like a rag doll. I pleaded for him to stop, but he wouldn't."

Barry is listening intently sitting opposite her, wearing a very concerned expression. "Go on," he gently urges.

"He pushed his way into my washroom. He then pulled the cabinet from the wall. The sliding glass doors shattered with the force. He went on to empty the vanity cupboard under the sink, leaving the contents strewn all across the floor."

"Did he say anything about his behavior at any point?" Barry asks.

"Yes, he kept apologizing, but told me it was my own fault as he continued to kick the contents around the floor with his dirty big boots." Lisa pauses for a moment twisting her engagement ring around her finger. She twists it three times before silently, and deliberately, removing it. She places the ring carefully in her breast pocket.

Barry is tempted to say something at this point but by keeping silent, he hopes this will encourage Lisa to talk some more. She looks up in the hope that Barry will start a conversation. He raises his eyebrows and gives her an encouraging sympathetic look. She is acutely aware that Barry's time is very valuable, but remains silent. He feels compelled to ask, "How did you get so dirty today then?"

Her reply comes slowly from her slightly bruised lips. "Seamus pushed me out of his way and I fell into a mound of you-know-what, but he didn't hit me if that's what you're thinking. I think he was angry as he had borrowed my car yesterday and he saw footprints on the dash from the soles of my riding boots. I think he thought somebody had been in the car with me. What happened was . . ." she starts to say as her voice trails away.

"No, no, no. You don't need to explain anything to me. It is your business"

"Yes, I do," she says, "I want to. What had happened was, yesterday I felt extremely tired and I had gone back to my car during lunch break to have a snooze in the passenger seat. I put my feet up on the dash. That was all, but he didn't believe me."

"Lisa. Just listen to what you are saying," he says.

"Oh, what should I do, Barry?" she asks hesitantly in the hope her boss will have all the answers for her.

He looks at her thoughtfully before replying, "Only you can decide that, Lisa, however, we both know that violence of any kind is wrong. If Seamus is showing frustration and anger now, what will he be like after you are married?"

Deep down, Lisa knows Barry is correct in what he is saying. He walks over to the window and slowly pulls up the blind to look outside. She stares out of the large window towards the yard which is now a hive of activity. She sees several horses being led by their grooms from the pasture back to their stalls, their hooves creating clouds of dust as they pass by. Realizing what time it must be when she sees the spectacle before her, she rises on her unsteady feet, thanking her boss for his advice and time. Barry moves towards her to give her a hug, trying not to breathe in during the process. A grateful Lisa rushes out to her rusty old bicycle standing against an old horsebox used to store hay. With adrenaline still pumping through her veins, she throws herself onto her bicycle as if it is a pony and pedals for all she is worth without so much as a backwards glance.

Barry looks in the mirror and rubs his fevered brow, suspecting that his hair is receding slightly. Closer inspection confirms his suspicions. Shrugging his shoulders at his reflection, he walks towards the door and removes the sign before asking Ethel, "Please close up for me. I am going to seek out Seamus and I will be going home directly after I speak with him."

"Will do Barry," his assistant replies. "You can depend on me as always. One question before you go, do you want Jay-Jay, Kate, and Joe to see to Miggles' Retreat or the Old Barn tonight?"

"Good thinking Ethel. Ask Kate to choose and then get the other stable hands to deal with the other building. It is time she took more responsibility in the scheduling of chores. One other thing, I need a vacant stall prepared in case of new clients dropping by without an appointment, which can happen, as we all know. Some people do it deliberately thinking they will catch you on the hop."

"Consider that done, Barry. You can fill me in about Lisa tomorrow," she says hopefully, lowering her head and looking over her glasses.

"You know the confidentiality clause here, same as everybody else, Ethel."

"But I'm management!" Ethel retorts with a smile.

"Good night, Ethel."

She thinks, when I get home, I am going to bake Barry his favorite chocolate cake and bring it in for a treat tomorrow. Maybe he will let something slip.

*   *   *

Deep in thought and with a spring in his step, Barry strides towards where Seamus is working. He finds him sitting on an upturned pail biting a piece of hay between his uneven teeth. On spotting Barry coming towards him, he springs to his feet and proceeds to groom Perrah. "Hi, Barry, how are you this evening?" he enquires unaware that Lisa has already spoken to him.

"I am well, thank you, Seamus. However, we need to talk right now. Please put Perrah in her stall and meet me at the picnic bench over here," he requests politely.

Seamus, now wearing a panic-stricken expression, realizes the trouble he could be in. He hands Perrah over to Joe who is passing and is already behind in his daily duties. "Barry needs to speak with me. Can you finish grooming Perrah before putting her in her stall?" he asks nervously, "Her feeding requirements are posted on the wall."

"Oh, I suppose so," is Joe's sluggish reply. "I have enough to do without this as well."

Choosing to ignore Joe's lack of enthusiasm and team spirit, Seamus joins Barry on the picnic bench. Before he can even open his mouth, he fears Lisa has spilled the beans about the previous night's events. He chooses unwisely to go on the attack, "Look, this is between me and Lisa. It is absolutely none of your business, so back off," he snarls at his employer.

"Sit down right now and remember who you are talking to!" Barry orders, before lowering his voice. "I understand you are upset, but whether you like it or not, I am your boss, for the time being at least. If a member of my staff is unable to continue with his or her duties, then it does become my business."

Jumping quickly to his feet, Seamus snaps back, "I have had enough. Lisa is always looking at the other stable lads. She even had the cheek to call me 'hop-a-long' the other day. She never used to be cruel or torment me in any way about my limp." Barry's temper eases slightly as he witnesses the pain in Seamus' eyes. "Walk straight, pull your leg up, do this, do that. I just can't take any more of it," Seamus continues.

Seizing the opportunity to speak, Barry reassures Seamus by saying, "Lisa loves you just the way you are. To my knowledge, she has never known you without a limp."

Calming down slightly at this thought, Seamus remarks, "I know what you're saying."

Barry continues, "I think it would be a good idea for you to take two or three days off, on full pay, of course. That will give you time to cool off and think things through."

"Full pay, you say?" Seamus enquires.

"Yes, full pay. You are an important cog in this wheel, Seamus. You are greatly respected here by everyone, but particularly by Grampy and me. I know he will be fine with my decision."

"Hmm," Seamus agrees gratefully. "Thank you, sir. I accept your kind offer." He shakes Barry's hand, "I assume Lisa must have spoken to you?"

Lowering his head, Barry nods in agreement. "Good night, Seamus."

"Good night Barry," he replies sheepishly as he turns to go home.

Oh boy! I do not know how this is going to pan out, Barry thinks as he opens the door of his Hummer to go home after what has been another long and tiresome day. He toots the horn, waving to Ethel in the driveway as he passes her. She has stopped to stroke Pixie, lovingly pulling up some grass for the pony. Flossie and Alfie trot towards Barry as he lowers his window as he passes them. What a cutie Alfie is, he thinks as he bids Ethel a good night.

CHAPTER 31

Kate's grumpy scowl greets Barry the following morning. The fog and drizzle does not help lift his mood either. "Good morning, cheery face. What's up with you?" he teases.

"Well for a start, Lisa and Seamus haven't turned up. Nigel came in to see his horses and told me to remind you about your appointment tomorrow morning."

"Yes I have that in my diary, thanks. Seamus will not be in until next week. Lisa should be here, though. I did not give her permission to take time off. Has she not phoned?"

"Not that I'm aware of," Kate snaps. "You gave Seamus permission to take time off?" she asks with anger in her voice.

"Yes I did. It is nothing for you to worry about. Leave it with me and I will get back to you when I find out what's happening with Lisa."

Kate continues, hand on hip, her eyes blazing, "Now Nigel wants me to exercise both his horses this weekend, on top of all my other chores as he is going to Anti-go-somewhere-or-other for a long ride, so he can't be here to ride his horses as he normally would be."

"Oh, I know the town you mean," Barry says laughing loudly at her inability to pronounce the unusual name correctly, which irritates Kate even more.

"I don't give a flying toss how you pronounce that stupid place. The point is he is not going to be here. What use is that to me?"

"None whatsoever, sweet pea," he replies trying to keep his face straight. "I hate to remind you, but you are paid to look after the customer's horses."

Quick as a flash, she retaliates with, "Yes, but there are only so many hours in a day. I am not able to do everything." She tries to disguise a smile creeping onto her freckled cheeks. She nods her head, tossing her gorgeous (auburn and blonde streaked) hair forward in an attempt to cover her face.

Barry suggests, "Just do your best and let me know what you are not be able to complete. I will get others to help you. As you know, I am seeing Nigel tomorrow, so I will ask him if he minds another stable hand or a jockey to pamper to his horses' every need. How does that sound to you, Kate?"

The reluctant stable girl grudgingly mumbles, "Thanks Barry. You're a great help, I suppose." She mounts her tethered horse and trots off towards the Racing Snake to continue with her busy day. Today can only improve, he thinks, as he checks his full diary.

Ethel arrives a few minutes later carrying a large cake tin, Barry notices. Oh no! He strongly suspects this is a bribe. "Sorry I'm late," she cries at the top of her voice. "I'll put the coffee pot on and cut this cake I made especially for you. I hope you haven't had too big a breakfast." Before he has a chance to reply, Ethel pats his shoulder, exclaiming, "Now you can tell me all about yesterday!"

"Ethel!" he quickly replies. "We talked about this, but I would like to take you up on the offer of coffee and cake. Now let's try and make up for the time we lost yesterday." A disappointed Ethel purses her lips tightly, reluctantly having to admit defeat, for now at least.

The chink of spurs echoes around the vestibule. Barry looks up on hearing the quick footsteps. A fond smile forms on his thin lips as the sound reminds him of Nanny when she used to come in for a coffee after a ride many moons ago. The office door bursts open and a tall gentleman dressed in a heavy tweed suit enters. He appears to be the "old school tie" type. To complete the look, he sports the most magnificent handlebar moustache Barry has ever seen. It complements the checked shirt he is wearing to a tee. He is also wearing a luxurious pair of soft shiny leather riding boots. Feeling almost compelled to stand to attention, Barry extends his hand towards the distinguished looking gentleman standing before him.

"Captain Huntington-Church," he says, introducing himself, taking Barry's small hand in his rather large muscular one, squeezing it so hard that Barry is unable to reply.

Barry musters a tiny smile before retracting his now bruised hand. He inspects it briefly and manages to say in a tiny voice, "Good morning, sir, please take a seat. I'm Barry, how may I help you?"

Ethel flounces into the room wearing a large grin on her face. Barry glances over at her thinking, is she seriously flirting with him? He is well out of her league. The Captain totally ignores Ethel's looks of admiration and takes the offered seat. "Any chance of a drink around here?" he asks brusquely to nobody in particular. Barry is rather taken aback by his forwardness, however, he feels there is no choice but to offer this potential client a drink, "Would you like tea, coffee, or would you prefer a cold drink?" he asks politely.

"You can keep them," the Captain quips, "A gin-and-tonic would be more in keeping." Ethel stares at him in astonishment, as if he has just said, "Ethel, you are the most beautiful woman I have ever had the good fortune to encounter."

Barry has to think quickly on his feet, and he then agrees. "What a great idea. I will phone Annie and ask her to bring gin, tonic, ice, and lemon over to us." Ethel makes the phone call to the house. Annie agrees readily, hoping Barry will offer her a glass too. She tells Ethel, "I will be there in two minutes."

"I am not going to beat around the bush," states the Captain, "Liz Smith assures me that you are by far the best livery stables in this province, and I respect her judgment. I require you to look after My Little Muffin. This horse is my entire life and I require her to be looked after to the very highest standard." Before Barry can utter a single word in reply, the Captain continues, "I shall require a list of your trainers and all staff who will be handling Muffin. I shall also require references and résumés from each of them, so that I can check them out personally." Barry looks across the desk quizzically, in disbelief at this ludicrous list of demands. Ethel is looking on adoringly, totally smitten by the Captain.

Annie hurries into the office carrying a silver tray with crystal tumblers, a small ice bucket, a bottle of Bombay Sapphire Gin, and some tonic water. She pours both men a drink. Ethel, wanting to keep her wits about her, politely declines Annie's offer of a drink. Annie leaves the office as quickly as she entered.

Barry takes a large gulp of the refreshing drink to steady his now shattered nerves. He shakes his head as politely as he can without showing disapproval and total disbelief at the audacity of this potential client. "I can put you on the waiting list," he offers in an authoritative voice. "We do not have any vacancies for a horse of that caliber at present." He can see that the Captain is stunned by his announcement. It had never crossed his mind that there might not be a vacancy at Hope Farm. Vigorously twirling his moustache, much to Ethel's amusement, the Captain starts to fidget uncomfortably in his chair. Barry adds, "People's circumstances change and a vacancy may arise at any time."

The Captain jumps to his feet in anger, slamming his drink down hard on the table, splashing some onto Ethel's sensible suede shoes. His nostrils flare, resembling a pony's, as he twirls the other side of his moustache in anger. He says, "If that is your attitude, I will take my business elsewhere."

The Captain storms out of the office, breaking wind as he pulls the heavy door shut behind him.

"Now do you still think the sun shines out of his you-know-where, Ethel?" asks Barry. Both burst into fits of laughter. "All that glitters is not gold. How I wish Nanny had been here to witness this. I know she would have given a very good impersonation of him within ten seconds of his leaving, without a shadow of a doubt." After a moments' hesitation he adds, "And she would have finished his drink!"

"Let's try to get on with the rest of the day," Ethel says, pausing slightly before adding, "I didn't think people like him made rude noises like that."

"Ethel, get on with your work and forget about him altogether," Barry advises her, trying desperately not to start laughing all over again. "Thank goodness we don't encounter many people like him. Just wait until I get my hands on Liz Smith. I don't know what she was thinking."

"Maybe she set the meeting up for a joke," Ethel offers.

"She wouldn't do that," he replies. "She knows we are all rushed off our feet and that we are too busy for time-wasters."

"Well, I know that she doesn't get much attention at home, so I suspect she takes any opportunity to mess people around for devilment, thinking it is funny."

Barry looks up in surprise. "How do you know that?" he asks his assistant.

"Oh, I'm sorry. I should not have said anything. It's none of my business."

"Sure thing, Ethel. No problem. We all need to vent our feelings from time to time." The phone rings and Barry answers. It is Paddy on the line informing him that Jay-Jay has called to report what he thinks there is ringworm in the Old Barn. "You were busy, so he called me directly."

"Okay, that's fine, Paddy. I will go there and check it out now."

"I will be with you in half an hour," Paddy informs him. "Ask Ethel to put the kettle on, please.

CHAPTER 32

Tawny and Katherine are sound asleep, perched high in the rafters of the Old Barn after an uneventful night flight when Paddy drives up in his brand new bottle-green Jeep. "Hi, everyone," he calls brightly, pushing his oversized bronze-framed glasses up his nose, only for them to immediately slip down again. "Jay-Jay suspects that Lady Jane has ringworm. Let's take a look," he says walking into the barn to meet Barry and Jay-Jay who are standing beside Lady Jane's stall.

Kate pops her head around the door, "Hi Paddy, I'm just disinfecting the saddle pads and all her grooming equipment. I've removed all her old bedding and Joe is going to burn it in a few minutes."

"That's good to hear," he replies. After a thorough examination Paddy announces, "I can confirm Jay-Jay's diagnosis was correct." Turning to him, Paddy jests, "You should have gone to veterinary school instead of messing about, Jay-Jay."

"No chance! I can hardly read," he replies, laughing at the thought. "You do your job and I will do mine, Paddy."

Kate interjects, "How can you tell that it is definitely ringworm?"

"Her hair has fallen out in circular areas, as you can see here on her hind quarters," Paddy tells her, pointing to the infected area. He asks Barry to instruct the team to check her vitamin A intake and suggests an increase of selenium in her diet. "That should do the trick," he assures them. "I will check on her in a few days' time. You caught it early and did the right thing by phoning me. You have most likely stopped an outbreak on the farm. Well done," he addresses everyone. Patting Jay-Jay on the shoulder, he reminds him to inform the owner.

On his way out, Paddy stops to pet Pixie who is grazing happily in the field along with Alfie. Pixie whinnies at the top of its voice as it recognizes him as he steps out of his vehicle. It swishes its tail vigorously and throws its head up and down in delight at the attention. Pixie trots all the way down the field beside the driveway as Paddy departs for home.

Barry asks Jay-Jay, "Do you have a couple of hours to spare? I will pay triple time tonight."

"Triple time plus a pint?" he asks hopefully.

"Deal," Barry replies gratefully.

"What do you need help with that I can do?"

"Don't underestimate your abilities, Jay-Jay. I need you to check all the equipment against the back numbers, which need double-checking. I also need help with the entry forms for the three-day event next month. I have quite simply run out of steam as well as time. I'm just so tired right now, I'm afraid I might miss something important if I try to do it all by myself."

"No problem, we'll get it done together," Jay-Jay assures his manager. "Before I forget, when you have a moment, can you please have a word with Joe?"

"Slow Joe I assume?" Barry enquires.

"Exactly," he promptly replies. "Only, now, the entire team at Miggles' Retreat is affected by his ineffectiveness."

"Yes, I will speak to him again, but between you and me, Joe will soon be out of the picture."

"Oh!" Jay-Jay replies. "That is music to my ears."

They work extremely well together. Barry is the more experienced of the two and he works methodically. Jay-Jay knows every piece of equipment inside and out. He also knows the number of trunks that are required for a three-day event. This makes life easier for the riders. They can then give their full attention to their mounts. He turns to Barry, asking, "While I remember, do you mind if I experiment by introducing a rubber snaffle to the young horse we purchased last month? I believe she would benefit greatly from using one."

"Do whatever you think is best. It is worth a try. Let me know how you get on. Technically, you do not have to ask my permission for any change in tack. I trust your judgment implicitly, Jay-Jay."

"Okay. Cheers, I will bear that in mind in future," he responds happily.

"I assume you are referring to the little bay we named Lucky?"

"I am indeed," replies Jay-Jay, nodding.

"Well actually, I'm not convinced that it has the correct temperament for the special class. That is why we purchased it originally. I observed it myself several times in the last two weeks. What is your professional opinion on her, Jay-Jay?"

"She needs longer to settle in before I can comment further. We'll see how she responds with the snaffle."

"You can take Lucky under your wing if you'd like."

"Yes thanks. I would like that. The horse definitely has potential. We will soon see if Lucky becomes more cooperative. Here's hoping anyway."

"You know I'm in favor of experimentation, trial and error. Let me know in two weeks' time how she progresses. Let's get cracking with this paperwork as I have a surreptitious meeting at the bank tomorrow morning."

"With Nigel?" Jay-Jay asks as he sorts the entry forms into alphabetical order.

"Yes," is Barry's prompt reply, hoping Jay-Jay will not ask for any details.

"Did you know he has four granddaughters?"

"He can't have! He's too young to have four grandchildren."

"Two sets of twins, apparently."

"Gosh! Better him than me. He did briefly mention that he has grandchildren, now you come to mention it," Barry remarks, before quickly changing the subject. "I have noticed Kate has come on leaps and bounds in dressage."

Jay-Jay smiles and nods in agreement. "I think she stands a good chance in the upcoming competition if she manages to keep her concentration long enough. Liz is very accommodating in allowing her to practice on Lady Jane. She feels sorry for Kate as she knows she still hasn't got over Jumper's untimely demise."

"Do you know if Kate has all the kit and tack ready that she will require?" Barry asks, knowing full well what the answer will be.

Jay-Jay bursts out laughing. "Kate organized? Are you for real? She expects everyone to get everything together for her. She needs someone to wave a magic wand to get her equipment ready in time. Mind you, after having said that, she is showing a marked improvement."

Jay-Jay then observes the owls flying around and around the outside of the building. "I wonder what's up with them," he remarks. Just as the words tumble from his mouth, Katherine flies by about three feet away from where the men are standing by the office window. Tawny quickly follows her. Both men decide to step outside for some much-needed fresh air. They lean against the freshly painted rails, watching the birds swoop and dive for a few moments before they fly through the gap in the wall into the Old Barn. "Let's follow them," Jay-Jay suggests. "I have a feeling they are up to something."

"Not this time, Jay-Jay. I must phone Nigel; another time maybe. Perhaps on a lunch break. That would give us enough time to watch them in peace."

"Sounds like a good plan," Jay-Jay quickly replies. "I will hold you to that. If there's nothing more I can do for you, I will go and finish off the stables for the night."

"We're finished here. I am going home now. Will you have about another hour's work to do?"

"Probably between one and two hours," Jay-Jay replies shrugging his shoulders.

"Good man. I appreciate your efforts. I will see you tomorrow after my meeting."

Jay-Jay wanders off, deep in thought of how he can complete his tasks quickly before falling into bed. He does not know if he will have the time or the inclination to eat.

Unbeknown to him, at this very minute, Katherine and Tawny are taking care of all of his duties. On his arrival at the stables, Jay-Jay's jaw drops in astonishment. He looks around, shouting, "Hello! Hello! Is there anybody there?" The only sounds in the building are the snorting of horses together with the low hooting of owls in the distance. He double-checks every stall in total confusion as the entire barn is spick and span. A huge sense of relief floods through his entire tired and sore body. He dims the lights before locking the door, and then he heads for home, stopping for a pizza on his way.

CHAPTER 33

The traffic in town is heavy and slow moving. About as slow as Joe, Barry thinks to himself as he mentally urges the vehicles in front of him to move more quickly. "Oh come on, come on! I'm going to be late for my appointment," he says addressing the line of cars in front of his Hummer. Beads of perspiration begin to break out on his lined forehead. The traffic moves slowly but surely forward. Checking his wristwatch, he reassures himself he will make the scheduled appointment in time. The toot of a car horn and a friendly wave comes from the driver in the next lane on the bridge. "Oh no, I don't believe this is happening. It's Grampy on his way into work. I thought he started an hour ago." Barry puts on his biggest smile and waves back. Grampy acknowledges the gesture but looks puzzled; his forehead appears even more furrowed than normal. Barry can tell from his expression that he is surprised at seeing him here at this time of day. I will have to make up some excuse about urgent farm business now, he reluctantly decides.

Barry manages to avoid a collision with a bus as it pushes into the lane directly in front of him. He narrowly avoids hitting it, but does not avoid Grampy, who has not only reached his destination, but also for his cell phone. Barry thinks the best plan of action is to ignore the call, for now at least. In doing so, he buys himself some time; however, a disgruntled Grampy is suspicious but cannot do anything about it at this particular moment. He sounds anxious as he leaves a voicemail message for Barry to call him at lunchtime. Grampy, understandably, hates being uninformed of any farm business.

Barry carefully parks his Hummer in the harbor car park. He has to run up the hill so that he is not late for his appointment, making it with two minutes to spare. He quickly visits the washroom to perfect his hairstyle before splashing his face with cool water. He delves into his laptop case to refresh the already slightly overpowering aroma of cologne.

On seeing Barry enter the bank, Nigel stands up from behind his desk. He had left his office door ajar on purpose to see him.

"Good morning, Nigel," Barry says accepting the offered handshake. "How are you?" Barry cannot believe a man of Nigel's age still sports such a ramrod straight back. He carries himself so well. It gives him such an air of authority, Barry decides.

Nigel greets him with, "Top of the morning to you my man," his faint Irish accent trickling through, despite his having left his homeland some twenty years ago. He appears tense and is visibly uncomfortable as he gestures for Barry to take a seat, closing the door behind him. Barry settles into a chair as Nigel twists the wand to close both window blinds. Sensing a change in the atmosphere Barry also begins to feel uneasy. "Would you like a coffee?" Nigel enquires politely.

"No, thank you," replies Barry, as he settles into the swivel leather chair. Nigel furtively unlocks his filing cabinet, removing a beige file containing photographs and a few photocopies of some documents. "What is this all about, Nigel? I've never seen you act like this before."

Nigel nonchalantly tosses the folder onto the desk for him to inspect. As he reaches forward to pick up the file, Nigel begins to explain. "I feel very disloyal showing this to you. I know I shouldn't. Doctor McCormack is a very valuable customer, but I feel it is only right to let you make up your own mind. I was rather hoping it wouldn't come to this, but due to the engagement I cannot remain silent any longer." Nigel strokes his old school tie which always boosts his self-confidence. He always wears it when he knows he has to conduct a difficult meeting. It is his security blanket. Ignoring the intrigued and worried expression on Barry's face, Nigel continues, "I really feel obliged to divulge the information I have regarding Beth. I regard Hope Farm, Nanny, when she was alive, Grampy and you, as good friends. I know you are all valued customers."

Turning to look directly at Barry over his bronze, metal-framed glasses, Nigel enquires, "Have you perchance heard anything in the past about Beth's husband to arouse any suspicion?"

"No, I haven't. However, I do know that everyone on the farm despises her. Rumor has it that she is also horrendous to work for due to her volatile temperament."

Nigel's voice becomes a little squeaky with nerves due to the uncomfortable situation. "You don't say. Can you imagine what it must be like being barked at all the time, instead of being spoken to? I suppose you just have to get used to it, or perhaps you might not even notice it after a while. Maybe you just have to accept it." Nigel suggests. "It wouldn't be me," he says wiping a trickle of sweat running down his well-trimmed left eyebrow with his silk handkerchief. "In her defense, I'm reliably informed Beth is a good practitioner, but, as you can imagine, she is belligerent most of the time. I personally find that both tiresome and offensive."

"Me too," Barry agrees, before adding, "I find that to be the most annoying thing about her. I find myself biting my tongue on so many occasions when I have to have a conversation with her. Anyway, Nigel, please fill me in on the mystery of why you called me here today. My curiosity is killing me!" Barry adjusts his suede vest, loosening the bottom two buttons before crossing his legs in anticipation of this taking some time.

Nigel silently studies Barry from the opposite side of his desk. Clearing his throat, he begins his story. "I knew Beth back in my university days." He hesitates slightly before continuing, "She was an awkward and argumentative student. The only time that she was quiet, I am reliably informed, was when everything was going her way. She did win several awards and yes, she studied extremely hard, but she made most of the staff and professors very wary of her. Beth would argue any point to try and persuade others around to her way of thinking."

"How could she argue with a text book?" Barry asks in wonder.

"Beth always thinks she knows better than everyone else, typically dismissing what she doesn't want to accept. I clearly remember the day her sister shouted across the campus 'Go home, Beth, you ruin my life, you are so anal.' I have no idea what the argument was about, however her sister's statement must have touched a raw nerve. After that comment, Beth would ask anyone who would listen, 'Do you think I'm obsessive or anal?' Depending on the reply she received, the tone for the day would be set. Many people were afraid of her. She intimidated everyone she met. They would lie to her repeatedly just to keep the peace. She is a force to be reckoned with. It is so sad that she has such an unfortunate nature."

"No surprises so far, Nigel." Barry is showing signs of irritation at Nigel's procrastination in this meeting. He has so many chores requiring his attention back at the stables. He is acutely aware of time passing quickly.

Nigel slowly sips his mineral water, clears his throat once again before blurting out, "She was involved in her husband's so called accident."

Barry's head tilts a little to the right, his eyebrows rising slightly. "Oh, yeah?" he says urging Nigel to spill the beans. "The information has to be accurate, you do realize that, don't you Nigel?"

"Of course I do. I witnessed her tampering with her husband's horse tack myself. Is that good enough for you, Barry?" enquires Nigel, a little irritated by the previous remark. "Beth graduated with honors, achieving one of the best final grades that year. She was a very attractive woman then and she still is, as you know. Her expressive eyes with their flecks of green twinkled in a certain light. Everyone used to comment on them."

"You just happened to notice," quips Barry.

"I did indeed. Beth always struggled to maintain any relationship one way or another, until the day Alexander McCormack was introduced to her. He was studying oceanography at the same university. He was a year below her, but they seemed to enjoy each other's company. They immediately clicked. Surprisingly, they could challenge one another without argument most of the time. The bond between them became stronger as they both shared a love of horses."

"Both were accomplished riders, I assume?" asks an intrigued Barry.

"They certainly were. They were both horse owners as well. I think Beth mentioned that she had owned a pony as a child. She and Alexander used to compete on a regular basis at a competitive level. While other students would be out doing what students do, Alexander and Beth would be studying furiously or, as far as I can remember, they were in the company of the equestrian fraternity."

Barry ponders this for a second. "Hmm, very interesting Nigel, do go on," he urges, glancing at his watch.

"I must admit they were a striking couple. I'm reliably informed Alexander's family was self-made. They owned a construction company which had gone from strength to strength over the years. They had been in the right place at the right time, plus they were hard workers and had reliable staff."

"A winning combination," Barry comments with a wide grin spreading across his face.

"Indeed. Alexander's father was in a horrific car accident and passed away after being bedridden for many years. Although he did have insurance, there wasn't anything like the coverage he should have had, and that's putting it mildly. The cost of his medical requirements after the accident was astronomic. Unbeknown to his wife, he had remortgaged everything apart from a few horses and a small stable block. He had to do this, along with many other people, because of the recession caused by nine-eleven. When he died he left an enormous amount of debt."

"How sad," Barry interjects.

"Alexander's mother couldn't live with the shame. She had never known what it was like to want for anything. She could not cope after her husband passed away, so sadly she took her own life." Nigel pauses briefly to take another sip of his mineral water. "Beth thought her husband was not just rich, but very rich indeed when they married. The truth was revealed after she became pregnant with her first child."

"Her first child?" Barry enquires. "I wasn't aware she had any children. I guess it never came up in conversation."

"She has three actually," replies Nigel, "Twin boys and one daughter. As far as I know, the boys are married and live in Germany. Her daughter, who is an academic genius incidentally, runs a riding school in the south of England."

"Oh, really? You do surprise me," his eyes widening at Nigel's revelation. "I have never heard her make any reference to any of them."

"I remember one time being at a dinner party at Beth and Alexander's house. She was trying to impress her medical colleagues, amongst others. Typically, Beth would invite the local minister, the bank manager, plus the school principal, always a good one. It resembled a board meeting more than a social dinner party. You know the score."

"I sure do," Barry chuckles quietly, while uncrossing his legs. "I can just picture the scene."

"I used to go just to get a fabulous meal. I must say, Beth is a fantastic cook," Nigel admits.

"Did she do the cooking or did she get caterers in?" Barry jests.

"She possibly did. I never thought on that. You are wicked," giggles Nigel. "Their children were never spoken of as such, but the oddest thing I noticed when I was there was that considering both her boys are married, there was not a single wedding photo on display in any of the main rooms. I don't know about you Barry, but I find that very odd."

"That says it all," Barry looks down at the office floor shaking his head at the thought of how hurtful that must be for all concerned. "So getting back to the tampered tack part of the story, what happened next?" he asks, looking directly at Nigel.

"At the Willowvale summer competition, Beth was standing beside the Chef de Keep at the edge of the arena, watching her husband intently. I did not know what she had done to the saddle and girth until it was too late. Had I known the chain of events that took place afterwards, I would not have allowed her husband to enter the arena. I can never forgive myself for that as I knew something underhand had gone on."

"What happened next?" Barry asks gently.

"Alexander kept pulling his helmet forward so I immediately knew he was having a problem with it. Then I noticed he looked lop-sided in the saddle after the water jump. He took five strides instead of his usual four at the dry ditch, which confirmed to me that he was in big trouble. His horse was snorting and blowing, but the rhythm of the canter was good. He then proceeded to the vertical wall, knocking the top block off which was most unusual for him. You could see him pushing down hard with his right leg trying to straighten the saddle, all the while pushing his helmet forward. Slowly but surely he was losing control of the animal. It was throwing its head much more than normal and it was obvious Alexander was extremely uncomfortable as he turned to face the triple jump."

Barry looks silently at Nigel, nodding slightly urging him to continue. "He jumped the first part of the fence well, considering," Nigel recalls, "however his helmet flew off before his horse's hooves had even touched the ground. I think this was a contributing factor to what happened next. I think it spooked the horse and it stumbled, throwing Alexander from the saddle which was now obviously loose. I glanced over towards where Beth was standing. She was staring with an odd expression on her face. I found it suspicious that she did not show any concern whatsoever at the difficulties her husband was having in the arena. I also found it odd that the Chef de Keep did not utter a single word to her either. It was as if they were witnessing a well-rehearsed play. Alexander crashed headlong into the left hand side of the second part of the triple, scattering poles in every direction. The horse stumbled, then bolted. His saddle slipped under the horse's tummy before falling off altogether. Without thinking, I ran into the arena signaling for the paramedics to follow me. Alexander was lying motionless with blood trickling from his right ear. I glanced in Beth's direction again and could not believe that she was still standing in exactly the same spot, only this time she was alone. She had not made any attempt to attend to her husband or catch his horse."

"You mean she didn't go into the arena at all?" Barry asks, extremely concerned by now.

"Not at this point she didn't," Nigel replies. "The announcement came over the P.A. 'Doctor Elizabeth McCormack, please meet the ambulance at the main entrance immediately.' Beth then proceeded to show massive concern in front of the gathering professionals. I looked straight into her eyes noticing the lack of emotion in them. Eventually the horse was caught and was led back to the stable block, shaken but otherwise unharmed. I could not help but notice that a man from the crowd picked up the fallen saddle. I happen to know who that person was."

"Who was it?" he asks.

"It was Inspector Whipton."

"I thought he retired years ago, didn't he?" Barry asks rhetorically, thumbing through the newspaper clippings in the file, without actually reading them.

"Yes," Nigel replies with a frown. "It struck me as odd at the time, and it strikes me as being even more suspicious now. It was a strange coincidence, was it not, that the inspector was right there at that particular moment. I happen to know he doesn't even like horses. The paramedics carefully carried Alexander into the ambulance with Beth dutifully at his side. Alexander suffered a fractured skull, amongst his many other injuries. He slipped into a coma for about two months as I recall. Beth became the dutiful wife, visiting at every opportunity, bringing gifts to the hospital staff. She was full of the joys of spring. Not what you would expect from a woman whose husband was at death's door. When people enquired how he was progressing, you could see the joy in her eyes even though her mouth delivered the appropriate response every time without fail. I remember he appeared to be coming out of his coma at one point. Beth became agitated instead of being delighted with his progress. She appeared angry and disappointed. Poor Alexander proceeded to have two heart attacks within a week of one another. Beth appeared more relaxed than ever after that happened. She must have known what was most likely going to happen to him next. She was becoming adept at playing the merry widow."

"Oh Nigel, that's an awful thing to say, but I'm enjoying this story. My dilemma now is how, when, and if I tell Grampy about this?"

"Well I can't help you with that one. I felt obliged to give you this information, and it is entirely up to you what you do with it. A word of warning, though; I would not mention the tampered tack. That would open up a completely new can of worms," Nigel warns.

"There is nothing I would like more than to see that woman behind bars. I would even be delighted to visit her," Barry laughs at that very thought.

Nigel smiles before continuing, "The only time I detected her voice waver, even slightly, was when she phoned me to tell me he had died of pneumonia and complications."

"Oh, my goodness!" Barry exclaims, "This is about the last thing I expected when I walked in here today. I thought it might be about our business loan, although business is brisk, thank goodness."

"Don't ever worry about that," Nigel reassures him, "but if you could get your clients to pay on time, especially ones with a title, it would help," he says with sarcasm dripping from his tongue. Barry notes there isn't a flicker of a smile on Nigel's face, despite the dry comment. "Here's the best bit, Barry." Nigel teases, taking another sip of his water, before asking him if he would like another drink.

"Nigel, please stop it! You are deliberately throwing verbal grenades then waiting for the after effects. You know I will get you back! Get on with it, or I will have no option but to leave."

"No you won't, this true story is too juicy."

"Okay, you win, but I promise you, I will get my revenge."

Nigel concludes his story. "There was very little left over from what the insurance money Alexander had once the medical bills, equine debts etc. were all paid. Beth went into a deep depression and was unable to work for quite some time. She had to employ a locum doctor. I suggested she sell some of their horses to ease her financial burden, but she refused. Her melancholy mood lasted a long time, during which time she drank heavily. She did other things that Grampy is unaware of, but I will not go into that. That is her business."

"Do you know that for a fact?" interjects Barry.

"Yes, I witnessed it many times but I don't want to elaborate on the subject."

"Okay, fine," Barry nods in recognition of Nigel's discretion.

"She is a very discontented, obstreperous woman at the best of times."

"No chance of you getting together with her then?" Barry asks, moving his chair back.

Nigel glares in both amazement and amusement, his cute little nose twitching at the thought. He is unable to think of a sharp reply. Eventually he says, "Touché." They shake hands, and Barry thanks Nigel for the most entertaining and informative meeting he has had all year. Although the last hour has been extremely exciting for him, he realizes one way or another that this is going to have an enormous effect on Hope Farm. An unburdened Nigel returns to his everyday duties, deciding to do a review on Doctor McCormack's accounts.

CHAPTER 34

Ethel is in full flow as she organizes the daily schedules for the farm staff. She is distracted by a small mail van pulling up outside. She does a double take as she sees the driver getting out. He rifles through his bag as he walks towards her. Opening the door with mounting excitement she asks, "Conrad Burke? Is that you?"

The stunned mailman looks up from the contents of his bag, staring at her as recognition slowly dawns on him. "Ethel Hartlin, is that really you?"

"It is, and I'm still a Hartlin," she replies with a fond smile. "Well goodness gracious me! How are you, Conrad? I haven't seen you for," she pauses for a second, "it must be nearly thirty years."

"I'm good, thanks," is his chipper reply. His eyes sparkle in the morning sunshine. "It's thirty-one years, not that I'm counting."

Taking the bull by the horns, as she realizes time is running out, she launches herself straight at Conrad, kissing him fondly on the cheek. Conrad steps back in surprise, his jaw dropping with delight. His face lights up like a Christmas tree. They briefly look into each other's eyes, before he delves back into his bag, producing an envelope addressed to Barry Gordon. Ethel signs for the delivery, hoping Conrad will arrange some type of meeting to catch up on their lost years.

He looks Ethel up and down, telling her she looks well. Conrad then recalls a night when he and Ethel had attended a dance at the legion. "Do you remember the night I was walking you home from Tommy's party at the legion, Ethel? You fell into a ditch beside the road."

A horrified Ethel remembers the night in question all too clearly, but pretends not to, in the hope it will minimize her embarrassment. Conrad begins to laugh as he recollects them coming out of the door, tripping and falling into the bushes. The beautiful flowerbeds were ruined by their fall. The flowers were part of a memorial that had been planted by local seniors. "We ran away as quickly as we could. I turned to you to take your hand, but you were nowhere to be seen. You'd slipped into the ditch beside the road."

"Oh, I vaguely remember something about that," Ethel says, lying through her teeth. It was a night she had never been able to erase from her mind.

Conrad continues, running his hand over his bald head, "I pulled you out and carried you in my arms across the road. You phoned to thank me the following day asking if I had your cardigan, which you had dropped by accident. I borrowed my brother's motorbike to go back to the legion that afternoon to retrace our steps. There was nothing in the ditch. However, I clearly remember finding a grey cardigan with huge tire marks on it, lying like a dead raccoon at the roadside. I decided to leave it there, as it was completely ruined."

Both burst out laughing at the mental picture he had conjured up. "It's nice to see you again, Ethel. I hope to see you again before another thirty years pass." A disappointed Ethel bids him a fond farewell.

Beth, riding Rupert, trots past Ethel, totally ignoring her as if she is invisible. The steam is rising from Rupert's back. It looks like mist rising from the water, Ethel thinks. I wish I had my camera with me. It would make a most unusual and beautiful photograph, even with that rude moron on its back! I could Photoshop her out. Grampy is welcome to her. She heads back to the office, trying to contain her disappointment about Conrad.

The owls bask in the sunshine, perched on the apex of the roof at Miggles' Retreat. Beth dismounts, throwing the reins in the direction of a waiting Kate. "Deal with him," she demands, "I am going to be late for my work."

Not my fault you can't organize yourself, Kate thinks, admiring Beth's beautiful silk scarf draped casually around her neck. Kate dutifully cools Rupert down, lovingly catering to his every need before informing the doctor that she has already attended to Nellie. "Thank you, dear," Beth replies in a condescending tone, before throwing her beige suede jacket around her elegant shoulders. She looks a million bucks, thinks Kate grudgingly. I don't know how she does it.

Katherine and Tawny sit silently admiring the scene below them when suddenly, Tawny takes flight. A surprised Katherine is aghast at the unexpected departure of her trainee. This is not part of the day's plan. Tawny has her own agenda. Not caring about the consequences of her impending actions, she is more than willing to pay the penalties, regardless of what they may be.

Beth, having showered and dressed, is ready to start her shift at the practice. She strides confidently from the side door of Miggles' Retreat towards her Mercedes. Tawny seizes her opportunity, knowing that there is no room for error, she skillfully defecates a large amount of excrement hitting the doctor right between the shoulder blades, ruining the expensive suede jacket. "Bull's-eye!" she hoots loudly, before returning to an angry but amused Katherine. Beth is stunned. She carefully removes her jacket, however, not carefully enough as some of the mess slides down onto her designer pants.

Kate, having witnessed the event from Nellie's stall, dives head first into the straw. Howling with laughter, she fumbles for her cell phone to tell Jay-Jay what has just happened. "This is one of the best days of my life," she tells him. She recounts what she has just witnessed.

"That's fantastic! I wish I had been there," he replies. "I can't wait for lunchtime to tell Barry and Ethel all about it. Do you have any idea what Annie and Yvonne have made for lunch today?"

"No, I like surprises," she says. "Tell everyone you meet about Beth's jacket."

"Will do," Jay-Jay replies, "see you later." He whistles the theme tune to 'Top Gun' much to Katherine's amusement as he heads off to complete his morning duties. Her anger and frustration with Tawny's actions lift considerably on hearing the tune.

"Come here, lady," she quite rightly demands of Tawny. Looking a little sheepish, Tawny waddles along the roof towards the wise old owl with a slight limp, Katherine notices. They look at each other intently for a few seconds, neither wanting to speak first. Eventually Katherine shakes her head in mock disgust.

Tawny looks down, observing Kate lunging Perrah in the yard. She sees Jay-Jay laughing to himself as he tries in vain to catch Alfie. The donkey is leading him a merry dance beside the duck pond. Watching the amusing scene, Tawny asks Katherine if she is serious in wanting her to be her replacement when she retires.

"I have had a long and successful career," Katherine tells her trainee. "I have had the privilege of being able to spread a great deal of magic over many years. I am acutely aware that it is time for me to step aside and let someone younger take over this privileged position."

A surprised Tawny replies without any hesitation, "Thank you for the kind offer, Katherine, and for the vast experience you have graciously passed on to me. However, and I surprise myself in saying this, magic is not for me, fun though it can be. I am a great believer in reality. I have decided that it is time for me to retire also. I hope my decision doesn't disappoint you too much. My wings are too sore, my eyesight and hearing are failing me, so I think you should give someone else the opportunity to continue your marvelous work."

"You do surprise me," Katherine responds, her voice tinged with sadness, "however I very much appreciate your honesty and all of your efforts. You don't always go about things in the correct manner, but I know you always mean well, and that you do your absolute best at all times. Do you have anybody in mind who could replace you?"

"I do, as it turns out," Tawny replies smugly. "Ella, the hummingbird!"

"A great choice!" exclaims Katherine. "My only reservation with that suggestion is she would most likely cause as much havoc as you have, but I'll give it my careful consideration. I will ask my superiors for their input before getting back to you with my decision." The owls hug each other with mutual respect. Katherine informs Tawny she is going to the Old Barn to rest. Tawny tells her that she will catch up with her later. She wants to check on Alfie before night falls. As both owls fly away in opposite directions, Katherine hoots over her right wing, "If I ever catch you dive bombing again without my permission, I will not be responsible for my actions. Do I make myself clear?" Loud hoots echo around the farm for several minutes.

* * *

On returning to his Hummer, Barry checks his iPhone. The display shows Ethel has been trying to get in touch several times, despite her knowing he was with Nigel. This must be important, Barry realizes with trepidation. Before returning to the farm, he decides that the best plan of action would be for him to call her, as he assumes that she must have unsolved troubles waiting for his attention. An excited Ethel informs him that Conrad, the new mailman, has delivered a registered letter for him from a legal firm in New Zealand. "New Zealand?" Barry enquires. "Are you sure? I don't know anybody over there."

"That's what the return address on the envelope states," Ethel assures him, after checking it three times. She holds it up to the light in the hope of being able to read the contents. "Do you want me to open it for you?"

"Nice try, Ethel. You know as well as I do it is illegal to open other people's mail. You will just have to wait until I get back," he says teasingly, knowing this will make her even more curious.

"Oh, go on, please," she pleads. "I've had to wait two hours already. Another hour will kill me."

"Well, it's been nice knowing you, Ethel. Thanks for everything," he says switching his phone off, laughing to himself, picturing Ethel's face at this precise moment.

Barry is aware of Grampy's impending lunch hour. He stops at the local Tim Horton's to get a coffee, giving him time to collect his thoughts. "Grampy or Ethel? Ethel or Grampy? Who do I deal with first?" he ponders. Out of respect, he decides it would be best to phone Grampy who is waiting patiently in the staff cafeteria for his call. "Hi Grampy," Barry says, his voice tinged with guilt. "I forgot to inform you last night that I had an appointment in town this morning."

"No problem," replies Grampy, in a friendly manner. "It's just that it is most uncharacteristic of you not to notify me if you have to leave the farm. You know I don't like it when one if us is not there at all times. That doesn't matter now, though, it's not a big issue in the grand scheme of things." He continues before Barry has a chance to reply, "I made one of the biggest decisions of my life last night. I am going to call off the engagement between Beth and myself. I will be telling her tonight if she is free."

Barry breathes a huge sigh of relief. He feels that there is now a chance that life at Hope Farm will return to normal.

Grampy lowers his voice saying, "I don't think a single person, other than me, will be disappointed by my decision."

Unsure of what to say in response, Barry realizes he must say something sympathetic to his unhappy boss. "I respect your decision, Grampy. You have my absolute assurance that I will do my best to keep the inevitable gossip to a minimum."

"Thank you, Barry," he says, quite simply. "I know I can rely on you. You are a true professional." He quickly hangs up leaving Barry to face an increasingly impatient Ethel.

* * *

Grampy phones Beth's practice asking her receptionist, Tina, to ask Doctor McCormack to get in contact with him on his cell phone as soon as possible. He stresses to her that it is of the utmost importance. "Consider it done," Tina politely assures him. Within ten minutes, his cell phone rings. He excuses himself from his colleagues to speak with Beth in the hallway. "I will keep this brief," he says curtly, "Are you free to come to the farmhouse this evening?"

"Yes. I can be there around eight."

"Good. I will see you then." He quickly hangs up, trying his best not to let his decision affect his afternoon's work.

* * *

An impatient Ethel greets Barry when he arrives at the farm. She is now feeling very unsettled after having met her teenage infatuation earlier that morning. She was unable to concentrate on anything that she attempted to tackle while awaiting his return. "Do you want a coffee?" she asks, trying to sound as casual as possible.

"No, thanks, I have just had one on my way back." Barry antagonizes her even more by saying, "I need to catch up on this morning's mail and phone calls. I need peace and quiet for at least half-an-hour."

Ethel looks at him in total disbelief. "Are you doing this deliberately?" she finds herself asking, the words flying from her mouth before she can stop them.

"What are you implying?" is his immediate response. "Would I do that to you, Ethel?"

"You absolutely would, you rat, at every opportunity!" she retorts.

"Okay, okay, I surrender. You are as bad, if not worse than my mother ever was, even at her best. I will give you five full minutes of my precious time Ethel. Use it wisely." Slightly taken aback, she silently hands him the registered mail. He looks up at her in surprise. You could hear a pin drop in the office as he leans forward to grab his gold letter opener. Carefully slicing open the envelope, he removes the mystery letter and begins to read it silently. Ethel is unsure of what to do next as she watches the color drain from her boss' face. He glances up at his PA for a few seconds in silence before giving the letter his full attention once more.

"Is everything all right?" she enquires, with a look of deep concern on her face.

He looks back at her, unable to speak as his mouth has gone dry. Ethel notices his hands trembling as he offers her the sheet of expensive headed notepaper. She begins to read the contents as Barry heads towards the door to lock it, ensuring their privacy. He then switches off the ringer on the phone, something he has never done before. The noise of Ethel's scream fills the room. Barry is shaking from head to toe as he slumps down in his big leather chair. They stare at one another in silence for several minutes before Ethel shrieks, "Oh my God! I simply do not believe it! This cannot be happening to you."

"It is, Ethel," he eventually manages to squeak. "It is real. I feel incredibly guilty, not to mention lucky, as I barely knew the woman. I remember my mother talking about her friend periodically over the years. I always thought she was exaggerating or fantasizing about this woman's enormous wealth. The stories Mom used to tell about her throwing hundred dollar bills around like confetti made me laugh. I know she kept in touch with Mom until she passed away. Together they had been through a great deal over the years." His eyes fill with tears at the memories. "You'll have to excuse me, Ethel. I think I need to lie down. Hold all my calls, and please do not breathe a word of this to anyone."

With sweating shaking hands, Ethel slowly replaces the letter in its envelope before carefully locking it away in the filing cabinet under 'personal'. "Incidentally, do you know that there is a sofa bed in the room behind the office?" she inquires.

A wry smile crosses his face. "Yes, I do know. That is exactly where I am going to go for a nap right now. I always knew about Nanny's hideaway, but she thought it was her secret. Until the bitter end I chose to let her believe that. If people ask where I am, with the exception of Grampy, of course, tell them you don't know. If Grampy asks, tell him I'll speak with him when I'm good and ready."

"Are you serious?" she asks, grinning from ear to ear.

"Never more serious in my life," he says slamming the door behind him.

*   *   *

After his snooze, Barry emerges rubbing the sleep from his eyes. Still suffering from shock, he reminds Ethel not to mention a single word about the letter, for now. "If anybody mentions the contents of it in any shape, manner, or form, I will know you have broken your promise. I need to sleep on it tonight. I will make my decision about my future, and yours, too, come to think of it, Ethel, tomorrow!"

"You have my absolute word, Barry. Have a good night's sleep," she says excitedly as they prepare to go home after an exceptionally eventful day.

Jay-Jay enters the office to sign out for the night, singing, 'What a difference a day makes,' while tapping on the desk in time to the beat of the tune. Barry stares at him in total disbelief thinking, if only you knew what a difference a day can make, Jay-Jay. As he closes the office door Barry smirks widely saying, "Good night, Jay-Jay. See you tomorrow, don't be late. I will be making an important announcement to everyone. Snooze and you lose," he says opening his car door, oozing with newfound confidence.

"Yeah, yeah," Jay-Jay replies as Barry's car door closes behind him. Just as he starts the engine, Kate runs across the yard, waving her arms in the air to flag him down. "Oh for crying out loud, what now?" he exclaims. Lowering his window, he asks her, "Can't this wait till tomorrow? I really need to get home now."

"I suppose it could," disappointed at his lack of interest. "The incident of the owl pooping on Beth's suede jacket might not be as funny tomorrow, though."

With renewed interest, he urges Kate to relay her story. She tells the tale once more with glee, relishing every single moment. Barry laughs in delight at the thought of Tawny dive-bombing Beth. He reminds Kate to be on time the following morning as he informs her that he has a very important announcement to make which will affect the future of everyone at Hope Farm.

"Tell me more," she says in wonder.

Deliberately ignoring her plea he cries, "See you tomorrow, everyone," waving his whole arm out of the car window.

CHAPTER 35

As eight o'clock approaches, Grampy paces up and down the hallway. After asking Annie and Yvonne to finish early, he fed and groomed the dogs before putting them out in their pen. An hour ago, he checked that Flash had everything he needed for his night shift before unplugging the telephone. At exactly eight o'clock Beth arrives at the front door. She knocks politely before letting herself in. This is out of character for her. Grampy notices she looks shorter than of late as he glances at her footwear. She is wearing a heel, which baffles him even further. He could have understood it if she had been wearing ballet flats. He also notices that her shoulders are hunched forward. It is apparent that she is not wearing her usual air of authority. "Hi," she says to him in a shy but friendly tone, using his real name instead of the usual nickname that people generally used. "How are you tonight?"

"Cut the pleasantries, Elizabeth. After a great deal of thought, I have decided I no longer want anything to do with you on either a personal or a professional level. Our engagement is over." She looks at him in total disbelief, her eyes widening as the reality of what he has said dawns on her. It hits home hard. "You are an insincere, obnoxious, controlling madam. You have the most unfortunate personality which is a great shame as you are a very successful businesswoman." Before she has the chance to reply, he adds, "You are also a very talented horsewoman. That is one of the many things which I used to find attractive about you."

"Is this because I owe Hope Farm a lot of money?" she interjects, hoping to resurrect the situation she now unexpectedly finds herself facing.

"It has absolutely nothing to do with that, although I would appreciate you settling your account within the next three months. How could you do this to me, Elizabeth? I think my offer of three months to pay is more than fair, don't you agree?"

"I guess so," she says visibly crestfallen. Panic begins to set in. She wonders how much Grampy really knows about her circumstances.

Taking a deep breath, Grampy feels in complete control of the situation. "I knew deep down that you and I were not really suited to each other. I also suspected that you were only after my financial stability, which you should have in your own right by now." Beth opens her mouth to argue as she normally would, but quickly closes it without uttering a word, realizing he has spoken the absolute truth, hitting the nail on the head. As she walks slowly towards him, he backs away, noticing the absence of her usual confident strut. The swaying of her shoulders from side to side used to annoy him intensely as she expected him to walk two paces behind her. Grampy is feeling empowered by her sudden lack of brusqueness, giving him even more confidence than he already felt prior to her arrival. Beth is dumbfounded and starts to cry in the hope he will relent and take her in his arms. "We cannot be happy together anymore," he continues. "We should never have been together in the first place. I think we were both just filling a void in our lives. As we are both in our golden years, you must go and be happy with whatever it is that you need."

"I suppose you will want the ring back?" she eventually asks.

"It was my gift to you. Sell it if you need to." Adding insult to injury he adds, "It can go towards paying off your outstanding debt to the farm," he spits out without any real regret.

Abruptly, she turns on her heels without further argument saying, "Thank you for the good times we had, and by the way, get over Nanny. She stands in the way of you moving forward with your life."

"That is the most sensible thing you have ever said to me, Elizabeth. You do have a point, though. She would have been unstoppable if she had been educated like you. Goodbye and good luck, Beth. Please see to it that you remove your horses as soon as possible from my property. If you do not arrange to clear your debts with us, I will take ownership of both Rupert and Nellie. I would hate to do this, especially to you, but it is your own doing."

"I understand. I will phone Nigel tomorrow to make the necessary arrangements. You will get my horses over my dead body."

"Don't tempt me to say anything further, Elizabeth," Grampy says as he closes the door gently behind her. From the lounge window, he watches her get into her car, slamming the door and roaring off at speed down the gravel driveway.

Grampy pours himself a drink before leaving a message on Barry's voicemail informing him that the engagement has now officially ended. "I am a free man at last," he says to his reflection in the washroom mirror. He finds it impossible to get to sleep as the sound of an owl hooting outside his bedroom window keeps him awake for most of the night.

CHAPTER 36

Dawn is breaking as Barry arrives at Hope Farm. He mentally prepares his speech and jots down a few notes on his notepad to remind him of the points he is going to announce. Wanting to catch Grampy before he leaves for work, he keeps an eagle eye on the farmhouse door. As it happens, he does not have long to wait.

Grampy's intention was to leave the house half-an-hour prior to anyone else arriving. However, Barry's recent good fortune foils his plan. "Morning Grampy," calls Barry, trying desperately to keep the smugness from his voice. "I got your message."

"Gosh, you're up bright and early," he replies. "I didn't expect you to be here at this hour."

"I am sorry to hear about your break-up. However, I am not going to be a hypocrite. In my humble opinion, you absolutely did the right thing. In fact, I think you had a lucky escape."

"I appreciate your honesty, so I assume you know something that I don't," exclaims Grampy, as the line between his eyebrows deepens.

"I do, as a matter of fact, not that it matters now. I guess it's now just water under the bridge. If you need an ear, I will always be here for you."

"Thanks, Barry. I will see how I feel later. I suppose I should inform my work colleagues today, or on second thoughts, I might leave it until they find out for themselves. Incidentally, why are you here so early?"

Feeling slightly uncomfortable, Barry replies, "I'm feeling guilty, as on the same day that you broke off your engagement, I received incredibly good news."

"That's my misfortune," Grampy remarks indifferently, "Do tell me about your news."

"Well, erm," begins Barry, "recently my mother's friend passed away. I have inherited her ranch in New Zealand. She had left it to my mother, but as she is no longer with us, erm, it means that I have inherited the entire estate, lock, stock, and barrel." He laughs at what he has just said. "Erm, can you imagine me as a Kiwi shepherd?"

"Definitely not," Grampy replies quickly, brushing his moustache nervously as he begins to lose his composure.

"The ranch covers approximately a thousand acres," he informs his boss.

Grampy stares in awe, brushing his moustache once again. The realization hits him that his employee of many years has now become richer than he is. He offers Barry his hand in congratulation at his newfound fortune. Barry immediately and gratefully responds by shaking Grampy's hand vigorously, relieved at his obvious genuine pleasure. "You don't want to buy my farm, do you?" Grampy asks him, partly in jest.

"I will give that my serious consideration," he replies in all seriousness. "It did cross my mind last night. If you are thinking of selling Hope Farm, I would be very interested."

"Really? I was only joking, but if you are serious, I will give it some thought. A big change is exactly what the doctor ordered, if you will excuse the pun. I have to go to work right now, but we will talk later. Are you going to tell the staff today, or is it a secret?"

"Erm, I am going to tell them all this morning. That is why I have come in so early, but I wanted to tell you first," he says nervously.

"Good luck with that. I will see you later," Grampy says with a smile, climbing into his Jeep as he throws his bag carelessly onto the passenger seat. "If you buy the farm, does that mean I have to call you sir?" he jests.

"I'll have to think about that one," Barry says with visible relief spreading across his face.

Due to the events of the previous twenty-four hours, Grampy has difficulty concentrating on the road. Many thoughts go round and around in his head. As he slows down on his approach to the harbor bridge, he suddenly revels in the thought of returning to his homeland. He also makes the decision not to tell his work colleagues about the break-up. It is after all, none of their business.

By the time morning break arrives, he is unable to concentrate fully on his work due to the turmoil in his mind. He decides to fake another migraine and head for home. He takes some marking with him by way of compensation, alleviating his guilt. By the time he sees Hope Farm in the distance, Barry has notified all the staff about his new circumstances.

*   *   *

There is understandable jealousy from some people, but most are very happy for Barry. Several ask if he is going to have a celebratory party. He assures them that he will arrange a suitable celebration as soon as his inheritance hits his bank account, and not a minute before. His promise keeps everybody optimistic about the future as the farm staff goes about their daily business, knowing that he will keep his promise.

Just as Grampy parks his Jeep next to the house, Jay-Jay pops his head around the office door, "Hey, moneybags," he teases Barry, "any chance of a company car so that I can get to work on time?"

"Oh, I shall see to it that I put it on the top of my list of priorities, Jay-Jay," Barry replies sarcastically.

"Are you serious? Do you promise, eh?"

Carefully considering Jay-Jay's request for a split second, Barry replies, "Erm, yeah, okay. I suppose you do deserve a reliable car."

A look of amazement spreads across Jay-Jay's face. "Gee, thanks, Barry. I was only kidding really."

"No, you weren't," Barry mutters under his breath before continuing with his long list of duties.

CHAPTER 37

A great many changes take place at Hope Farm in the following months. Like his dear departed wife's, Grampy's arthritis worsens, now hampering his daily life. He decides to take early retirement from his teaching job in town after coming to the conclusion that he did not want to be the richest corpse in the cemetery. He has no desire to meet socially with any of his work colleagues ever again.

Barry inherits an obscene amount of money, enabling him to buy Hope Farm from Grampy. As promised, he buys Jay-Jay a reliable car. He sponsors Kate to attend the prestigious riding school in the adjoining province, enabling her to pursue a promising career in dressage. He decides to buy a dappled grey dressage horse, giving Kate a fifty percent share. She decides to name it Jumper. He offers Ethel his old position of manager on the farm. After careful consideration, due to her advancing years, she politely declines, asking if she could keep her position as his PA. Barry is more than happy to oblige. He also tells Ethel to choose any horse on the farm to have as a gift—secretly knowing she will choose Pixie, which she does. Free livery for the life of the animal is included in his offer. He sends Annie and Yvonne, along with Flash as their chaperone, on a vacation to Turkey at their request, taking on temporary staff while they are away.

One of the most satisfying days of his life happens when he unexpectedly bumps into Doctor McCormack at an equine conference. On seeing him, she bursts into tears, and then promptly faints. Surprisingly, she does pay her debts to the farm in full. She still lives alone and probably always will. Barry offers Nigel his old position of manager at Hope Farm after Ethel declines the post. There are only three days left before Nigel must decide whether to accept the position or not.

Despite the huge amount of lottery tickets bought, the return is very small. Somebody from out west scooped the mega jackpot.

Neither Lisa nor Seamus returns to work at the farm. They end their relationship. Barry is delighted to give Lisa a glowing reference as she is offered a job in America. Liz Smith sells her beloved horses to Alistair before joining her husband in Dubai in yet another attempt to patch up their troubled marriage. Alistair promises her he will sell them back to her if she ever divorces her now ailing husband.

Grampy buys a small house in town for his daughter Victoria. She decides to stay and look after his dogs, which she dearly loves. Her intentions are to become a vet and she starts at the veterinary school in town shortly after the farm sale is completed.

Katherine casts her final magic spells. She sprinkles a veil of magic dust over Tawny's thick feathers, enabling her to become human once again on the next full moon. Katherine also casts a spell over Ella the hummingbird. Ella can then use her new magic powers periodically, for as long as Barry remains the proprietor of the farm. She becomes Katherine's replacement at Hope Farm.

The following evening, Katherine, the wise old owl, passes away peacefully in her sleep. Tawny is with her the entire time. They are huddled together in the trunk of the maple tree when Katherine takes her final breath. On the night of the next full moon, Tawny disappears. No one knows where she has gone. Her remains are never found.

Grampy bids a fond farewell to Barry and all the staff on the farm, thanking them for their many years of loyal and faithful service to both him and Nanny. Victoria drives him to the airport in what is now her pumpkin colored Jeep. He is looking forward to his new life, but also with a heavy heart as he has many happy memories, as well as some sad ones, attached to this country. Upon his arrival at the airport, a woman in the line-up at the check-in desk irritates him initially. She has many bags and he only has hand luggage. Grampy had shipped a few tea chests full of his possessions to his destination a few weeks earlier. He notices that the woman at the check-in desk has a beautiful Scottish accent. The way she leaned heavily on her cougar print cane grabbed his attention. Apparently, she had requested a seat with extra legroom but when she arrived at check-in, the airline has given her seat away by mistake. She is becoming more excited by the minute as the airline offers to upgrade her to business class.

She turns to Grampy to apologize for the holdup she has created. Her twinkly hazel eyes mesmerize him. Could it be? Her curly white hair resembles cotton candy after having being hit by a tornado. Feeling his impulsiveness taking over, he says, "Don't worry, and take your time."

"Do I know you?" she asks, with a huge smile forming on her plump face. "You look very familiar."

"So do you," he replies cheerfully. "Are you on the flight to Gatwick by any chance?"

"Well, I'm trying to get on it," she says in a soft Scottish voice.

"I couldn't help over hearing that you have been upgraded to business class. What seat are you in, if you don't mind me asking?"

She glances at her ticket before showing it to him. Grampy can hardly believe his eyes. He has to read her name twice before he notices that their seats were adjacent to each other. This is impossible, he thinks. How can she be alive again? With his heart pounding in his chest, Grampy asks her, "Where are you from?" only just managing to keep his face straight.

"Oh I can't keep this up," she says as she bursts out laughing. "We're too old to play this game now."

Feeling twenty years younger, he takes hold of her hand firmly, helping her to balance. He looks her up and down as she places her enormous soft leather purse over her shoulder. Turning to him she says, "I can call this a handbag now, not a purse."

"I can switch my mobile off instead of calling it a cell," Grampy tells her delightedly. "Can you pick up your cane, or can we call it a walking stick now?"

"Not until after we're in the departure lounge," she quips.

"Do you have a jumper in your bag in case it gets cold?" he asks his wife lovingly.

"While you are still in this country Grampy, and we are not out of it yet, you have to call it a sweater, do remember dear."

He starts to laugh pointing out, "You're not quite as quick as you used to be you know."

"Neither are you," she replies quicker than ever, making him laugh even more. "Let's go home, James. I can't take any more of this nonsense."

"Yes, let's go home, Jan," he says as he takes her arm, leading her towards the duty-free shop. "Your usual tipple, dear?"

"A liter of vodka will do for now," she says, looking deeply into his chocolate brown eyes.

Soon after, they board the aircraft. They settled into their soft leather seats as Captain Gower announces their departure. James turns to his wife saying, "What an adventure we've had, eh?!" They both look lovingly out of the aircraft window at the land they are leaving behind them, along with some wonderful memories.

"Remind me not to listen to you the next time you have a harebrained idea, please, James," says Jan with a serious expression. He nods in agreement. They look lovingly at each other and smile as the aircraft climbs into the clear blue sky as they head back to their homeland.

Who knows what the future has in store for them all? We will just have to wait and see.